GAT HEAT

My Cad was at the curb a few yards ~~from~~ the house. As I glanced toward it my gaze took in another car parked nearly a block away.

I tossed my eyes around the area, swung my head left fast.

I saw him then. But he'd seen me first. He already had a gun in his hand.

I went down fast and hard, one knee pounding a shallow depression in the grass, slapping my hand to the Colt under my coat. As my knee hit the lawn, he let go a shot at me, high, close but high.

I squeezed the Colt's trigger twice and missed the man both times. "Shell," I said to myself, "you're in trouble."

I dived forward, skidded on the lawn and rolled as another gun blasted. When I came up I saw that a second man was firing at me. He was a blur in my sight, not clear, but clear enough for me to know the sonofabitch was trying to kill me.

GAT HEAT
was originally published by Trident Press.

Other books by Richard S. Prather

Dead Heat
Dead Man's Walk
Kill Him Twice
The Kubla Khan Caper
The Meandering Corpse
The Trojan Hearse
Come Seven/Come Death (with others)

Published by Pocket Books

 Are there paperbound books you want
but cannot find in your retail stores?

You can get any title in print in:
Pocket Book editions • Pocket *Cardinal* editions • Permabook editions or Washington Square Press editions. Simply send retail price, local sales tax, if any, plus 10¢ to cover mailing and handling costs for each book wanted to:

MAIL SERVICE DEPARTMENT
    POCKET BOOKS • A Division of Simon & Schuster, Inc.
    1 West 39th Street • New York, New York 10018
    Please send check or money order. We cannot be responsible for cash.
    Catalogue sent free on request.

Titles in these series are also available at discounts in quantity lots for industrial or sales-promotional use. For details write our Special Projects Agency: The Benjamin Company, Inc., 485 Madison Avenue, New York, N.Y. 10022.

GAT HEAT

Richard S. Prather

PUBLISHED BY POCKET BOOKS NEW YORK

GAT HEAT

Trident Press edition published April, 1967

A Pocket Book edition
1st printing...........May, 1968

This *Pocket Book* edition includes every word
contained in the original, higher-priced edition. It is printed
from brand-new plates made from completely reset, clear, easy-to-read
type. *Pocket Book* editions are published by Pocket Books, a division
of Simon & Schuster, Inc., 630 Fifth Avenue, New York, N.Y. 10020.
Trademarks registered in the United States and other countries.

L

For Tina, my wife

1

"Sex," she said.

"Yep," I said.

"Sex. That's what."

"That's what, all right. You hit it that time. Couldn't have said it better myself."

"Sex . . ." she repeated, lingering over the word as one might linger over the olive in one's first martini.

Maybe I'd better tell you about this kid before you get the wrong idea. Kid—hah. I'm only thirty years old myself, not exactly a kid, but this babe could have been my father.

You could say she was so thin she had to wear a fat girdle. You could say she appeared to be wearing a lifeless bra. You could say she had no visible means of sport.

But even that wouldn't say it.

Her complexion was the delicate tint of poisoned limeade; and her expression was that of one biting down, all unaware, on thirty-two cavities. I had seen that light in her eyes before: in glass eyes. I had seen those curly locks on her head before: on drugstore dummies. I had seen—well, I had seen enough.

Her name was Agatha Smellow, and to put it gently, she simply was not my kind of tomato; thus this was—at least—an unusual circumstance for the one man of the one-man firm, *Sheldon Scott, Investigations*. That's me, Shell Scott. And I wished I was dead.

"Well, Aggie, old girl," I said—she had asked me to call her Aggie—"here's to nothing."

We clinked glasses. And she smiled her pearly smile, fluttering her eyelids.

Friends, in my years as a private investigator in Los Angeles, I have looked upon death and destruction, blood and urp, split brainboxes and disemboweled oxen. But I have seldom looked upon anything less appetizing than Aggie fluttering her bald lids at me.

An explanation—I hope—is in order.

I am a fairly large fellow, reasonably agile, healthily tanned from much Southern California sun. The face is bearable, even if it is not the one I might have chosen if given my pick of a half-dozen gorgeous ones; what poetry of feature it might once have possessed having since been edited into disrhythm by numerous individuals who bore me no good will—guys, that is, who socked me and kicked me and jumped on me and sapped me and even shot off a piece of one ear.

The head to which all that was done is topped by inch-long white hair springing upward, as if trying for an inch and a half, and sharply-angled cotton-white brows, which I now suffer bravely, having learned as a mere boy that despite the exercise of much ingenuity and even mustache wax I could not straighten them out.

Despite all this, I generally look forward to whatever life brings —even if, as sometimes happens, it's death; for the blood does not creep in my veins, but rather, I like to think, sings and sometimes yodels in splendidly harmonious arteries.

More, in my yodeling blood are several pounds of iron filings, each ounce of which is magnetically attracted to what I think of, fondly, as toothsome tomatoes. I have, in fact, a fondness amounting virtually to dedication for lovely lasses with lissome curves and eyes like silk, with smiling lips and boastful cleavage, with fire in their glances—and all that.

Why, then, was I here?

Here, talking about sex?

Sex, with *Aggie?*

Listen, and I shall tell you a tale which will split your toenails . . .

2

THEY WERE ALL NAKED. IT WAS THAT KIND OF PARTY. EVEN the dead guy was naked.

Clothes were scattered around, as if a hurricane had hit the wash basket. None of the guests I glimpsed were jumping about vigorously, at least not at first, but all of them looked as if they'd really been living.

Except for that one guy. You couldn't really say he was living.

Nobody seemed to be paying any attention to him. Of course, he wasn't actually right out in plain sight, being half hidden among bushes and ferns and big-leafed tropical plants, which lined a narrow winding path. Also it was night, after ten p.m. on a balmy Friday evening in July; but there were plenty of garden lights spilling reds and yellows and blues and greens all over the landscape, and it was difficult to miss him entirely.

Even so, I walked past him myself, thinking he was passed out, or sleeping and dreaming sweet dreams. But I have seen a lot of dead guys, and there was something about the way he lay on the grass under a hydrangea bush. . . .

I didn't spot him right away.

I'd come in the side gate into the six-foot wall, through the radiantly-blossoming garden, and walked over a white gravel path to the side of Mr. Halstead's big hilltop house in the Hollywood Hills, and stopped for a moment near the forty-foot long free-form pool. So the first person I saw was the gal in the pool.

3

I knew it was a gal right away.

I can usually tell gals from other things without much difficulty, but the deduction was made easier because she seemed to be wearing the standard outfit here: nothing.

She was swimming lazily in the pool, sort of swirling around like a sleepy otter, and for a moment I wondered if I should take off my shoes—at least—and jump in and rescue her. There was a chance she was drowning.

Only a bare chance maybe, but it was worth considering.

In a matter of life and death you can't overlook anything.

I knew I'd never forgive myself if a gorgeous babe like that drowned right in front of my eyes.

But then she saw me and said, "Hi."

"Hi," I said. "You couldn't be drowning, could you?"

She swam toward me, reached the edge of the pool, and climbed out. *"Whoo!"* I said.

She said, "I couldn't be what?"

"Never mind, you've answered the question. Boy, I hope to shout you've—"

"What was that other thing you said?"

"What other—oh, you mean *Whoo?*"

"Yes. Was that it?"

"Yeah, that was it. Well, I was just making conversation."

She seemed to expect me to say something else. So I said, "Ah . . . Uh . . ."

This gal was quite a number. Quite a lot of numbers. Like, maybe 66 inches tall, 125-130 pounds, 39-24-37, and 25-30 years old; and her parts added up to more than the sum of her numbers.

Finally she asked, "What are you doing with all your clothes on?"

"Beats me."

"I don't remember you. Should I remember you?"

"Not yet."

"I didn't think so." She looked me up and down attentively. "I think I'd remember if I had. Who are you?"

"That's not important. Whoo are you?"

"I'm Sybil Spork."

"Sybil Spork? That's . . . ugh. Well, I'm pleased to meet you, anyway, Miss Spork. Or Sybil. May I call you Miss? I mean, may I call you Sybil?"

"Why not?" she said. "Only it's not Miss. I'm Mrs. Spork. Did George invite you?"

"Mr. Halstead did."

"Well, he might have *told* somebody! Who are you?"

"I'm Shell Scott."

That shook her up. She stifled a yawn, squeezed her eyes shut, then stretched langorously and let her arms flop to her sides. "Well, see you around," she said.

Then she walked past me and headed for the house.

It was a long, low pink job that looked sort of Spanish-Mediterranean, with thick cement arches and a red tile roof, about thirty yards away and half hidden behind clumps and masses of Southern California flora. I watched Sybil until her delectable Southern California fauna disappeared in the masses of flora, then I started after her.

I had to go to the house anyway. There, presumably, was where Mr. Halstead would be awaiting me. Probably soused to the gills. Passing a hydrangea bush, I walked past a heavy-set and hirsute individual lying face-down on the grass, three or four feet off the path; and I took two more steps before I stopped.

Then I turned around, looked at the guy again, went back and knelt by him. No pulse. No heat, no electricity, no zip. No more parties for this one.

Somebody let out a lusty whoop. From where I squatted I could see one small segment of the swimming pool and the blue-tiled deck next to it. As I looked toward the whooper, he came into view pursuing a short, shapely redheaded gal who dived into the pool. The man, a tall, large boned, dark-skinned egg with an enormous amount of black hair waving over his scalp, stooped and picked up a red and green beach ball. When the gal swam to the edge of the pool, he let out another whoop and whomped the beach ball down on her head. Then he jumped in at her. She climbed out and raced away. He climbed out and raced after her.

The dead guy lay with his legs extended toward the path on which I'd been walking, his head and shoulders half hidden by drooping shrubbery. A white bath towel was crumpled near him. I moved alongside him until I got a look at his head. He had a lot of wavy dark hair, but it was crushed in at the base of his skull. So, of course, was the base of his skull. There was quite a bit of blood.

I moved back to the path and walked toward the house again, wondering if this explained why Mr. Halstead had called me. It seemed a logical deduction. At first. A little more than half an

5

hour earlier I'd been in my apartment at the Spartan Apartment Hotel, relaxing with a bourbon and water while watching the tropical fish frolicking in the community tank, when Halstead phoned. He'd sounded somewhat unraveled and, speaking very softly after identifying himself, had merely asked me if I would come to his home on a matter of the "greatest urgency," and as speedily as possible. He hadn't told me what was so urgent, explaining only that it was a matter of "peculiar delicacy."

Which made me wonder if me wonder if my deduction was so logical after all. A man with his skull bashed in wasn't what *I* would have called a matter of "peculiar delicacy." Moreover, thinking of the people flitting nudely about, I had a hunch the party was supposed to have ended at least half an hour ago. But Halstead had told me he would meet me in his den and there explain everything in detail, so I let the hunch simmer.

This was the rear of the house, so—following Halstead's instructions—I walked to the end of the path and over a bricked patio to the rear door, through it and inside. Stairs rose on my left, and I went up them to the closed door opposite the head of the stairs. I knocked, waited, knocked again, and then went in.

It appeared to be the den, all right: large, masculine, with a dark cork ceiling and cedar-paneled walls, two small bookcases, a few hunting prints, and a hideous etching of some dead ducks. The carpet was shaggy and brown, and the couch and several chairs were big, squat, heavy. There was a desk in one corner, a few papers on its top, and a TV set glared from the wall. But that was all. No Halstead, nobody.

I went downstairs again, out the back door and stood for a moment, thinking about that hunch. In a few seconds there was the soft pad of feet behind me. As I turned, the door opened and out came a gorgeous naked tomato. It was the same one who'd been alone in the pool.

"*Whoo!*" I said.

She was eating a big, red, juicy-looking apple. "I still don't know what that means," she said.

"Well," I said, "ah . . . Uh . . ."

"Want a bite?"

"Don't mind if I do."

She handed me the apple. I handed it back. "No, thanks."

"But you said—"

"I changed my mind. I thought it was a tomato."

"You don't know *what* you want, do you?"

6

"I wouldn't say that. Where's Mr. Halstead?"

She lifted her brows and rolled her eyes, thinking. "I don't know," she said finally. "Haven't seen him for a while."

"How long a while?"

"Hour or so."

"How about Mrs. Halstead? Do you know where I could find her?"

She turned and pointed with her apple. And quite a lot of tomato. "Right down the hall there," she said. "Second door on the right." Mrs. Spork—or, as I preferred to think of her, Sybil —added, "At least she was. I saw her go in there a while ago."

Then she took a big crunchy bite out of her apple and walked past me. I watched her till she reached the pool and jumped in feet first, apple and all. You aren't supposed to swim right after eating, I thought. But, then, these people seemed to do lots of things people aren't supposed to do.

Musing thus, I walked down the hall to the second door. It was open. The room was a bedroom, and at first I thought there was nobody in it. But there was one person, a woman—presumably Mrs. Halstead—in the bed. I walked over there.

She was sleeping in the nude beneath a pink sheet and spread, both of which had been pushed, or slipped, down to her waist. She was a strawberry blonde about thirty years old, with a pretty face and at least half of a splendid figure.

It was a jolly sight, but you don't stand around staring at sleeping tomatoes when their covers have slipped. Not much, you don't. But it didn't seem right not to let her know somebody was here—especially under the circumstances.

So I cleared my throat. Not very loud. In fact, I couldn't hear it myself, which proabably explained why she didn't wake up.

I cleared my throat again, then hummed a jazzy little tune. Didn't do any good. So I reached over and waggled her shoulder a bit.

She opened her eyes, blinked.

"Hello," I said brightly. "Are you Mrs. Halstead?"

She said something like, "Glammbl," and her eyelids went up and down about eight or nine times, very slowly, and the last time were either staying down or moving so slowly I couldn't detect any movement whatever.

She knew I was there, though. I was still kind of shaking her shoulder. "Hey," I said. "Hey. All sorts of things are going on around here. Things you ought to know about. Hey."

She got her eyes open again.

"Are you Mrs. Halstead?" I said. "You better be. I'm not going to look much longer. I'm going to say the hell with it, and go for a swim or something."

"Who are *you*?" she said, sort of mushy.

"I'm Shell Scott."

"I'm Mrs. Halstead."

"How do you do?"

She made a little effort to cover herself up. Not much. She sort of plucked at the pink sheet, but not very pluckily.

"There's a dead guy out there," I said, pointing.

"What?"

"A dead guy. He's out there near the path. Under a hydrangea bush."

"A what?"

"A hydrangea bush."

"No—there's a *what* out there?"

"A dead guy. I thought you ought to know about it."

For some reason, I counted the seconds as she stared with her eyes—finally—wide open. You know the way you count seconds; that's the way I was doing: *One*-two-three-four; *two*-two-three-four; *three*-two-three-four; *four*-two-three—that was all.

By my count, it took three and three-quarters seconds, and then *zowie!* She was standing about fourteen feet from the bed —behind me, even—sort of in a crouch and yelling, "Dead? DEAD? *Dead?*"

I'm not certain I even saw her move. One moment I was looking down at her, kind of waggling her shoulder, and then she was behind me making an awful racket.

"You ought to at least put some shorts on," I said. "I don't know what's going on here, but I sure like it."

She looked down at herself.

One-two-three-four; *two*-two—*zowie!*

Yeah, back in bed. Covers up under her chin. Couple more of those and she'd be wide awake. Or clear over the hill and halfway down the next valley. Never did see a gal move like that.

"Who's dead?" she asked me.

"Beats me. I just got here. Your husband phoned me about half an hour ago and asked me to come out. But I'm beginning to doubt—"

"George phoned you?"

"That's right. Didn't you know?"

She shook her head. "Why would George phone you? Especially tonight . . ." She let it trail off. She got a kind of tortured look. After a few seconds she said, "Did you . . . see anybody else outside? Or—inside? Any—people?"

"Some."

"What . . . ah . . . how did they look?"

"Naked. That's the best one-word description I can think of. I suppose that's what you meant. Aside from that, well, they looked . . . happy, I guess."

She blinked her eyes some more, rapidly this time. Then she said, "Who did you say you were?"

"Shell Scott."

"Why did my husband call you?"

"He didn't explain. He was going to tell me the details when I got here. I'm a private investigator, and he merely—"

"You're a detective?" I nodded, and she said, "My God. What in the world would George want with a *detective?*"

I shrugged. Mrs. Halstead was wide awake now, and apparently trying to think about three or four things at once. In a moment she said, "Dead . . . Were you *serious?* Somebody's *dead?*"

"Yes, I was serious."

"Shouldn't we do something?"

"Sure we should. That's why I came in here and waggled you."

"Waggled?"

"I'll turn my back if you want to put on a robe or something. Of course, if you don't give a hoot—"

She gave a hoot. I turned my back, and in half a minute she was clad in a rosy-pink bathrobe and following me down the path outside.

"There he is," I said.

She stepped off the path, parted the shrubbery, and looked down at the dead man.

Then she turned and stepped back by me. "That's George," she said. "It's my husband."

Her tone was level, soft and apparently controlled. Her features weren't twisted into an expression of pain or shock. But I waited a few seconds before saying anything. And then there was no need to say anything.

Her lips puffed very slightly as breath pushed through them. Her head rolled to one side. Then she collapsed and fell suddenly, loosely, like an empty sack.

But I'd had a hunch she might keel over, and was able to catch her as she fell. Which made two of my hunches, so far, which had been proved correct.

I carried Mrs. Halstead into the house, laid her gently on the bed, and waited for her to come around again.

3

Twenty minutes later Mrs. Halstead was not only back almost to normal, but she was my client.

She claimed to be extremely curious to know why her husband had phoned me—if he really had, as she put it, which gave me something else to wonder about—but also, and naturally enough, she wanted me to do everything I could to find out who had killed him, and why. I told her there was probably little I might come up with that the police wouldn't get to first, but that I'd certainly do what I could.

By then I had called the police and they were on their way from the Hollywood Division, but I'd delayed my call briefly in deference to my client's wishes.

When she'd recovered enough to talk intelligently, she had asked me to please, *please* refrain from filling the premises with all kinds of cops until she could arrange for her guests to get their clothes on.

It seemed a reasonable request, so I told her, "O.K., but I'll have to tell the police some of the, ah, clues have been covered up."

"You wouldn't!"

"I've got to."

"You mustn't!"

"Look, Mrs. Halstead, first of all I'd tell them anyway. If that seems like betrayal, fire me. But in the second place, the police will find out whether I tell them or not—and it's better for all concerned if I do tell them."

"I don't understand."

"When the officers get here and find everybody clad in the height of fashion except the ... the victim, this will give them pause. They will query the guests—and you—about this unusual circumstance. And they will find out precisely what the score was, believe it or not. Contrary to opinion bruited about in some areas, the police are just as bright as the rest of us—and in some areas, a good deal brighter. You want them to find out their own way and land on your guests—and you—like a ton of bricks?"

"Oh. Well . . ."

"Yeah. So, O.K., tell the people the party's over—just so long as nobody, but nobody, leaves here."

She agreed. In fact, even before she passed the word around —caught me a little off guard there, by the way—I had her give me a list of the names and addresses of all the people present.

It turned out there had been, aside from the host and hostess, five other married couples enjoying the Halsteads' hospitality. They were the Warrens, Pryers, Smiths, Bersudians, and Sporks.

I went along with Mrs. Halstead while she rounded up the guests. She made a lot of racket, yelling names and things like "Lookout!" and "Yaah, here we come!" as we walked, which I thought interesting.

Even so, we found dark-skinned Mr. Bersudian with red-headed Mrs. Warren; they were sitting in a brightly-striped canvas-covered swing, but they weren't swinging, merely looking about blankly and breathing through their open mouths.

We found Mr. Warren and Mrs. Pryer lying on their stomachs, side by side on green grass beneath a weeping willow tree, plucking industriously at the grass, as though they were uncontrollably superstitious and each blade was a four-leaf clover.

Mr. Pryer came out of the house with Mrs. Bersudian, hand in hand, he saying over and over, "Wuzzamatter?"

And Mr. Spork, the old fuddy-duddy, was in the pool with, curious to relate, Mrs. Spork.

Perhaps more curious to relate, we found no Smiths. Mr. and Mrs. Smith were not on the premises at all.

Since I was now working for Mrs. Halstead, I took the opportunity to question Mr. and Mrs. Pryer, once they pulled themselves together, so to speak. Mrs. Halstead was still looking for the Smiths. I stood near a green chaise longue, on which Hugh and Betty Pryer sat.

He was in his middle forties, a short, solidly built man with thinning brown hair and long sideburns, good teeth and dark brown eyes that would probably have been intelligent and alert if he hadn't been so stewed. His wife was a few years younger, a slightly plump woman with small blue eyes and the faint beginning of a double chin, but with a rousing good figure nonetheless. She was quite sober.

So I talked mainly to Hugh Pryer.

They knew George Halstead was dead—they and everybody else here; Mrs. Halstead had blabbed that at the top of her lungs before I could stop her—and for the first minute or so, the Pryers merely expressed their shock and total ignorance of anything and everything connected with the homicide,

Finally I said to Mr. Pryer, "What about the people who aren't here now? What can you tell me about them?"

He shook his head, as though trying, unsuccessfully, to clear it, then said thickly, "Well, lessee. The Whists and Rileys dropped out. The Kents and Nelsons weren't here at all tonight, though. That's—"

He chopped it off because little Betty Pryer got him pretty good in the ribs with her elbow. It was neatly done, hardly noticeable at all. But I noticed it.

She looked up at me, smiling sweetly. "The Smiths?" she said. "That's John and Nella. I haven't any idea what—"

Hugh looked at her. "Smiths?"

"Yes, you ... dear," she said. "That's who Mr. Scott is asking us about. John and Nella, who were here earlier, but who aren't here now."

"I didden even know they left," he said.

His wife was right, I had indeed been asking about the Smiths. But I was now more interested in Hugh's woozy response, so I tried to keep him going. "You say two couples dropped out earlier? You mean they were here tonight?"

He looked at me blankly.

"Whists and Rileys, wasn't it?" I encouraged him.

He began shaking his head again. "No, they weren't. They weren't here."

"You said—"

"No," he broke in. "Ackchully, they weren't. I must've been thinking about another part—another time, somewhere." He squeezed his eyes shut for a couple of seconds. "I mus' confess, I had a little to drink, had a couple. Couple thousand, it feels like. You mus' excuse me, Mr. Scott." He paused. "Smiths, huh? I didden even know they left."

Then the first police car arrived, without siren.

George Halstead's body was on its way to the morgue, and the police were still taking statements when I decided to leave. I'd told them all I knew, and they would efficiently cover everything to be done here.

Also, if they came up with anything significant, I knew I could probably get the info tomorrow. Not only am I on very good terms with the Hollywood and Los Angeles police, but Captain Phil Samson, head of Central Homicide downtown at the L.A.P.D., is my best friend in town. So I led Mrs. Halstead aside and told her I was going to take off.

She was pale and unsteady, not in very good shape, her large green eyes dulled with shock, but holding up well enough under the circumstances. I knew she wanted to take a sleeping pill and get back into bed, but there were a few questions I had to ask.

I told her what Hugh Pryer had said, but she merely frowned and shook her head.

"I don't understand what he could have meant, Mr. Scott. John and Nella were here. The Smiths. I've no idea what happened to them. But neither the Whists nor Rileys was here at any time tonight. I haven't seen them for, oh, weeks." She smiled wanly. "No telling what Hugh meant—or thought. I've never seen him so drunk."

"Yeah."

"Hugh seldom drinks more than a highball or two," she assured me. "But he did tonight. Of all nights." She chewed on her lower lip. "In fact, most of us did. The party got . . . well, a little out of hand. If you know what I mean."

"Uh-huh."

"George made a punch. I don't know what he put in it. But it must have been . . ." She finished with an expressive shrug of her eyebrows.

I didn't say anything.

She went on, "It was awfully good punch. And everybody . . . It's embarrassing to talk about it . . ."

"So forget it," I said. "You don't have to explain anything to me, Mrs. Halstead." I smiled. "After all, I'm supposed to explain things to you."

She smiled slightly again, and I said, "In which connection, I

14

would like the addresses of those couples Mr. Pryer mentioned."

"I told you, none of them was here tonight."

"I know. But the person we're looking for was either somebody present, or—perhaps more likely—somebody *not* known to have been present. Someone who simply walked in." I paused. "It's just for a check. You never know where a lead might come from."

She nodded, then gave me the names and addresses from memory, and I jotted them in my notebook.

She had already told me, and the police as well, that she knew of nobody who might have wanted to kill her husband, no possible motive for the crime. So far as I'd been able to tell, that was the same story the rest of the guests were giving the officers. George Halstead had apparently been extremely well liked by almost everybody. But, clearly, not by everybody.

So, simply as routine, I asked, "Was this the first marriage for both of you, Mrs. Halstead?"

"For me, yes. George was married before."

"His former wife live out here?"

"Yes, Agatha lives in Culver City now."

"Agatha?"

"Agatha Smellow. She and George were married for, oh, twelve or fourteen years, I guess. She later married a man named Smellow, but he died after a year or two."

Agatha Smellow, Culver City. Probably not worth much, but you never know. "Mr. Halstead and his former wife were still friendly?"

"Not very. He couldn't stand her. And she *hated* him."

"Oh? Hated?"

"I don't mean *hated*. I shouldn't have said that. They still saw each other occasionally after she divorced him. There was a lot of bitterness connected with the divorce, though."

"She divorced him?"

"Yes."

Mrs. Halstead's face was virtually without expression, like a mask of wax, but right then I noticed the shimmering softness of her green eyes. They filled with tears, and the tears spilled silently, and glistened down her cheeks.

I had kept her talking about it long enough—too long. I looked around, caught the eye of a police lieutenant I knew, and jerked my head toward the house. He nodded.

I took Mrs. Halstead's arm and led her to the back door. There I said, "Sorry I kept digging at you."

"It's all right. I want you to—dig. I want you to . . ."

She stopped speaking, leaned her forehead against my shoulder and sobbed quietly, her arms hanging loosely at her sides.

After a little while she said, "Good night, Mr. Scott."

"Good night, Mrs. Halstead."

She turned and went into the house.

The lieutenant—a tall, bald man named France—was leaning against a white-stone outdoor barbecue grill when I walked over to him.

While he lit a cigar I asked him how it looked.

He puffed a couple of times, then said, "You ask me, nobody in this bunch busted his head in. They're shook up. Which is natural enough. But I can't smell anything else, Scott."

"What about this John and Nella Smith?"

"Another team's checking them out now. Haven't heard yet. You got anything else we can use?"

"Nothing important so far. Except what I told you."

"Yeah. Naked as jaybirds. Bloody nudists." He shook his head, looking around. "This is how the rich live, huh?"

"I guess. Some of the rich, anyhow."

"Jaybirds of a feather," he said. "Looks like every damn one of them's in the excruciatingly painful tax brackets. Where I wish I was."

"Yeah, it hurts so good."

"You coming downtown?"

"I'll be in. Tomorrow O.K.?"

"Yeah, if you don't have anything special to add."

"Not yet. When I do, you'll know it."

"That's a good fellow, Scott. See you."

I nodded, walked back toward the side gate I'd come in earlier. Near the pool, seated in metal-frame chairs laced with strips of plastic webbing, were Sybil Spork and Mrs. Angelica Bersudian. Sybil looked extremely delicious in clothes, too. She was peeling an orange and licking her fingers.

Mrs. Bersudian had looked quite a bit better naked. In clothes she appeared fat. She wasn't fat. Angelica Bersudian was a tall, bosomy, healthy-looking gal, thirtyish, with thick black hair and heavy lashes drooping over slumbrous eyes. She

16

was speaking to Sybil in a low, humming voice as I walked by them.

Sybil dropped a handful of orange peelings into a redwood wastebasket, then looked up at me.

As she caught my eye she smiled slowly.

"Whoo," she said.

4

DRIVING HOME, TOP DOWN ON MY CAD CONVERTIBLE, THE thought kept coming back: I wonder what she meant by that?

I was also wondering why her name had to be Mrs. Spork. Spork was bad enough, but the *Mrs.* ruined it entirely.

I was wondering about a number of other things, too. From brief talks with some of the Halsteads' guests and a chat with Lieutenant France, I had a few other facts. George Halstead's skull had been bashed in with a smooth, heavy rock—there were small boulders all over the place, lining paths, in decorative clumps, and scattered in and among the plantings—which had been found in a clump of dichondra about ten yards from the body, near an outside phone apparently used by swimmers around the pool. So either Halstead had been clobbered where he fell and the stone tossed away, or he'd been struck and then dragged to where I'd found him. The police hadn't come to a decision on that when I left.

Halstead was worth a couple of million dollars, perhaps more. All the guests present were, at least, well-to-do. Or "Jaybirds of a feather" as Lieutenant France had said. He'd also said he doubted that anyone present had banged Halstead in the brains, and if that's what he thought, I was inclined to go along with him. Which left the disappearing Smiths, whom the police were now checking on, and the others Hugh Pryer had mentioned: the Whists and Rileys, Kents and Nelsons. Plus, of course, any one of perhaps two or three million other people.

Even so, it was possible that by the time the police finished

18

their investigation tonight there'd be no further investigating to do. Often it happens that way, and a case is closed shortly after it opens. But until and unless that happened, I was interested in talking to a few people myself, particularly the Whists and Rileys.

I was remembering Hugh Pryer's mention of them and the not-so-sly dig in the ribs from his wife. It has been my experience that when a husband says something apparently innocuous and his wife instantly gets him a good one in the ribs, the comment may well be considered nocuous. So, while driving to Hollywood Boulevard I checked the addresses I'd jotted down as Mrs. Halstead gave them to me.

The Rileys lived in Pasadena, farther then I felt like driving at this hour—it was after midnight. But the Whists were living at the Norvue, which was in Hollywood and only a few blocks out of my way. So when I hit Hollywood Boulevard, instead of turning at Vine and continuing on to North Rossmore and home, I kept going to Highland Avenue and swung left toward the Norvue, three blocks ahead.

It was a new building, twelve stories of swank apartments and suites built around an enclosed pool-and-patio area and outdoor dining room and expensive as hell. I'd never been inside the place. The Whists were in 12-C, which I presumed would be one of the four penthouse suites on the Norvue's top floor.

As I turned to park in the curving drive before the lobby entrance, I noticed something mildly disturbing. Or, rather, noticed it again.

Checking traffic and keeping a casual eye on my rear-view mirror has become a habit with me, so before pulling into the Norvue's drive I glanced at the mirror, fingering up the turn indicator to signal for a right turn. The only car behind me was half a block back, but the left headlight was a little cock-eyed and tilted up slightly, so that its beam glared more than the right one. It wouldn't have been important, except that I'd noticed that same cock-eyed light behind me a few minutes earlier.

By the time I'd pulled into the drive and started slowing to a stop, the car had gone on by, and I didn't get a good look at its make or color. It was a dark sedan, but that was all I knew.

I turned off the ignition, left the Cad where it was, and went into the lobby.

It probably wouldn't have looked more expensive if they'd

19

built the furniture out of new money. The carpet was off-white, thick, spongy, probably fifty bucks a yard—and there were a lot of yards. The furniture, divans and chairs and even "love seats," was a little spindly for my taste, but it looked as rich and as modern as Mars flights. A bank of elevators was on the right; and on my left behind arcs and planes of black steel bands and rich red woods the shade of vitamin-enriched blood stood, at alert attention, a thin man with a kindly face.

He was dressed in a black suit, an unobtrusively patterned white shirt, and a white silk tie, and he stood there beaming kindness at me.

I waded to the desk and said, "Good evening."

"Good evening, sir. May I aid you?"

They didn't just help you here. They aided you. That was probably good. "I'd like to see the Whists. Ed and Marcelle."

Mrs. Halstead had told me their first names, so I tossed them in, probably thinking that my casual familiarity with penthouse dwellers might make up for the lack of class of my chops. But that was a pretty sneaky thing to do, I immediately realized, so I added, "Actually, I don't know them. Not intimately. Not even personally, that is."

"No matter."

"What?"

"No matter, sir. They are not here."

"Oh? They're out for the evening?"

"I know not," he said.

"You know not? Don't you work here?"

"Yes, sir," he said. "But Mr. and Mrs. Whist have not been in residence for nearly a month."

"They moved? Checked out?"

"No."

"Then where are they?"

"I know not."

It may be that I am not the most patient chap in the whole wide world. I flipped out my wallet, flapped it open to my private detective's card and dangled it before the desk man's eyes; then I leaned on the counter, maybe even a foot over the counter, and said, "Look, friend, maybe you've got nothing else to do, but I should like enormously either to see the Whists or determine before the dawn where the hell they have got to. So will you give it to me all in one gob?"

He grinned, and seemed to stand at ease. "Why didn't you say so?"

I grinned back at him. "I know not."

"They took a six-month lease on their penthouse," he said. "It expired night before last, but—" He broke off, flipped through some cards, then went on, "Last night they were here was four weeks ago."

"They didn't check out? Didn't give up the suite, I mean?"

"No."

"Skip out on the bill?"

"No, nothing like that. They paid the six months in advance. I recall asking the bell captain about them a few days ago. He said that when the Whists' luggage was taken to their car, Mr. Whist, after presenting him with a handsome gratuity for his aid, indicated they were going on a short vacation."

"I don't suppose they said where."

"No."

"Well, if their lease has expired, what about the stuff still left in the suite?"

"Nothing is left. They took everything with them."

"All? Clothing, the works?"

"All. Which, I presume, is why Mr. Whist presented the bell captain with such a handsome gratuity."

"I heard you—" I smiled—"the first time."

He smiled. "Splendid. The night they left, that was the night of the fire in their bedroom."

"The night of . . . in the *bedroom?*"

He nodded.

"What the hell were they doing?" I paused, held up a hand. "I know—you know not. What kind of a fire? Huge conflagration? Sheets of flame leaping and crack—"

"No, no. The bed burned, that is all."

"That's all, huh? Did it discomfit the Whists?"

"They were not in the room, not even in the suite. According to Mr. Whist, when he and his wife returned from dinner in the Tongolele Room, here in the Norvue, they discovered the fire. Apparently it began in a nearby wastebasket, into which he had emptied an ash tray before leaving the suite. It would seem there was still a cigarette smouldering in the ash tray."

"Only the bed was damaged?"

"The mattress and bedclothes were ruined and the bed frame was charred. One wall was scorched considerably. That was all, other than a little smoke damage. Members of the staff were able to prevent the blaze from spreading." He paused. "Mr.

Whist was very apologetic. Of course, he paid handsome—paid for all the damage."

"Good for him. And then they left, huh? On this—vacation?"

"Yes, later that same night."

"Maybe they wanted to sleep in a bed that hadn't burned up."

He agreed that was possible.

"You haven't seen them since?" I asked.

"No."

"And you've no idea where they are now?"

"No," he repeated.

I shrugged. That was enough for the moment—especially since I was probably wasting my time to begin with. So I thanked the desk man and left. Left—after, of course, presenting him with a handsome gratuity.

I tooled the Cadillac back down to Vine, took a right and followed Vine into North Rossmore. The Spartan was only a block ahead on my left when I noticed that cock-eyed light again. At least I thought I did.

A small Corvair was directly behind me, but a block or so back one car had pulled out to pass another and then pulled in behind the small job. It was the second car back now, but when the driver had pulled into the left lane the headlights bounced on my rear-view mirror, and the left light was high, glaring.

I felt that queer, cool-nettle prickling beneath the surface of my back, as if the temperature of my spinal column had dropped a degree or two; I reached under my coat and rested my thumb on the butt of the Colt Special, handy in its clamshell holster there.

Then I slowed down, let the Corvair creep up on me, creep up and pass. I went on past the Spartan to Beverly Boulevard, pulled up at a stop sign there. The other car idled behind me, but I wasn't able to see who was at the wheel. I didn't delay overlong at the stop, just sat there a few seconds and then swung left into Beverly, as if heading back toward L.A.

The other car—it was a dark sedan, a late-model Dodge Polara—turned right, away from me. That wasn't what I'd expected. I drove on slowly, watching the Dodge as long as I could. It kept going straight up Beverly. Then I turned, headed back to the Spartan.

So, maybe I was nuts. Maybe it was a coincidence. Or even a different car with a cock-eyed headlight.

And maybe not.

Home is apartment 212, three rooms and bath complete with two tropical-fish tanks, Amelia—jazzy nude in bold oils—on the wall, yellow-gold carpet with thick shag nap on the living room floor; and on the carpet a low, chocolate-brown divan, two leather hassocks, the much-scarred coffee-and-booze table. and in the air—faint but still detectable by an expectant nostril—the scent of soft, and sweet, and spicy, and slinky perfumes and sprays and lotions.

Or maybe I imagined it. Lots of memories in that room. In all the rooms.

In the kitchenette I mixed a short bourbon-and-water nightcap, then showered, wrapped a towel around my middle and went back into the front room. For ten minutes I sat before the two aquariums, watching the little devils dart after the threadlike tubifex worms I fed them, and thinking about the three or four hours just past, the murder, nudity, people, motive, means, opportunity, Sybil, Mrs. Halstead, a car with a cock-eyed light.

After ten minutes of watching and thinking, I'd come to one firm conclusion. I was going to have to hospitalize the inch-long *Microglanis parahybae* bouncing himself on sand at the bottom of the community tank. Apparently he'd picked up some *Ichthyophthirius*.

5

I YAWNED OUT OF BED WHEN THE SECOND ALARM EXPLODED clangorously, planted my feet on the bedroom's black carpet, and swore dully.

One reason I like to stay up all night is because awakening is such a severe shock to my nervous system, and probably to my spleen, kidneys, and bladder. And one reason it's such a shock is because I so often stay up all night.

I pressed my hands against my head and sort of molded it back into shape, put the coffee pot on to perk and prepared to face the new day, slowly gathering my strength. For breakfast I had three bites of gummy mush with four cups of coffee. And began feeling almost alive.

This morning, after ablutions and shaving and such, I dressed in a lightweight, pale blue-green suit which, I knew, shimmered in the sunlight like clabbered electricity—which is more gorgeous than it may sound—added an appropriately lichenous tie, combed my hair with three fingers, and then checked my gun.

Ordinarily I carry an empty chamber under the .38's hammer since I would hate accidentally to shoot off a chunk of my latissimus dorsi or something even more desirable; but this morning I dug a box of cartridges from the dresser drawer and slid a sixth fat pill into the cylinder.

It wasn't that I had a premonition.

There was no creepy "feeling" that I might need to use even one, much less six, slugs during the hours ahead. At least there was no conscious awareness of any below-the-mind's-surface whispering.

Oddly, though, I felt more comfortable, a little more at ease, when I pressed the fully-loaded Colt Special back into its holster.

Then I phoned the L.A.P.D., got Homicide, and talked to Captain Samson for a minute. He knew about the Halstead murder, of course, but said there wasn't much on it yet. I told him I'd be down within the hour, and hung up.

On the way out I checked the two aquariums again. All was well in the small guppy tank, but my inch-long catfish in the big tank was clearly unwell. It was the Ick, all right: I could see the little white specks on his fins.

Trouble, trouble. I was going to have to give a treatment to the whole damned tank. If I wasn't careful, the little beggars could wind up with *Saprolegnia*. Then I *would* be in a pickle.

I netted the brown and pinkish-gray scavenger and put him in a separate temperature-controlled bowl, added a teaspoonful of two-percent Mercurochrome to the water in the community tank and a couple drops to the sick bay, then turned the thermostat up a couple of degrees and headed for downtown L.A.

Phil Samson, Central Division Homicide Captain, is more than just a good cop—though he is that, he for sure is that. He is also one of the most rigorously principled and finest men I've know in my thirty years. He's hard-boiled, yes, tough, at times unrelenting; and he takes no guff from anybody. And he will give a hood not an inch or even a quarter of an inch if the hood deserves no extra measure. Thus he would not by today's standards be judged compassionate, and today's counterfeit Solomons would—and have—reviled him as "unfeeling" and brutal.

There is not, however, a brutal or calloused cell in his big, hard body. He is simply efficient, dedicated, and abysmally honest, a man who believes justice is a virtue.

Probably he'd had his usual five or six hours of sleep, but Sam nonetheless looked wide awake. And—as usual—as if he'd just finished shaving, his pink face healthily glowing, brown eyes sharp and alert.

"And there he is," Sam said, looking up from stacks of papers on his desk as I came in. "There he is, the only private detective-nudist in the Western States."

"My, you're giddy this morning," I said. "What happened? Some crook actually get sent to the slammer?" I pulled a wood-

25

en chair over, sat down straddling it and leaned on the back. "Besides, *I* was not one of the nudists, Captain."

"Got the reports right here—"

"I was *not*—"

"Sheldon Scott, once again caught with his pants down—"

"No, that was the other citizens. Me, I was the one who broke it up. Where were *you* while I was acting as the city's conscience—"

"You're working for the Halstead woman?"

"Yeah, that's why I'm up so early. Lieutenant France told me last night a team was checking the Smiths—the couple who left the party early. They get anything?"

Sam rubbed his iron-gray hair vigorously. "Doesn't look like it. Rawlins was out to see them already this morning, just called in. He agrees with Lieutenant France they look clean."

Rawlins was a sharp, good-looking lieutenant who worked out of Central Homicide, one of Sam's top investigators. I not only liked him, but had a high opinion of his ability and judgment.

"What was the Smiths' story?" I asked Sam.

"Simple enough. Wife saw Halstead's legs sticking out from under some bushes, and thought he was snoozing, or maybe just resting up, so she tickled his feet."

Sam scratched his hair, then stuck out his chin—which closely resembles the back end of a dump truck—and scratched under it. "Tickled his feet. What kind of people are these?"

"Darlings," I said. "So, she tickled his feet. And?"

"Naturally he didn't let out a giggle or anything. So she gave him a yank."

"No."

"Yes. Grabbed one of his legs and yanked it."

"Yeah, they're a playful bunch. About then she must have begun getting the impression something was amiss, I'll bet."

"It looks like she figured out all of a sudden he was deader than a mackerel. Well, she didn't quite faint, found her husband and told him they had to leave right away, convinced him; they hightailed it out, and it wasn't till they were maybe halfway home—with him chewing the hell out of her, I gathered—that she told him what happened."

"Sounds straight enough. About the way it would've happened, I'd guess, if one of those gals stumbled over the dead host. Either that or lots of screaming. So they just forgot about it?"

26

"Something like that. Afraid to get involved. After awhile they figured out somebody would find the body before long, and realized they shouldn't have taken off in such a rush. Might look suspicious; they *were* involved just by having been there."

"Must have been about then the Hollywood police drove up to their house."

"Right. The woman had a small attack of hysterics, almost went up the walls. But Mr. Smith filled the officers in. Same story they got from the wife. Once she came down from the ceiling."

Sam scratched under his chin again.

"You got the Ick?" I asked him.

"Ick? What the hell's Ick?"

"It's what you and my catfish have got, I think. If you start breaking out in little white spots, be sure to take some Mercurochrome and raise your temperature ten or fifteen degrees—"

"I am impressed," he said, "with the sudden deterioration of your brain. I shaved too close this morning."

"No, it's the Ick—"

He scowled fiercely—which was something, since often when he smiled it was a fierce thing—and pulled a long black cigar from his middle desk drawer. That was ominous.

Those cigars were dandy cigars just as long as he didn't light them. But once lit, the odor of decaying mold and flaming skunk gas replaced all oxygen in the near atmosphere, whereupon I inevitably left.

"I was kidding," I said. "Sam, I'll be gone in a minute."

"You bet you'll be gone in a minute."

"Anything else from Hollywood—or Rawlins?"

"Odds and ends. Victim didn't seem to have any real enemies, nobody that stands out, anyway. Pretty well liked. Successful investor, owned a lot of blue chips and several thousand shares of speculative aerospace stocks, good marriage, lots of friends." He shrugged. "Something'll turn up."

"Yeah. How about the party? Had they been sneaking up on the deviltry for a year and a half, or was it just—"

"Spur of the moment. The Halsteads had a couple named Bersudian over for bridge, got to drinking and called the Smiths. A little later they phoned Mr. and Mrs. Pryer, and it happened two other couples were with the Pryers. So they all went over."

"No friction anywhere in the bunch, huh?" I paused. "Of course, I didn't get the impression they despised each other."

Sam shook his head, stuck the cigar in his wide mouth and growled around it, "Haven't turned up a thing yet. Maybe he threw the rock 'way up in the air, and when it came down—"

"Uh-huh. Well, I see no advantage in having a police department at *all*—"

Sam lit a match.

"Don't, Sam. Ah, have a heart, old buddy—Sam."

Holding the match poised, he said, "You have been milking my brains, yet have not even once told me how to solve the case. Or that you have already overcome its perplexities. This isn't like you, Shell."

"I know. Well, there are two or three little tidbits you might want to check on." I paused. "I might have stumbled on something that wasn't repeated after the police arrived." He'd blown the match out, so I continued, "I told the officers about the dandy nudist camp, didn't I? I'll admit they probably would have, ah, uncovered that intelligence themselves, but I saved them a little time, didn't I? Maybe a week? Besides, I left out how it must have happened. The way I figure it, they were all sitting around in the house watching TV commercials, some of those real *good* ones, and they all got so charged up—Sam. Sam —don't. There were some *other* couples who maybe were at the party earlier last night. Before I got there. Maybe. Also there's an intriguing item concerning people named Whist."

"Well, hurry up," he said.

I told him all I knew. It didn't take long.

At that point Sam lit his cigar. But by then I was ready to leave anyway. And Sam, of course, was aware of that.

Mrs. Riley came to the door when I rang.

I still hadn't found any trace of Mr. and Mrs. Whist, though I'd tried. I'd put some lines out among individuals who'd proved efficient at digging up odd bits of info for me in the past, but without luck so far. I had, however, already talked to Mrs. Bersudian, and to Mr. Warren in the plush offices of his law firm. I had also called at the Sporks' residence, but found nobody at home; Sybil hadn't even been in the back yard.

I'd come up with nothing concrete, that is, nothing I hadn't learned last night or from Samson this morning; but one of the case's intangibles had taken on a little more importance in my mind.

It was so intangible that I didn't even know what the hell it was. But it had become increasingly evident that nearly all of the people I'd talked to were twitchier than bats in the moonlight. It was difficult to get anything out of them except an impression that they weighed every word at least twice before reluctantly using it.

That's not uncommon when people talk to an investigator, but this was something more; and I had the feeling that nobody had yet told me all that could be told. Mrs. Riley wasn't much different from the rest of them. But, at least, before the interview was over I'd learned one item of exceeding interest.

I hadn't phoned before dropping out—I rarely do when on a case since an individual unprepared for interrogation has less time to prepare a possibly phoney story—so at the door I identified myself and told Mrs. Riley why I was there.

She was pleasant enough about it. Sometimes you find a door slammed in your face, or get hit with a mop. But Mrs. Riley smiled and asked me inside.

She was a handsome gal about thirty, or perhaps two or three years over the mark, slim and curvy and with a lazy, languid way of moving. She was wearing a simple but bright print dress and had a pink bandanna over her hair, which appeared to be put up on those big plastic curlers, judging by the lumps in the bandanna. Either that, or she had a very funny head.

"Well, come along inside, Mr. Scott," she said. She sounded like a Southern gal. It wasn't accent so much as the easy, drawly way she talked.

I went along inside, and we got seated in the living room, she on an emerald-green couch and me on a big greenish-blue ottoman near it.

I asked her if she knew about Mr. Halstead, and she said, "Yes, isn't it a terrible thing? He was the sweetest man." She shook her head. "I just can't conceive of anybody wanting to kill him like that."

"I was hoping maybe you could, Mrs. Riley. I mean, that you might know of someone he'd had trouble with, friction, business problems. Anything that might help explain why he was killed."

She shook her head some more.

I went on, "That's the trouble. So far, I get the picture of a man everybody liked, a man with no real enemies."

"That's the way he was."

"Yeah. Only somebody, obviously, failed to share the general opinion of Mr. Halstead."

"Are you working for the police, Mr. Scott?"

I'd showed her my wallet card at the door, but I said, "I'm a private investigator. Mrs. Halstead hired me last night while I was at her home. By the way, what time were you and Mr. Riley out there last night?"

"Last night?" Her eyes widened. "Why, we weren't there at all. We haven't even seen George and Ann for—oh, for weeks now."

"That's funny."

"What's so funny about it?" she asked, just a little snappish.

"I heard you'd dropped out there, that's all. You and another couple, the Whists."

"Well, you certainly heard wrong . . . The Whists?"

"Yeah."

She gave me a very funny look. "What did you mean by that?" she asked finally.

"Nothing stupendous. A guy simply told me you'd been at the Halsteads', that's all. I think. Granted, he was about eleven sheets to the wind and changed his mind very speedily. In fact, he said he must have been thinking of some other time."

"Who was it? Who said that?"

"One of the guests."

"Who?"

"One of the guests," I repeated.

"I'll bet it was Gregor."

Gregor was Mr. Bersudian. I didn't tell her it hadn't been Gregor. Instead I asked, "Why him?"

"He drinks like a fish. Like a whale. It was him, wasn't it?"

"What difference does it make? Apparently the guy was full of beans as well as booze. Look, I'm not accusing you of anything, Mrs. Riley. I'm simply trying to determine the facts. If you and Mr. Riley were at the Halsteads' place last night, fine. If not, also fine. Just tell me—"

"We were *not* there."

"That's all I wanted to know."

"Maybe the Whists were, but *we* weren't. I wouldn't know about them." There was something a bit snappish in her tone again.

"O.K.," I said. "That settles that. I'd also like to ask the Whists, however. Can you tell me where I might find them?"

"They live at the Norvue."

"Not any more, they don't."

There she went again, giving me that glittery eye. "They don't? They've moved?"

30

"Yes."

"Where to?"

"Beats me. They didn't leave a forwarding address. I'm not even certain they've moved. All I know is they're not at the Norvue now."

"It doesn't surprise me." Her lips curled a bit. "No, it doesn't surprise me."

"Oh? Why not?"

"Never mind. It's not important."

Here we go, I thought. She seemed to withdraw, sort of retreat inside herself. It was that bats-in-the-moonlight bit again. And it was beginning to sour on me.

I stood up. "Look, Mrs. Riley. *Maybe* it's not important. I'm not here bothering you just for fun, but because George Halstead got slammed in the head and died suddenly of scrambled brains. We're talking about a murder."

She winced slightly when I said "scrambled brains," and then looked at me as she bit on her lower lip.

I went on, "If you truly don't know a thing I might be interested in hearing, O.K. I'll get out of here. But if you do, if you even think maybe you do—"

She interrupted me. "It's just that . . . well, I don't think their name is Whist. That's all."

"It might be plenty. What makes you think that?"

"Well, I'm not really sure. And if I'm wrong, I'd hate to—"

And so on. I told her not to worry, that I'd check everything out, but it took another minute of coaxing and even getting a little red in the face before she finally gave voice to her suspicions.

They had met the Whists—"*if* that's their real name"—four or five months ago. They went out together several times, then one afternoon the Rileys had picked them up at the Norvue to take them to lunch.

"We went to the Beverly Hills Hotel," she said. "For some reason, they didn't want to go there. But we'd reserved a table and had a special lunch prepared and all. So we went anyway."

"How do you know they didn't want to go there?"

"They said so. Said they'd rather go somewhere else."

I nodded.

"While we were having lunch, a Mr. Edward Walles was paged. That's Walles—W-a-l-l-e-s—Edward Walles," she said.

"Hold it a minute. This was over the p.a. system?"

"One of those cute bellboys walked around saying there was a phone call for him."

"Well, either way, how could you tell the spelling of the name—particularly an odd one like that—just from hearing it pronounced?"

"Oh. I must have left something out."

"I'll bet you did."

"Two or three weeks before then, my husband and I were over at their place for dinner. At the Norvue, I mean. We, well, we were playing bridge. I was dummy and went to the bathroom. And I happened to see a stack of mail, two or three letters on the dresser. They were addressed to Mr. Edward Whist—only one of them wasn't. It was addressed to Mr. Edward Walles."

"Uh-huh. So maybe it was delivered by mistake. It happens. I've got mail meant for people named Wangler and even Barshfergenweis. Occasionally the post office—"

"But the letter had been opened. He wouldn't open it if it wasn't for him, would he?"

"Not if he's a nice fellow. But if it revealed some dark secret, I wouldn't think he'd leave the thing lying out in plain sight."

"But it wasn't. The letters were in the bedroom."

She stopped.

I waited.

Finally I said, "In the bedroom, huh?"

She gazed at something depressing in the corner of the room. I looked, but couldn't see it myself.

In a moment she went on, "Did I say bedroom? Well, that's because . . . because the letters were there. On the dresser. You see, the prettiest bathroom is just off the master bedroom. You have to go through it to get to the bathroom. Does it matter?"

"Not to me, it doesn't."

"There's more than one bedroom. And I just happened to see the letters. My eyes just happened to fall on them." She paused. "I wouldn't want you to think I was an old snoop."

"Perish the thought. What else about the letters?"

"That's all. I'm explaining how I knew the spelling of the name when I heard Mr. Walles paged."

"Got it. O.K., go on."

"After they paged Mr. Edward Walles—we're back at the Beverly Hills Hotel now, all right?"

"Swell. Incidentally, when was this?"

"Oh, about two months. Yes, almost exactly two months now."

"O.K. You're ready for lunch."

"Yes. Well, when they paged this Walles, Ed and Marcelle *looked* at each other. You know."

"I'm not certain I do. You mean, that ... told you something?"

"It was the way they looked. Like they weren't really looking at each other."

"What does that mean?"

She was disappointed in me, I think.

She eyed me for a second or two, then said, "It was—oh, goodness. A *woman* would know. The important thing is right after that Ed excused himself and left the dining room."

"Maybe he had to go to the, ah, the master bath?"

"No, he didn't. I had to go myself, and on the way I saw Ed picking up one of the house phones. So he was taking that call for Edward Walles."

"It's certainly a possibility. One of approximately three-point-two thousand possibilities."

"It's what he was doing, you can bet. After all, there was that letter to him at the Norvue."

"Yes, you've got a point there."

She did at that.

I mulled it over, then looked at Mrs. Riley. "O.K. You make a pretty fair case. So why, if their name is Whist, would they claim to be named Walles?"

She shrugged.

I said, "Or it could be the other way around. Why, if their real name is Walles, would they tell you it was Whist?"

She shrugged again. "For all I know, their real name may be Bargenshwaffer ... or whatever you said."

"That might be it—I just made it up. Well, I'll check on this, Mrs. Riley. Who knows, it might be very important." I paused. "You don't like the Whists much, do you?"

She frowned, and I thought she wasn't going to answer. But then she said, "Oh, Marcelle's nice. I liked her. But I never did *really* like Ed. He's pleasant and certainly good looking enough. But there was ... oh, just something about him. Something I felt."

"Uh-huh. By the way, do you happen to have a picture of them?"

33

She sure gave me a lot of twangy looks, this one. "Why did you say that?" she asked me.

"Well, I know roughly what he and his wife look like, but a photo might help me find them. As the Chinese say, one picture worth ten thousand word."

"Do the Chinese say that?"

"Ah—somebody, who cares? I just want to make things as easy on myself as I possibly can, since there is something very twitchy in the air ... Never mind. I thought, perhaps you and the Whists, or Walleses, or Fergenbashers, or whoever they are, while getting snockered in a nightclub might have paid one of those leggy camera girls to preserve for all time the memory—"

"Oh, no. We never did that. I don't have any pictures of them. I'm sorry."

"It's all right. Can you think of anything else about them—or other friends of the Halsteads, for that matter—that perhaps I should know?"

She couldn't.

On the Pasadena Freeway, heading back toward L.A., I reached under the Cad's dash and grabbed the mobile phone, checked with information for a phone in the name of Edward Walles. There wasn't any listed, so I put a call through to my own number in the Hamilton Building.

Hazel, the cute and bouncy little gal on the switchboard down the hall from my office, answered, "Sheldon Scott, Investigations."

"Oh, it is not," I said. "It's Hazel, down at the end of the hall."

"I'm surprised you remember my name," she said. "It's been so long since I saw you here at work, I thought you'd died."

"You poor kid. How you must have suffered—"

"Actually, it was kind of a relief. What do you want, Shell?"

"You, You, you, you! Don't I keep telling you? Hazel! I—"

"Shell, it's time I told you the truth. I'm still a virgin."

"O.K., I'm trying to find a guy named Walles." I spelled the name, adding, "Edward Walles, wife's name Marcelle. Maybe. These might be people who use half a dozen names."

"Are they in Los Angeles?"

"You've got me. I'm hoping they're still in the L.A. or Hollywood area. Last-known address the Norvue, registered as Mr. and Mrs. Whist. Left there about four weeks ago, present address unknown."

"All right. Hospitals and morgues?"

"Might check the morgue. Don't waste time on the hospitals for now."

"It's an unusual name. That might help. Where will you be, Shell, if you're not in the car?"

"I'm not sure at the moment. Keep trying the Cad—I'll call again if I'm going to be gone for a while." I paused. "Hazel, you *must* be kidding."

She pulled the plug.

It took her half an hour.

During that time I stopped at the Norvue, but didn't learn anything more. None of the people I talked to had an address for the Whists, and the name Walles didn't mean a thing to any of them. From there I drove on out Sunset to Beverly Hills and the Beverly Hills Hotel. I didn't find my quarry, but I did at least pick up the scent.

Mr. and Mrs. Edward Walles had occupied a suite at the hotel for five months, and had checked out two months previously. More precisely, three days less than two months.

Clearly, just about the time of the Rileys' luncheon there with the "Whists."

It was becoming interesting.

Especially since—if the Whists were also the Walleses—they'd been paying for a suite at the Beverly Hills Hotel even while living, at least part of the time, in the Norvue.

When the attendant brought my car I climbed in and let it roll down the curving drive to its end, stopped and waited to swing into the traffic on Sunset.

I'd noticed the guy standing at the right edge of the drive, lighting a cigarette. But what the hell, he was just a guy lighting a cigarette. At least he was then. But not when, as I gawked to my left eyeing the traffic stream, he opened the Cad's door and slipped onto the seat.

Then he was a small, thin-faced and thin-lipped guy with a history of youthful chicken pox mapped topographically on his young-old face and a heavy gun in his right fist—the usual gun, the big one, the cliché gun, a Colt .45 automatic. Cliché, maybe, but not comical. They can just about cut a man in two.

And I knew Kestel—that was the creep's name, Lester Kestel, commonly called Bingo for some reason I never took the trouble to discover—had cut up a few.

He pulled the Cad's door shut with his free hand, and I felt my breath stop as I waited for the moment to take him—or to try to take him.

He saw my eyes flick from the automatic to his face, and said quietly, "You better look behind you, Scott."

6

SOMETHING IN KESTEL'S TONE CARRIED CONVICTION. MERELY his gun carried conviction, but it wasn't likely he'd have been standing there alone without a car nearby. A car and somebody at the wheel. Even before I looked I heard the soft swish of brakes being pressed and the faint sound of springs creaking.

A heavy black sedan, a new Lincoln, had pulled up on my left in the driveway. A hook-nosed, meaty-faced man was at the wheel; another guy sat on the driver's right, looking at me through the open window. I couldn't see all of his gun, only about an inch of the barrel and the fat round doohickey screwed over the muzzle. It was a silenced heat, a dumb-gat.

I looked back at Kestel. "Yeah, that big one of yours would make a lot of noise, wouldn't it?"

"Prob'ly hurt our ears," he said.

"What the hell is this?"

"Questions, questions," he said. "Grab a left into Sunset."

I looked back at the Lincoln. I didn't recognize the driver, but I knew the short, thick, square-faced sonofabitch smiling at me over his silenced pistol.

"Hello, Stub," I said. "I kind of hoped the worms had got you by now."

His smile didn't change. But it hadn't been much of a smile to begin with. He had an eyetooth out on the left of his smile. Stub Corey could afford to pay a dentist for repairs to his chops, too. I guess he was just a slob. Hell, I know he was a slob. Anyhow,

37

that eyetooth had been missing, to my knowledge, for two years.

That was how long it had been since I'd had anything to do with these guys. More than that. Even then we hadn't tangled head-on, hadn't shot at each other or even pounded on each other. I'd tagged one of their friends on a grand larceny rap and he was, so far as I knew, still doing his bit at Q.

He'd been a minor cog in the group to which Stub and Bingo belonged, not much loss, and there'd been no real friction generated. Just a lot of words, a few threats from the boys. Of course, it hadn't made them love me more.

I turned back to Kestel. "How's Jimmy these days?"

"Mr. Violet to you, Scott."

"Mr. Manure to me," I said. That's a loose translation of a most unpalatable comment, but when with hoods you talk the hoods' lingo, the language they understand.

He turned the gun's muzzle away from me, and let me look at its flat side. "One more crack and you get it in the teeth, Scott."

Most likely he meant it. But if he swung that heater at me I was going to pop him. And very likely get shot in the back of the head. Nonetheless I was going to pop him.

"Sunset," he said.

I put the car in gear, eased down on the gas pedal and took a left, rolling along close to the divider in the middle of the road.

"Right lane for now," Kestel said.

It was O.K. with me. For the moment, at least. I wanted a little time to think. I eased into the right lane, wondering what the hell. Why were these creeps and musclemen hard-boiling me—after all this time?

Also, how had they happened to pick me up here at the Beverly Hills Hotel? Tipped by somebody? Or on my tail for a while? I didn't expect Bingo to tell me all of that, but maybe he'd tell me a little.

"Nice morning for a drive," I said. "Where we going?"

"Questions, questions. But it ain't no secret. Don't worry. We ain't gonna kill you."

"I'm glad to hear it."

"Not unless you get jerky. But I like the way you're taking it, Scott. Just tool along nice and easy like this, and we won't kill you."

"Bag the bigmouth, Bingo. You should know by now it

doesn't impress me. If it's no secret, tell me where the hell we're going."

"Jimmy wants a little gab with you."

"So why didn't he call up and ask me?"

"You wouldn't of come."

"Yeah, you're right. I'd come to his funeral, but that's the only— Don't do it, Bingo."

It was pretty close. He'd hauled the gun back, and maybe was going to swing it. Maybe. He wasn't quite right in the head. Anyway, he didn't.

"So Jimmy Violet wants to see me, huh?" I said. "What about?"

"He'll tell you."

I saw the amber light start glowing on the dashboard. I did not, however, reach for the phone. Not just then.

First I said, "Let me tell you something, Bingo. I never had any reason to build a real gripe against you. Not before today. But you have now earned a spot near the top of my list."

"I just wet my pants."

"Hell, if the smell's a clue, it happened before you got in the car."

He started swearing in a high-pitched voice that got even higher. He was burning, on the edge—which was where I wanted him. On it, not over it.

"Hold it," I said. "Look at that, Bingo." I moved a hand—slowly—and pointed at the phone light.

Breath hissed between his teeth, but he didn't say anything. He really wasn't right at all in the head.

"You know what this is, Bingo? It's a phone. Radio-telephone, under the dash."

"So what?"

"So I'd better answer it."

"In a pig's rear end, you'll answer it."

"Listen, try to use your brains just once today. I know who the call's from, I've been expecting it. It's from my secretary—not really my secretary, but Hazel Green, the gal on the switchboard in the Hamilton."

He hissed a little more. "So? So what?"

"Use your conk, you saphead." I stretched it a little. "She knows I'm in the car—knows I'm *driving* the car, for that matter. If I don't answer she'll also know something's wrong. She'll know I've got trouble, or somebody else is driving the heap—"

"Shut up, lemme think."

"That'll be the day. If I don't answer she'll sure as hell tip the fuzz—"

"Shut up."

"O.K." I grinned at him. "If that's the way you want it, Bingo."

He wavered for maybe three seconds, then said, "Answer it." As I reached for the phone he added, "But make it fast. *Fast*, you get it? One wrong crack and she'll hear the shot herself."

I put the phone against my ear. "Hello."

"Shell, I got it. Edward Walles, a home on Beverly Drive in Beverly Hills." She gave me the number—clear up at the north end of Beverly, barely inside the city limits—then went on, "I checked the utility companies. Do you realize they've got electricity, and gas, and hot and cold running water in Beverly Hills?"

"Yes."

"So it's their home. In the name of Mr. and Mrs. Edward Walles."

"Fine," I said. "And thank you, Miss Green."

Then I hung up and looked at Bingo. "O.K.? That suit you?"

He was squinting his eyes, and his hand was so tight around the gun's butt that his knuckles were bloodless, but he said, "Sounded O.K. Yeah . . . O.K."

I'd figured it would sound O.K. to him. Bingo would certainly know I didn't have a personal secretary, and he probably knew there was a gal on the switchboard in the Hamilton. He might even know her name was Hazel.

But he wouldn't know about the way we usually yacked on the phone.

And very likely he didn't know her last name was not Green.

Bingo liked it that I was driving carefully, and slowly. Well, I like it too—now. So I continued to drive carefully, and even slowed down a little more. The slower the better from here on, as far as I was concerned.

"Jimmy still at the same place?" I asked Bingo.

"What's it to you?"

"Just making conversation."

"Well, don't. We'll be there soon enough."

"He put piranhas in that lake yet?"

"What's perahnus?"

"Little fish. You go swimming with piranhas, and they eat you up. Eat you alive."

40

"You're sure full of it, Scott. Jimmy didn't do nothing to the lake. It's like it always was. What's it to you? You planning to swim in and see him?" He laughed.

"I'm not planning to go at all."

He laughed at that, too. "You're going," he said.

One police car had passed us so far, traveling in the opposite direction on Sunset. The driver had taken a long look at my car —the sky-blue Cad convertible is pretty well known in the L.A.-Hollywood area. The radio car didn't turn around or come after us, but it was a start.

We drove into the Strip, past the swank nightclubs and restaurants, the small shops, hole-in-the-wall cafés and strip joints, the black Lincoln behind us all the way. But there seemed to be more police cars passing us now, in both directions. And a plainclothes car was a few yards ahead in the left lane. I knew it was a plainclothes car because I'd recognized two of the men— the four men—inside it.

The outcome was only a matter of time. What I didn't know was whether my getting shot in the stomach would be part of the outcome. My stomach—that's where Bingo held the .45 pointed with a sort of what-the-hell air. I suppose from his point of view, what the hell, it was my stomach.

We were still on Sunset, but from the talk of piranhas and the lake and such I figured Jimmy Violet was living at the same place where he and his crumby pals had been hanging out two years ago. That was in a big dump on several acres well up into the hills between Hollywood and North Hollywood, less than a mile off Laurel Canyon Boulevard. So I figured we'd soon be turning north, probably on Laurel Canyon. I was right. Bingo directed me, and I signaled well in advance just in case anybody was interested.

Well, there was lots of interest. It happened about a minute after we started up Laurel Canyon. The plainclothes car was still in front of my Cad, and it slowed to a stop. At the same time a black and white cruiser appeared a block ahead, coming this way. The black Lincoln was still right behind us, but there also seemed to be an unusual amount of traffic on this stretch of road, especially back there behind us.

"Hey, whatthehell," Bingo said as I came to a stop.

"You want me to crash into that heap?" I asked him.

"I don't want you should stop."

"O.K., wait'll I put the wings on, and we'll fly over—"

"Don't do nothin', that's a cop . . . Oh-oh."

You wouldn't believe how fast it happened. At least, Bingo didn't believe it. He just about had time for one more "Whatthehell," and then there were cops all over the place.

All four officers in the plainclothes car had poured out and were on their way back toward us, but the black and white cruiser had already braked to a stop on my left and, at the same time, a man yanked open the Cad's right-hand door.

Bingo jerked his head around, but before his chops had moved an inch I'd grabbed the .45 with my right hand and then swung my left in an increasingly speedy arc, which ended with a most satisfactory *chuncck* on the side of his jaw. Satisfactory. but not as lethal as I'd have liked, since I didn't really have opportunity to set myself and plant my feet, but it addled him. He didn't go clear out, but he slumped down in the corner and said, "Buh," or something like that. Then he shook his head slowly and said, "Whuh."

"The black Linc behind us," I told the guy who'd yanked open the door.

He shook his head. I glanced back and saw a plainclothes car, a black and white cruiser, and two motorcycles around the Lincoln. There were cops—and guns—everywhere you looked. I guess there were at least a dozen policemen, and I figured that was approximately the right number.

Stub Corey and the driver were getting out of the Lincoln, leaning forward with their hands on its top as the officer shook them down.

Bingo straightened up, rubbing the side of his face. "Where'd they all come from?" he said wonderingly.

The officer who'd pulled the door open was a detective sergeant, and I handed him the Colt .45.

"Here's Kestel's gun," I said. "He was—"

Bingo didn't let me finish. "Gun?" he said. "It ain't my gun. I ain't got no gun. Gun, you crazy? What would I be doing with a *gun?* Why, Scott and me, we was just takin' a drive. Then you guys started beatin' me up."

I looked at the sergeant and he looked at me. Neither of us said anything. There was no need. That was Kestel's story and he'd stick with it. And it was eight to five he'd be on the streets again an hour after he was booked. Hoods have expensive lawyers. And the hoods' expensive lawyers have read, with delight, all of our omniscient Supreme Court's decisions defining and clarifying the rights of hoods.

42

"Why don't you confess, Bingo?" I asked him. "Hell, it can't do you any harm."

"Confess what? I didn't do nothin'. Here we are, takin' a little ride and cops come out of the bushes. You beat me up. *Everybody* shoves me around—"

"You want me to sock you again, Bingo?"

He shut up.

I got out of the car and went back toward the Lincoln, A lieutenant named Dan Peterson, a gray-haired detective working out of the Hollywood Division, was standing before Stub Corey and the pudgy-faced driver with the hook nose and speaking to them as I walked up next to him.

I'd heard the refrain before. So, undoubtedly, had Stub and the other hood.

"—that you have the right to remain silent," he was telling them politely. "Anything you say can be used against you in a court of law. You have the right to the presence of an attorney to assist you prior to questioning and to be with you during questioning, if you so desire. If you cannot afford an attorney you have the right to have an attorney appointed for you prior to questioning. Do you understand these rights?"

Corey smiled, exposing the hole in his row of teeth. "What?" he said. "Would you say that again, officer?"

Peterson's jaw muscles bulged slightly, but he said, "Will you voluntarily answer my questions?"

"Why should I do that? You some kind of nut or something, officer?"

Peterson looked up at the sky, then stepped back, turned his head and nodded to me.

"Thanks, Dan," I said. "Spread my very large thanks around among the boys, will you?"

He smiled. "Stub Corey and Little Phil here," he said. "Who's the other guy?"

"Lester Kestel."

"Old Bingo, huh? What was going on?"

"He had a .45 in my gut. The boys were escorting me out to see Jimmy Violet."

"What for?"

"Nobody told me. I'll probably ask Jimmy after a while. I suppose you got Corey's silenced pistol. That should count as at least a misdemeanor—"

"Pistol, yeah," he interrupted. "No silencer on it, though."

He showed me the gun. There were grooves around the

43

barrel's end, but the bulky cylindrical silencer wasn't on the gun.

I swore—knowing we'd probably never be able to prove he'd ever had a silencer. Possession of which is a felony and thus illegal. Even today. And he just might have a permit to carry the heater.

I said, "It's probably around here, somewhere close. Stub must've had time to give it a toss before you grabbed him."

Peterson called over a uniformed patrolman, told him what to look for. He found it in a minute and a half. Stub Corey of course expressed great amazement when shown the silencer. "What in the world," he said, "is dat?"

Lieutenant Peterson quietly screwed "dat" over the bore of the gun he personally had taken from Stub Corey.

"I wouldn't of believed it if I hadn't seen it," Stub said, once again showing us the empty space in his grin.

I took a step toward him. "Stub," I said, "I think you need a tooth out on the other side. In the interest of harmony, balance, and beauty—"

Lieutenant Peterson grabbed my balled fist in his hands. "Easy, Scott. You want to get us all tossed in jail?"

"Yeah, that's right," I said. "At least I got to hit Bingo." I paused. "I just hope he doesn't sign a complaint. Hell, let me hit Stub, and they can both sign complaints."

"Be a good fellow, Scott," he said wearily. "We got enough troubles. O.K.?"

"O.K." I sighed. "Well, here's what happened."

I told him and then followed the gang down to the Hollywood jail and told it again to a stenographer. I signed the statement, jawed five minutes, and left. It was my guess that I was getting out of jail about half an hour before Stub Corey, Little Phil, and Bingo.

But even half an hour, I figured, would give me time to get to Jimmy Violet's hoodlum sanctuary before his boys were sprung.

44

7

I TURNED OFF LAUREL CANYON BOULEVARD, DROVE TO THE one-lane asphalt drive leading uphill to Jimmy Violet's home.

On the way I'd been worrying the knot of perplexity which had started growing when Bingo Kestel first slipped into my Cad outside the Beverly Hills Hotel.

I am not unacquainted with hoods. On the contrary, because my business is crime and criminals, the law and lawbreakers, hardly a day passes when I don't have some kind of contact with cons or ex-cons, gun-toters or musclemen. But I couldn't think of a solitary reason why Jimmy Violet would—all of a sudden—be interested in me.

It was that suddenness which perplexed me.

In the last month I hadn't been on a case which, even by a pretty good stretch of imagination, could be considered as in the area of Jimmy Violet's interests. Those interests were primarily such enterprises as gambling, extortion, prostitution, and "legitimate" investments into which he'd poured hot money. And the only case I was on at the moment was the job Mrs. Halstead had hired me to do.

Any connection between the Halsteads and Jimmy Violet struck me as extraordinarily unlikely. But the timing intrigued me more than a little. I'd taken the Halstead case late last night, and Jimmy's boys had braced me before noon today. It seemed an odd coincidence. And I'm a guy very leery of coincidences.

When I'd been talking to Bingo about Jimmy Violet's lake, it had not been just a play on words. The guy actually did own a lake. It wasn't anything like Lake Superior, but it was a respectable little body of water for a man-made job, approximately seventy-five by a hundred yards. Violet's house sat on an artificial island in the middle of the lake and could be reached only by the road I was on. Unless you wanted to climb a ten-foot-high fence and swim in—or maybe wade; I didn't know how deep the water was.

I didn't particularly want to know, either. If the lake was deep enough, there were probably already some guys down there tied to anvils. Jimmy wasn't known as a particularly forgiving fellow. It was said he didn't stay mad at a guy long, though, since he held no ill will for the dead.

The road ran out over the water to the roughly circular island, actually more like the end of a small peninsula including the road. From the air I imagine the picture would have been much like half of a dumbbell, which seemed appropriate, since there were usually half a dozen dumbbells on the premises. You couldn't just drive out to see the dumbbells, though. First you had to pass through a heavy gate made out of what appeared to be two-inch steel pipes. And to accomplish that, you had to get the approval of a guy at the gate, a guy named Fleck who looked like Gargantua, and who appeared to be made out of four-inch steel pipes.

Fleck, at any rate, was the boy who used to be on the gate. Yes, he still was. Opening and closing it probably taxed all his creative powers to the utmost, but at least he was good at it. You might almost say of him that he was that most fortunate of men, one who had found his niche. Of course, presumably his duty was not merely to open and close the gate for invited visitors, but to kill anybody who wasn't invited.

He'd lumbered into view from behind a green hedge near the gate's pipes and stood on massive legs, his thick arms dangling at his sides. His resemblance to the Missing Link was remarkable. His head sort of came to a point in front, between his little red eyes, and his chin looked like something Samson might have slain the Philistines with. At the end of his dangling right arm, like a toy in the huge hand, was a large gun, which he seemed to dangle toward me as I got out of the Cad and walked to the gate.

"Hello, Fleck," I said agreeably. "Open up."

"I remember you," he said. "Don't I?"

"Man, if you don't know, how would *I* know? Shell Scott, I was here a couple years ago."

"Couple years." He shook his head.

I knew what he was thinking. *Couple years,* he was thinking. *How long is that?*

He'd heard my name though—recently. If Jimmy had been expecting me and the boys he would have told Fleck.

"Yeah," Fleck said finally. "Jimmy says . . ."

He stopped and looked carefully at my Cad. Then he looked behind it. Then he looked all around. Clearly, no boys were anywhere about. Finally he looked way up in the air.

"Fleck," I said, "are you looking for Stub and Bingo and Little Phil?"

He fixed the red eyes on me again. "Well, yeah, I was."

"They'll be along later. Open up."

"Well . . ."

"I had quite a talk with Bingo. Open up. Didn't Jimmy tell you I was coming out?"

"Yeah, but . . . But . . ."

"Well, O.K., if you don't want me to see Jimmy. See if I care," I said. Sometimes it helped to talk to him like that.

He shook his head. Then he opened the gate.

I climbed into the Cad again and drove past Fleck, who was still shaking his head, and on up the asphalt drive, which curved in front of the house and ended at a wooden two-car garage, which was past the house and near the water's edge. The garage door was open and two Cadillac sedans were visible. I braked to a stop a few yards behind them.

On my left was a small strip of grass growing from the edge of the asphalt down to the water, and on my right was the home of Jimmy Violet. It was a two-story brick and wood job, very attractive on the outside. Inside, it was a dump. At least it had been the last time I was here.

On that occasion I'd called upon Jimmy Violet at my own request, trying to get information about the lad I'd tagged on the grand larceny rap. I hadn't got any info; and I had found Jimmy Violet a nauseating host, but we'd each learned to know the other a little better. We'd each learned we loathed the other.

The place was a dump not because it hadn't originally been rather tastefully furnished, but because there was dust and all kinds of slop around. Jimmy wasn't married—I understood he had once been years before—and lived in the house with some of his hoodlum associates, none of whom was any more neat and tidy than Jimmy himself.

I walked to the front door, but it opened before I reached it.

47

The guy looking out at me—and at the emptiness behind me—with an expression of vast suspicion was one I hadn't seen before. He was tall and broad shouldered, with a sharp chin and ledges of bone over his eyes, but I didn't know who he was.

He knew who I was, though. At least he did after looking me over, checking the white hair and brows, giving me the head-to-toe perusal.

"You're Scott, huh?" he said.

"That's right."

He didn't ask about my three recent companions. "O.K. Come on in."

I walked past him and turned.

He said, "I suppose you got a gun on you."

"Yeah."

"I'll take it."

"You'll play hell."

The chin slid forward slowly and his brows lowered.

I said, "Jimmy wanted to see *me,* remember. I didn't have to come out here."

"You didn't have to? What . . ." He let it trail off.

"I suppose you're wondering," I said, "about Bingo and Stub and Little Phil. The sooner you escort me to mine host, the sooner I can tell him about them."

"What about them?"

"I'll tell Jimmy."

He chewed on the inside of his lip for a moment, then shrugged. "Come on," he said.

We walked down a carpeted hallway toward the back of the house and stopped before heavy double doors on our left. My escort knocked twice, then went on in, leaving me outside. After about a minute he opened the door and motioned me in. I suppose he had to explain to Jimmy that I'd arrived without company and presumably armed to the teeth.

Jimmy Violet wasn't alone in the big room, which was some kind of den with a polished mahogany bar against the right wall. Two other guys—beside my escort—were sitting in upholstered chairs drinking beer from bottles.

Jimmy slouched on a gray couch across the room from me, legs crossed and one hand behind his head. He didn't get up when I came in.

"Hello, Jimmy," I said. "You wanted to see me?"

"Where the hell's Stub and Bingo and Phil?"

No Hello, no How are ya, no nothing. No graciousness at all.

You could almost tell by looking at the creep. He was what you might find in a cemetery at Full Moon, near a newly-opened grave. Tall, rangy, cadaverous, he had the look of mortuaries, winding sheets, and shrouds. In his own way, he was just as cute as Fleck out at the gate.

He was an inch or two taller than I am and weighed maybe two hundred pounds, but he looked wasted, as if he'd been a heavier man but was sickening of a disease. His eyes were dark, dull, with sparse brows above them; and his hair, black streaked with gray, was thin and limp and lay flat on his round skull. His lips were fat, cupidlike, but not rosy; they were a kind of pinkish-gray, not quite as ashen as his face. I guess his nose was the only reasonably nice thing about that face, a bit long maybe, but straight and possessed of only two nostrils.

There was an empty overstuffed chair a few feet from the couch on which Jimmy Violet lounged, so I walked toward it.

"Mind if I sit down?" I said.

"I asked you a question."

"I heard you. Mind if I sit down?"

"Ah, go ahead and sit. Sit on your head if you feel like it."

The guy who'd brought me in here had walked over to stand near the two men already in the room. I turned the chair a little so it not only faced Jimmy Violet but afforded me a view of the three other men, and sat.

"Where the hell's the boys?" Jimmy asked.

I grinned. "What's the matter, you think I shot them?"

"You bastard, don't give me no lip—"

I interrupted him. "Don't call me names, Jimmy. I get upset when creeps call me names. And I'm more than a little upset already."

"I don't give a gahdamn what you are," he said. "I asked you —"

"Stow it. You wanted me to come out here. O.K., I'm here. Tell me what you've got in mind, and maybe I'll tell you what you want to know."

He opened his mouth, then closed it. "O.K. It won't take long. I figure you got enough sense to know a word to the wise when you hear it. So here's the word. Lay off the Halstead thing. Just drop it. I'll see you don't lose no money about it; that's on the one hand. On the other, well, guys get killed every day making dumb mistakes."

It really jarred me. Not the threat—that was par for the Jimmy Violet course—but his blunt reference to Halstead.

True, I had toyed with the idea that there might be some kind of connection—because I couldn't think of any ot_er reason why Violet would want to see me—but I hadn't really believed it.

"Halstead?" I said. "The guy who bought it last night?"

"Who else? There some other Halstead?"

"What's your interest?"

"My interest is, you lay off, you get it? It's simple. Just forget it. You won't lose nothing by it—"

"Save your breath."

"Look, don't be a jerk. I'm giving you a good out—"

"I said, save your breath."

The dull dark eyes seemed to get even duller. He took the hand from behind his head, slapped his thigh with it. "I shouldn't of tried it this way," he said finally. "That's what I get for trying to be a nice guy."

I laughed.

"All right, what's with the boys?" he said.

"Bingo and Stub and Little Phil are enjoying one of the sights of Hollywood which they seldom see, namely the Hollywood can. The clink, the slammer, the jail. In fact, if you haven't got a call already; the phone should soon be merrily ring—"

He didn't let me finish. He uncrossed his legs, leaned forward, started getting to his feet. "You're lyin'!" he yelled. "You dumb crud, they ain't in jail. Where they at?"

I closed my eyes, shoved my teeth together, then opened my eyes. "I'm not going to tell you again about the bigmouth, Jimmy. Your boys picked me up and tried to do your bidding, but I managed to tip the fuzz, and the boys are indeed in the can. Temporarily, at least. I hope, of course, that they get electrocuted or something infinitely worse, but they're being booked, mugged, and printed, at least."

He stalked over the carpet, stopped before me and leaned down, his face a couple of feet from mine. "You dumb sonofabitch," he yelled. "Who the hell you think you are? You stinking son—"

That was all he said for a while.

I got him on his nice nose. Well, reasonably nice. Before I got him on it, that is. It was practically the same situation as when I'd popped Bingo in my Cad: I wasn't able to get set, get any real leverage or power into the blow. But I did my very best, and threw my left arm up, turning my body and pressing with my left foot against the floor in front of my chair; and all in all it was a fairly satisfactory operation.

50

My knuckles covered his nose and upper lip and made a surprisingly loud and meaty sound when they landed. He did not quite do a back flip. But his head snapped back and he traveled about nine feet, arms flailing, before he fell with a thump to the floor at the end of the couch where he'd been sitting.

All three of the guys on my right were reaching, two of them for their hips and one for the gun under his coat, but while I may not be the most brilliant fellow under the heavens only an idiot could have failed to anticipate that development. So I was a little ahead of them.

As soon as I'd clobbered Jimmy with my left hand, I'd grabbed the Colt Special in my right and flipped it out to cover the three men.

One of them—the tall broad-shouldered guy who'd met me at the door—almost didn't stop, almost yanked out his heater anyway. But he decided against it at the last moment. Just as my finger was tightening on the .38's trigger.

Then he relaxed.

"You don't know how close you came to it," I said.

He licked his lips but didn't say anything, pulling his eyes from my gun to look at Jimmy Violet.

Jimmy was still on the floor, but he wasn't unconscious.

Well, maybe I hadn't knocked him clear out, but I'd done his nose no good, and the event had given me a lot of satisfaction. Even if I did seem to be losing my punch. I'd had enough of his bigmouth to begin with. And I guess you know, ever since Bingo slid into my Cad I'd been itching to hit somebody. Most important, however, I do not cotton to guys who send me invitations at gunpoint.

I glanced at the door on my right and partly behind me. It was still closed, and nobody else had come into the room. If anybody had, I presume I would by that time have been shot in the skull. But all was—for the moment—under control, so I turned most of my attention to Jimmy Violet.

His legs were moving, and he was clawing with his fingers at the carpet. In a few more seconds he managed to sit up. Blood from his already swollen nose smeared his mouth and chin. It was pretty messy, but at least it gave his face a little color.

He was so mad he wasn't thinking straight. Or else he wasn't seeing straight, and couldn't see the gun in my hand. He sat there on his duff and reached under his coat and grabbed a

51

small revolver. He had it out of the shoulder holster when I let one go right past his ear.

The blast of the shot was loud in the room, and his ears, if not his eyes, must have told him he was embarking on the wrong course. I didn't even have to tell him to drop the gun; he let go of it while his hand was still moving and the small chrome-plated pretty—a lady's gun, I would have called it—bounced across the floor toward me.

It was quiet.

I glanced at the three men.

Jimmy pushed a hand over his mouth, then leaned forward and spat on the carpet. Slowly he got to his feet.

And the phone rang.

It was on the bar top, behind the three men. I walked over there and answered it.

A high-pitched voice said, "Gimme Jimmy, quick."

"O.K. Who's this?"

"Bingo. Get Jimmy . . . who's talkin'?"

"He'll tell you," I said. "At least, I imagine he will."

"Is—is it Scott? It can't be. Crud, it can't be."

I looked at Jimmy Violet and pointed to the phone, then put it down and moved back to my easy chair.

"Yeah," he growled into the mouthpiece. "Yeah, this is Jimmy." He listened a moment. "Yeah, it was, all right. Yeah, so he's nuts. Sure he's nuts, who's arguing? Yeah . . . yeah . . . huh. Right . . . I'll see you here, then. You sure did a fine job, sweetheart. I can really count on you, can't I? Well, hurry it up."

Jimmy put the phone back on the hook, wiped his nose gently with a handkerchief, then glared at me. "Blow," he said. "We got no more to talk about."

"I hope you don't have any idea it might be fun to let one of your boys shoot me on the way out. You just talked to Bingo. So you must know—or can guess—that six thousand cops are aware that I'm now calling on Jimmy Violet. They'd love to get something on you. Especially a murder rap."

He glared at me some more. "It'd almost be worth it."

"But you know better, don't you, Jimmy?"

He stared at me for a few moments longer, then looked at his three men. Slowly he nodded. He was telling them they couldn't kill me, even if they got the chance. Not right now anyway.

It changed the situation enough that I stopped covering the

men with my gun. But I didn't put it away, just let it rest on my thigh.

"Tell me, Jimmy," I said. "What's your interest in George Halstead? One of your boys poop him?"

"Don't be a jerk. I got no more to say to you."

Well, maybe he'd said enough. But I hadn't. There was one more thing I wanted to tell Jimmy Violet.

"All right," I said. "But listen to this, you spook, and listen with both your big ears. If you ever send any more of your paid muzzlers after me, I'll come here again. Only I won't just bust you in the hook, James, I'll wipe you out."

The gaze he laid upon me combined the best of Dracula bending over a fair neck and Wolf Man with the scent of boiling blood in his nostrils, but he spoke gently. "I don't believe," he said, "I shall invite you again." He was quite grand at that moment, I had to admit.

I got up and walked to the door, not watching the door, however. The boys didn't twitch. I went out into the hall and waited ten seconds, then peeked back into the room. The four of them stood in a huddle, jabbering. But they weren't coming after me.

So I said, "That's the stuff," and left.

I drove to the gate with my left hand on the steering wheel and my right hand holding the Colt just out of sight below the door. But there was no trouble.

Gargantua swung the gate open, and even smiled at me as I drove through.

I put my gun away and headed for Beverly Drive in Beverly Hills.

8

So far in this case none of the houses I'd been in could have cost less than fifty thousand bucks, and a couple of them were surely over the hundred-thousand mark. Add to that the Norvue and Beverly Hills Hotel, and I was certainly traveling among the moneyed.

So it didn't surprise me that the Walleses' home was a big, low, ranch-style house behind an extravagant amount of well-watered and tended green lawn, a chunk of real estate worth at least a hundred to a hundred and fifty thousand clams.

I pulled into the gray cement drive and parked in an open carport near the front door, walked to the door and gave the bell a push.

Chimes played a pretty tune inside the house.

In half a minute the door opened and Edward Whist—or Walles—looked out at me, a pleasant expression on his tanned, good-looking face.

I was satisfied that this was the man I'd been looking for, even though I hadn't turned up a photograph of him, because he clearly fit the descriptions I'd got from several of the people I'd interviewed.

It was difficult to guess his age. Between thirty and forty somewhere. He was about six feet tall, maybe an inch less, well put together, with good, muscular shoulders and lean hips. He was wearing sandals, blue Bermuda shorts, and a white T-shirt. His hair was light brown, almost blonde, wavy and thick. Good

54

chin, a happy-go-lucky mouth, and vivid blue eyes—a very good-looking man.

I went ahead as I'd planned it on the way here.

"Mr. Edward Whist?" I said.

"Whist?" His brown eyebrows puckered, then he smiled slightly. "Well . . . yes," he said.

"I'm Shell Scott." I showed him my identification.

He nodded. "Sure, I've heard of you. What do you want with me, Mr. Scott?"

"I'm working for Mrs. Halstead. I suppose you know about George Halstead's death."

He nodded again. "Yes, I do. Read about it this morning, then called Ann right away. Hell of a thing." He paused. "But I still don't understand what you want with me."

"Well, I'm a little puzzled. Is your name Whist—or Walles?"

He smiled that oddly amused smile again. "It's Walles, actually. I—well, I used the name Whist for a while."

The guy puzzled me. I'd been prepared for belligerence, possibly even a violent reaction. But he didn't even seem embarrassed by my knowledge of his dual identity. Or whatever it was. He appeared to be more amused than anything else. Which certainly didn't strike me as the attitude of a man guilty of any fiendish crimes.

"Maybe you'd better come inside, Mr. Scott," he said.

"Thanks."

The house was cool, faint hum of air-conditioning—or smog-filtering—equipment audible. We went into a living room as big as some houses, thickly carpeted in a pale blue. There were a couple of divans facing each other with a low heavy table between them, the table top of gold-marbled mirrors. There were two or three chairs, a small table, and another table with a huge pink lamp on it against the wall near the divans. Against the far wall was a low custom-made stereo set. It was a pleasant room, not too much furniture, and all of it rich-looking.

We sat opposite each other on the two divans and I said. "Were you at the Halsteads' last night, Mr. Walles?"

"No, haven't seen them for some time, three or four weeks, at least."

"Incidentally, I'd like to talk to your wife, too, if you don't mind."

"I don't mind, only she's not here. Having her hair done downtown." He got to his feet. "If it's important, I can call her."

"It's not that important. Not at the moment, anyhow. You can probably tell me all I need to know."

"Well, as long as I'm up, I think I'll fix a drink. Join me?"

"Yes, I will, thanks."

"Scotch, bourbon, brandy, gin, vodka, you name it. Cointreau, Drambuie, rum, beer—"

"Bourbon and water sounds just right."

He walked to the stereo set, raised a segment of its top and pulled out some bottles, glasses, and even ice cubes. Well, I thought, that's one way to make music. In a minute he was back carrying two glasses.

He handed me my drink—dark with bourbon, but not too dark—and said, "You must have got the Whist bit from the Halsteads . . . Mrs. Halstead, I mean. But where'd you get onto my real name?"

I'd figured I would have to be very sly and clever—if possible—in order to worm from him the dark truth about all those names; but here he was attacking the problem himself. A private detective could hardly ask for more cooperation. I kept wondering where the hook was.

But I shrugged and said, "You're right about Whist. I dug up your real name—well, just legwork. For example, I know you had a suite at the Norvue under the name Whist. And one at the Beverly Hills Hotel in the name of Walles." I swallowed some of my drink, looking at him. "I hope you'd like to satisfy my curiosity about all these names and suites—in addition to your home here."

"Sure, be glad to. If . . ." He stopped for a moment, starting to frown. "Wait a minute. I'm not under some kind of suspicion, am I? If so, suspicion of what?"

I shook my head. "Suspicion of nothing, Mr. Walles. I'm simply talking to all the people I can find who knew the Halsteads, either in business or socially, and who might know something which could help explain why Mr. Halstead was killed."

"Uh-huh. Well, I won't be much help to you, I'm afraid. Ever since I read the papers this morning I've been wondering about that myself. Why anybody would kill him, I mean. You never met a more easy-going, pleasant guy."

"I'm still curious. Of course, you don't have to tell me anything if you don't want to."

He put his drink down on the table and lit a cigarette. "No sweat," he said. "I don't mind. But . . ." He picked up his drink again, had a swallow. "Well, I will say this, when Marcelle and I

—Marcelle's my wife—met the Halsteads, it was in a nightclub. We were all having fun, and it was just Ed and Marcelle, George and Ann. You know, buying each other drinks, yacking it up. They didn't know our last names—we didn't know theirs, for that matter. Not then."

He got up, sipped at his drink again and began pacing slowly back and forth. "Well, we had a ball. Great couple. Traded phone numbers, and a few days later they called us. We went out to dinner and during the evening we all had quite a lot to drink. They invited us to, well, a party they were having. Party, booze, meet some of their friends." He paused. "Well, uh, the way it sounded, we—Marcelle and I—just weren't sure we wanted them to know our real name."

"Could you make that a little clearer?"

He grinned and came back, sat down on the divan. "I could, but I'm not going to. Hope you don't mind, but that's the way it is. Anyhow, we saw them a few times, met some of the people they knew, palled around a bit you might say. Even had them up to see us a few times—that was at the Norvue. But, after a while, we just decided we'd had it. Frankly, we simply decided to drop them, the Halsteads and the whole bunch, not see them any more."

"Was there an argument? Trouble—"

"No, no. Nothing like that at all. On the contrary, there never was any trouble, no friction. It's just Marcelle and I agreed we'd be better off . . . ah, in with a different crowd. I suppose you'd have to know a little more about them."

I had a slug of the bourbon and water. It was good bourbon. "Maybe I do," I said.

He raised an eyebrow but didn't say anything.

So far this Ed Walles had impressed me very favorably. He seemed straightforward, candid enough, and he was certainly convincing. Especially since I thought maybe I knew part of his reason for leaving some gaps in his story.

But I said, "It would help if you told me some more about them."

"Nope. That's all I've got to say, Mr. Scott. Hell, you'll probably dig around and come up with—with the rest of it." He grinned. "But you're not going to get it from me."

"You sure live in a lot of places."

He laughed. "Oh, that. No mystery there. We live here—obviously. You know this is our home. We took a suite at the Norvue to have a place where we could entertain the Halsteads

57

and some of their friends from time to time. It was . . . expected of us. They still thought our name was Whist, and we wanted to keep it that way for the time being. Besides, by then it would have been a little sticky explaining why we'd given them another name in the first place. It gets a bit complicated."

"Yeah, it does."

It also made a weird kind of sense. A few pieces were falling into the pattern; and I thought I was beginning to understand why Walles might have acted as he had. Yes, it made pretty good sense; and I was still wondering where the hook was.

He went on, without urging from me. "I'm in product development. That is, I deal rather extensively in new products—with housewife appeal, mostly—sometimes financing the inventor or patent-holder, sometimes buying outright. Also I'm in the market substantially. I kept a suite at the Beverly Hills Hotel for some months. Place to meet and entertain possible associates, investors, other developers. It's not everybody you want in your home—Marcelle hates the hostess bit anyway. Besides the front's damned important, you know." He smiled.

"I suppose."

"Before the Hills, we had a suite in the Hollywood-Roosevelt. Earlier, at the Ambassador. Wherever the action is."

"Kind of an expensive way to live?"

He tossed that off with the flick of an eyebrow. "That, fortunately, isn't one of my problems. You have to spend money to make money. It's a business expense, anyhow. Costs next to nothing when it's deductible."

"The Norvue deductible?"

"Nope, not that. And I'll not list it as a deduction when I bare my financial soul for Uncle—you're not a spy for the Internal Revenue Service, are you?"

"Ye gods, no."

"I knew there was something about you I liked." He finished his drink. "Have another?"

I shook my head. "One's about it for now, thanks."

"Well, maybe we can have the second one on another occasion. I'd like for you to meet my wife. Bring three or four of your girls." He grinned.

His comment had sounded like a casual dismissal, but I didn't get up and say thanks for a charming time and leave. Not just then. Instead I said, "One other thing, Mr. Walles. When I checked at the Norvue I learned you had a little fire there—just before you checked out. That why you left?"

58

"No, we'd planned to leave that night—we didn't check out, by the way. Just let the lease expire. About the fire ..." He twirled his glass on the table top. "Ah, can I tell you something in confidence? I mean, with the assurance that you won't repeat it?"

"If you're leveling with me. And—" I smiled—"not covering up evidence of any crime, anything I'd be interested in as an investigator."

"Well ... good enough. No crime, not really. Thing is, that fire wasn't an accident. Not entirely."

"Come again? You deliberately set fire to the bed?"

He laughed—he seemed a happy fellow. "Not the bed. *That* was accidental. Of course, if you ever see Marcelle, you might think ..." He let it trail off, but I figured I got the idea. "The thing is, we burned something up in the wastebasket. Deliberately. Got a little out of hand and the damn bedclothes caught fire, and we had to yell for help. That was the accident; but the original burning was done on purpose, which is what I wouldn't want the Halsteads—Ann, that is—or the others, to know. I told them the fire was accidental."

"What did you burn up?"

He shook his head, but didn't answer.

I had the feeling there were some other things I should ask him; but I couldn't think of any really vital queries. I was there another ten minutes, but during most of that time Walles was asking me about my job, the work of a private detective. His interest, which seemed genuine, was flattering—show me the man who doesn't like talking about himself and his work—but it wasn't getting the job done.

So I stood up, thanked him for his time, and prepared to leave.

He shook my hand and said, "Sorry, I couldn't be more help. But, if it's necessary, I'll be here in case you've *got* to know more."

"I'll see how it goes. Thanks again."

He showed me to the door and I went out. Went out, still mildly bemused. All during our conversation I'd kept looking for the hook. But I had not found any hook.

I took Beverly Drive down to Olympic and swung left, heading for Robertson Boulevard. I'd already checked by phone with the Hollywood Division, on the way to the Walleses', so I knew Jimmy Violet's three musclemen were out of the clink, probably now back at Jimmy's expensive dump, which I'd recently left. I had also phoned Hazel to sing her praises for so speedily getting word to the police that I was in some kind of trouble.

So this time when I phoned in it was merely to ask if anything new had come up.

"Can you be in your office at two o'clock, Shell?"

"I guess so. Why?"

"I made a tentative appointment at that time for you. It's supposed to be very important."

"Somebody come in?"

"Appointment was made by phone. About twenty minutes ago."

I suppose because I still had the thought of Bingo and Stub and Little Phil in my mind I smiled and said, "I don't suppose the caller said his name was Jimmy Violet, did he?"

"Nobody's named Jimmy Violet. Besides, it was a woman. Very sexy voice, by the way."

"Indeed. Who?"

"She wouldn't give me her name."

"She say what's so urgent?"

"It's something to do with George Halstead. She said you'd know what she meant."

"Uh-huh."

I had so far today talked to Angelica Bersudian and Mrs. Riley. Maybe one of them had thought of something she'd "overlooked." Or it could be Mrs. Halstead, Mrs. Pryer, Mrs. Warren . . . who could say? Maybe even sizzling Sybil Spork.

"O.K., Hazel. I'll come in. You supposed to call her back and confirm?"

"No, she said she'd call in again. But it has to be two o'clock. That would be the only time she could get away, she said. Whatever she meant by that."

I looked at my watch. It was a few minutes before one p.m. "I'm on my way out to see a woman named Agatha Smellow, in Culver City. I should make it back to the office by two."

"Don't pick up any more little men with big guns, Shell."

"I'll try not, Sweetie. But if I should, I know who'll fix his wagon. And as a reward, I'll never again doubt anything you say."

"Well, it's all right if you . . . doubt a *little*."

I smiled, and hung up the phone.

I'd checked on Agatha Smellow's address and was looking forward to calling on her. So far, I'd met a number of exceptionally good-looking gals connected with the case—Halstead seemed to have had a propensity or knack for surrounding himself with lasses ranging from adequate to stupendous in appearance and not visibly overburdened with inhibitions.

I do confess that I enjoy talking to good-looking tomatoes not overburdened with inhibitions, and Agatha, Halstead's former wife, might turn out to be the choicest of the lot, the jackpot.

So I idly mused, not having the least idea what was in store for me.

9

AGATHA SMELLOW WAS NOT THE JACKPOT.

She was three lemons, and you get arrested for putting a lead nickel in the machine.

Moments after I rang the bell at the front door of the middle-bracket-nice house on a tree-shaded street, curtains fluttered behind a window on my left. Peeking out at me, I thought. Probably this gorgeous babe is in there alone, I thought; nude, dancing around the room to flutey music, trailing a couple of veils maybe. She'll wrap a towel around her wild, naked body and come to the door and peek out, and say in a sexy voice— sexy voice! Maybe she was the one who'd phoned Hazel—"I don't know who you are, but . . . I've been waiting for you."

It has happened before. Gal in a towel, I mean. More than once. Neither of them said "I've been waiting for you," and like that—but it *could* happen. One of these days it *will* happen. I'm a very optimistic fellow.

The curtains had stopped fluttering.

The door opened a crack, and—yes—she was peeking out at me. Just as I'd had it pictured.

I smiled. "Hello," I said.

"Go away."

"What?"

"Go away. I don't want any."

"Well, I . . . you don't?" I paused, got my thoughts lined up again, tinged with a bit less imagination.

To be certain, however, I said, "Don't want any what?"

62

"Whatever you've got."

"Well, erum, that should cover it. Ah, are you Mrs. Smellow? Mrs. Agatha Smellow?"

"Yes."

"My name is Shell Scott, Mrs. Smellow. I'm a detective, a private investigator. I have been employed by Mrs. George Halstead—"

"Her! Hah. Hoo. Her!" she said.

It came out "Herhahhooher!" like one word. I got the impression she didn't like Mrs. Halstead.

"Fooey to her," she said. "She probably killed the old goat."

Yes, it was a very definite impression. Maybe I should go by my impressions instead of my imagination, I began to think. Barely in time, for if I'd still been dreaming of gals dancing to flutey music the next few seconds might have sent me a bit off base.

Because I said, "Well, that's what I'm trying to find out, Mrs. Smellow. Who killed George Halstead, and why. I'd very much appreciate a few minutes of your time. . . ."

And she opened the door.

"All right," she said. "I've got nothing to hide."

Boy, truer words might not have been spoken since the Gettysburg Address.

If this gal danced around naked twirling veils the world would undoubtedly tip off its axis. She wasn't what I would call a tomato. Not even one of those little green, bumpy tomatoes. She was more like a cucumber.

Agatha Smellow was five-nine or so, with a figure approximately the contour of her bones, all that charm covered by a simple plain gray dress reaching well below where her knees might have been, which was probably fortunate; for, if the rest of her was the shade of her face, you could plant her and be reasonably sure she'd sprout in a fortnight.

"Do come in," she said.

I sighed, and went in.

It was a nice house. That was the word which sprang automatically to mind. Nice. A little drab for me, but then I'm a guy who likes a bit of color. We went into the living room—from which she'd been fluttering the curtains—and sat in comfortable overstuffed chairs covered in a rough brown fabric, and on the chair arms were crocheted white doilies, or whatever they call those things which keep falling off chair arms.

There was a beige carpet on the floor, quite thick and with a good long nap. A large color-television set stared like blinded Cyclops from a corner. On the wall was a framed piece of cloth with green yarn spelling out, "Home, Sweet Home." I read it twice to be sure.

"I gather you know of Mr. Halstead's death," I began.

"Yes. I prayed for him, but it didn't do any good. I knew this would happen."

"You knew he'd be killed?"

"Not that, not in so many words. I knew he'd come to no good end. I told him. Oh, you can bet I told him."

I'll bet you did, I thought. We chatted inconsequentially for a minute or two. She said, yes, they had been married for several years. Fourteen and a half years. Divorced four years ago. Yes, she'd filed for divorce, and had been awarded the judgment. She had seen the signs long, long before then, long, long ago. She'd seen the signs. Satan was creeping up on him.

"Who?" I said.

"Satan."

"Satan, huh? You mean, the old . . . the old Adam? No, not that one—the devil, you mean?"

"Yes, him, the Evil One."

It seemed cooler in the house than when I'd first come inside. The curtains were drawn over the windows—not a lot of light in the room—and Mrs. Smellow gazed at me, gazed her glassy gaze at me.

"I knew," she said. "I knew what was happening. I warned him. I did, you can bet I did."

"Uh-huh."

She fell silent. But she kept gazing her glassy gaze at me. I made some mild comment about the divorce, without specifically asking her what the grounds had been, but even without real encouragement she told me. It was as though she wanted to tell me about it, all about it.

"He committed the most heinous, the most awful, the most sinful thing a man can do."

"He did? I suppose you mean . . ." I stopped. That covered a lot of territory. What did she mean?

She told me. "I mean he broke his sacred vows."

"How?"

"You know."

"No, I don't. Not precisely. There's lots of ways. I suppose. I'm not an expert, of course. How would I know?"

"You're a *man!*"

64

"Well, thank you, ma'am. That's nice of you ... Wait. You mean—"

"Of course."

I thought I had it. Or at least a piece of it. But I wasn't sure how to pin it down, how to get it clear as could be. "Ah, perhaps you mean that Mr. Halstead, during the course of your marriage, committed that most ... um ... heinous sin of ..." It was pretty tough.

"He broke his marriage vows."

"Yeah. I had it figured."

"I caught him with her."

"Her? Might as well come right out with it. Another woman, you mean."

"What else would I have caught him with?"

"Beats me."

"Under my own roof. Actually in the bedroom!"

"Oh. Well, that *is* foul. In your own bedroom—"

"Not mine. His. There they were—in his bedroom." She made some mumbling sounds. It looked like she was going to get sicker than a dog, just remembering.

But she didn't get sick. Oddly, she appeared almost to get healthier there for a while, as she dwelled on it.

In fact, she dwelled audibly on it a bit more than I really cared to have her dwelling. So about a minute later I said, "I see. Then he had his bedroom, and you had your bedroom."

Her eyes were quite wide, and I would have sworn her chest bones were rising and falling more rapidly than at any time since I'd entered the house. Her face had a bit more color in it, too, sort of a brighter green.

"Yes," she said, the consonant drawn out in a soft hiss. "Yes —we had to have separate bedrooms. He was always wanting to ... It was the only way I could keep him from ..."

She didn't know how to finish it this time, herself. I tried to help her. "Like he was a regular wild animal, hey?"

"Yes, that's it. You do understand. A beast, a beast ... I know I shouldn't speak ill of the dead. But he was a terrible, awful, fiendish, *immoral* man, may his soul rest in peace."

"Well, you've certainly helped me get an insight into his character, Mrs. Smellow. I was, of course, hoping you might be able to give me a lead to something I've been unable to dig up as yet. That is, an indication of who might have hated him enough to kill him ..." I let it trail off. So far, Mrs. Smellow was the only person who appeared to fit the description.

But I shrugged that wild idea off and continued, "A motive for the murder, or—"

"Sex."

"Hmm?"

"Sex, something to do with sex, that's the motive. You'll find out. Mr. Halstead was obsessed, sexually obsessed. He was enmeshed, mired, in the carnal life, a slave to Satan. That's why he died."

"I see what you mean. I guess. I was thinking of something more specific, like revenge from some egg he ruined in a business deal, or a guy who hated him because Halstead had exposed his evil machinations—"

She interrupted me again, which was probably just as well since I was on the verge of talking like Mrs. Smellow. But I was glad she'd interrupted me for another reason. By the time she finished, anyhow.

"There was bound to be violence, the way they all carried on. Mr. Halstead and his evil friends and those terrible parties. Sex and nakedness, evil, *evil*. All of them sinning, caught up in the grasp of Satan, sinning and naked. Naked, naked, naked!"

I leaned back away from her a little.

The juice was really pouring into her, and for a moment I thought she was going to light up like a Go signal. "You know about the party, then? Did you say *those* parties?"

"Yes, of course I know about them." She paused, and let her eyes glitter at me, then said slowly, "And you do, too, don't you?"

"Well, I sort of stumbled into one. But I assumed maybe it was just, well, one of those things. A sudden kind of casual, ah, flirtation with Satan."

"Nothing casual about it. It was like a—a ritual. A *habit*. They did it all the *time*."

"They didn't."

"They did. It was a regular club, a sex club. Every two weeks they went to somebody's house and . . . you know."

I did know. In fact, her rather vehement comment didn't exactly come at me like a bolt from the blue, considering what had met my eyes and ears when the case had barely begun. Still, it was a bit of a shock to hear the thought so bluntly expressed.

I said, "Wait a moment, Mrs. Smellow. That's quite an accusation. It may well be true, but it isn't the sort of thing we should guess about."

"I'm not guessing. I've seen them. More than once."

"Oh?"

Maybe she'd got a bit carried away, because she rolled her orbs around for a few seconds, then said, "Purely by accident. By accident. There's one place on a hill behind Mr. Halstead's home where you can look down and see part of the pool. And garden. I just happened to drive there one night. By acci—anyway, I saw."

"Uh-huh. I guess it didn't look like, well, just a pool party."

"I guess it didn't. Besides, I told Mr. Halstead about it when I saw him again, I warned him. You can bet I did. And he laughed." She let her tongue roam around inside her mouth, as though probing live nerve ends. "He just laughed. He admitted it, came right out and told me about it. He had the meanness to say he was making up for years of—"

She broke it off and chewed on her lips for a few moments. "You don't have to wonder if I'm guessing. I'm not. I *know*. They had a regular club. Haven't you heard about that sort of thing?"

"Well, yes, I have. But I just never got this close to the fact of the matter before."

"It's the times. It's nigh onto Armageddon. Just look around you, see, read, listen. Degeneracy, depravity, robbery, thieving, murder. It's all sex."

"Well, Mrs. Smellow, sex has been around quite a while—"

"Yes, it has," she said, as if wishing it hadn't.

"—even the little old atoms swinging around the nucleus; and the birds and bees—"

She had the floor, and I guess she intended to keep it. "The television," she said. "You can see it just watching the television. Naked women taking showers right out in the open."

"Oh, I don't think they're really naked. I think they wear pink overalls or something. Damn clever. You can't really tell —"

"Naked. Toothpaste, hair oil, automobiles, razor blades, toilet paper—"

"Oh, come on, not—"

"—soap, white tornadoes, wild men on horses, big lunging horses, deodorants, depilatories, debauches, cigarettes, pipe tobacco, toothpaste, hair oil—"

She was starting over again. So I tried to turn my mind off a bit, reached for a cigarette and flipped my lighter.

"Don't do that!" she cried.

"Huh?"

"Don't light a cigarette. You can't smoke in here. I don't allow smoking in here."

"Oh, sorry. I guess I wasn't thinking. I won't do it again." I put my cigarette back in the pack and said, "So, Mr. and Mrs. Halstead and a number of their friends had a club. That does explain quite a lot of things. Except who killed him. And maybe even why somebody killed him."

"Why? I've been telling you."

"I know, but it's barely possible—"

"There'll be more, hundreds, thousands. It was marked in the skies when the papers first wrote it up about wife-swapping. You read it; everybody read it. Nothing had ever been heard like it on the earth, not in trillions of years. I read it; I read all the papers on those days. And books. I know, I've kept my eye on it all. And I pray; I pray for the sinners." She paused and gasped a little and clasped her bony hands. "It's there, all there, the story of the world going to hell in the clutches of Satan." She unclasped her hands and waved one of them.

She was waving at something in the corner of the room. I followed her wave and spotted a three-shelf bookcase, seven or eight feet wide, against the wall. Probably a hundred hard-bound books and several paperbacks there, not a bad little library.

"Mind if I take a look?" I asked. Hell, I had to do something; couldn't smoke.

"Do," she said. "Do."

So I did. I got up and walked to the bookcase, ran an eye over the titles. She had a number of recent bestsellers, volumes of the excellent Readers' Digest Condensed Books, even some paper-back mystery novels with horribly stimulating art leering from their covers.

Then I noticed one segment of a shelf on which were a number of books, both hardbound and paperback, with titles more than a little reminiscent of what Mrs. Smellow had—either so lovingly or so hatingly, I couldn't be absolutely sure—been describing.

As I ran a finger over their spines Mrs. Smellow said, "That's it, they're the ones, that's it."

And she didn't even pause, just went on, "It's all around us, all around; it's in the air, choking, killing the land, the land and the people, killing," and her voice seemed to rise and fall, rise and fall, as if she were beginning to croon a song she had

68

crooned before. Maybe not to men, or even to women, maybe not to anybody but herself, but a song she had crooned before.

And as she crooned softly behind me, I looked at the books on the shelf.

The titles alone were something of an education: *The Erotic Revolution* by Lawrence Lipton; *Sexual Rebellion in the Sixties* by W. D. Sprague, Ph.D.; *Swap Clubs* and *The Swinging Set* by William and Jerrye Breedlove; *The Velvet Underground* by Michael Leigh. Between a very large hardcover book, *The Kama Kala*, and the not quite as large *Eros and Evil* by Masters, was a paperback, *Sex in America* edited by Grunwald. Then the *Kama Sutra of Vatsyayana*, *Koka Shastra*, and *Ananga Ranga*. Another paperback, *Lord Denning's Report—The Christine Keeler and John Profumo Affair*, and at least a dozen more.

"Hair oil and razor blades," crooned Mrs. Smellow.

I picked one of the books from the shelf, a thick volume bound in red buckram; picked it perhaps because it looked well-thumbed and worn, or perhaps because the author was an M.D. named Scott—Richard, Not Sheldon. Its title was *The Sexual Sixties: Extrapolation of the Prognosis*, a forbidding thing if ever I saw one.

It opened automatically to page 47 as I held it in my hands.

Several lines, I noted, had been underscored in lead pencil. I glanced at a few. ". . . in the Sexy Sixties, the decade of the Sexual Revolution, the old and long-cherished mores became the citadel under attack and soon the ramparts were crumbling. The fixed folkways were becoming the flexible . . ." I skipped a few lines. ". . . there was a ferment in the land, seething in the endocrines, the gonads, and ovaries of the twanging peoples."

The guy wrote like a nut, I thought. But I was interested, so I pursued the subject for a few more lines. "Concurrent with this —preceding it, of course, in the beginning—were innumerable sensory stimuli nearly as prevalent in the atmosphere as oxygen: advertisements in newspapers, magazines, on radio and especially on television, all either overtly or covertly Pavloved to produce sexual salivation. Products first named, and later designed, produced, and publicized to produce the maximum of erection in the male and hotsy-totsy tumescence in the female. Hair cremes for men were alleged to be more exciting . . ."

"Toothpaste!" cried Mrs. Smellow. She wasn't really crooning so much by this time as giving out with something rather like a battle cry. "Huge lunging horses!" she yelled.

I read on, choosing more of the underlined passages. ". . . lotions and salves and stickums and pretties with such suggestive names as: Seduction . . . Surrender . . . Take Me . . . Do It . . . Rape . . . Makeout . . . Orgy . . . Aphrodisia . . ."

"Stallions!" bellowed Mrs Smellow. "Anvils! Horseshoes! Soap and soup and cigarettes—"

"In this atmosphere, a sizable proportion of still zesty marrieds heeded the siren song of Madison Avenue, the coo of a mammary Mammon, the panting of Big Business, and, with the urgent, repeated and again-and-again-repeated 'Get with it . . . Swing! . . . Join the horny generation . . . Do it now!-now!-now!' reverberating in their ears, mumbled. 'Why not?' "

"Naked! Naked horses!"

She really had a thing about horses, she did.

But I wanted to see what the hell this guy was working up to, if anything, so I perused the page a bit more.

"A predictable consequence was the burgeoning of tribal groups which gathered privately for orgiastic conniptions tending toward libidinal unshackling eventuating in casual and part-time polyandry and polygamy, i.e., community fornication."

I shook my head. Yep, a true and legitimate nut. Worse, he wasn't *clear*. You couldn't tell if he was *for* it or *against* it. Probably had to publish the stinking book himself. I thumbed to the front of the book. Sure enough. "The Doctor Scott Medical Press." Well, you can fool some of the people some of the time, and all of the people—no, that wasn't it.

"All over the place! Everywhere. In your eyes, ears, noses—"

I mentally turned her off again. She was worse than Dr. Scott. Who, I noted, had produced this prize: ". . . subconscious banners emblazoned right and left with libidinous slogans, the dexter 'Give Me A Libertine Or Give Me Death!' and the sinister 'Better Copulate Than Never.' It began with whispers, with small reports in the tabloids of what was called with a titter, wife-swapping, then rumors of special groups, clubs, sex clubs, and swap clubs, a new breed of emancipated dizzies . . ."

"Everywhere, all over the place, here—there—"

I couldn't take much more of this without flipping. So I flipped clear to the back pages of the book.

"Thus, as one result of this revulsion against asceticism and denial, the pendulum had swung perhaps too far to the opposite extreme, to unbridled hedonism and voluptuous non-denial. No longer heeding the whisperings of virtue and admonishments of the chaste, they listened—and danced—to the song the senses sang . . ."

I closed the book.

Mrs. Agatha Smellow fell silent.

I went over and sat down in the rough brown chair again.

"You see, Mr. Scott?" she said.

"I see," I sighed. "Well, you've—helped a great deal, Mrs. Smellow."

"Have I? I hope so. Have I?"

"Yes, you have. So I'd better be on my way—"

"Oh, don't go."

"But I must—"

"I so seldom get to talk to—I mean, discuss important things. I . . . will you stay a little while longer?"

I peeked at my watch. "O.K., just a little."

"I know you must drink." She smiled, sort of. "I smelled it on your breath."

She had a great smeller. She could smell all kinds of things. But I said, "Yeah, I had a belt earlier."

"Once in a while I have a little sip, myself. Because it's so lonely." She didn't hit it hard, didn't dwell on it. In fact she went right on, saying. "And I'm so disturbed I think I'd like one right now." But, still, a coolness rippled up my spine.

"It's so lonely," she'd said, very casually, matter-of-fact. It was, I guess. Yes, I guess it was lonely for Mrs. Smellow.

"I know how to mix a martini," she said.

"You do, huh?" I said, without much enthusiasm.

"Would that be all right, Mr. Scott?"

"Sure. Fine, Mrs. Smellow."

"Oh, don't call me Mrs. Smellow. Call me Aggie. What's your first name? Sheldon?"

"Shell, Just Shell."

"You call me Aggie, and I'll call you Shell. All right? If we're going to have a sip of martini, it seems—"

"Sure," I said. "Sure, Aggie."

"It's almost like a party—" Apparently she realized the possible connotation of that comment, and gasped. "Oh, I didn't mean—"

"I know." I grinned stiffly. "Well, up and at 'em; let's stir those jazzy martinis. Uh, not too much, of course." I paused. "Would you like for me to fix them?"

"No, no. I have a prescription."

As she got up and reeled across the room, I raised my eyes

toward Heaven and groaned a little. Well, I could get one gagger down, I supposed. Had to get on my horse—into my Cad, that is—and zip to the Hamilton Building pretty quick. Two o'clock appointment, and I was cutting it thin already. Maybe you're not supposed to drink and run, but that's what I was going to do.

She doddered back with the drinks. We sat, and conversed delicately a bit more, and a time or two we clinked glasses.

This one was, sure enough, quite a horrendous babe.

But, oddly, there came a point when, for some reason undiscovered, Aggie for a moment looked different. Not much, but some. It wasn't the martini—and, strange to relate, it was a splendid martini. Apparently a wise doctor had written the prescription. No, it was simply that maybe for a second or two her expression was not that of one chewing cavities, but quite relaxed, almost pleasant.

She was still a horrendous babe. But I could almost imagine what once she'd been, or could have been. The eyes weren't really bad. It was just that very little life flickered in them; there seemed not fire but ashes there, and deep frown lines were heavily creased between them. Those cuckoo curly locks could have looked halfway presentable if fixed or put up or coiffed properly, whatever babes do to their hair. And it could have been a quite presentable mouth if not so pinched, not so twisted and almost torn with bitterness. Her smile was very stiff, too, as if she'd forgotten how to smile.

Well, maybe she had. Maybe life had kicked her in the teeth too many times. Of course, maybe she'd stuck out her chops and asked for it. Who knows? How would I know? I know from nothing.

Neither did Aggie. She'd been telling me if it weren't for sex, carnality, lecherousness, and all that, the world wouldn't be sliding downhill to Satan. And Mr. Halstead would still be alive. And everything would be as lovely as love. Once in a while she said things like that.

"Even the birds would sing more sweetly," she said. I believe she was half plastered on that one martini.

"Well, now, Aggie," I said, "those birds sing a lot in spring, you know. Don't forget that. Sing like crazy in the mati—nesting season. Can't be all bad. Got to have nests. Little beggars would fall out of the trees."

There had been so much sexy talk—rather, talk of sex—that

72

the subject was naturally in the forefront of my mind. Which was not, with me, a circumstance as rare as elephant feathers. Consequently, it could not be doubted that my thoughts on the subject were somewhat different from Aggie's thoughts on the subject.

Thus, the dialogue went:

"Sex."

"Yep."

"Sex. That's what."

"That's what, all right. You hit it that time. Couldn't have said it better myself."

"Sex . . ." she repeated, lingering over the word as one might linger over the olive in one's first martini. As though savoring it, trying to decide whether she really liked it or not.

But, that's the way it often is with olives. Especially your first few. They're like chocolate bonbons.

Some people take to them right off the bat, go through bottle after bottle saying "Yum-yum" all the time. Others just put up with them, maybe because they come with the martinis. And some people never *do* learn to like them.

I didn't like the way my thoughts were going.

Here we were talking about sex, and I was mentally maundering about olives. I knew I'd hate it if every time I looked at an olive I thought about sex. It could even work the other way —every time I looked at sex I'd think of an olive. Then where would I be? I might have to give up martinis.

It was time to go, sure enough. Even my watch told me it was time to go. In fact, I was late.

Aggie went with me to the door. After a parting comment or two she said, "I've enjoyed our talk, Shell. I hope you can come back sometime. And bring your wife next time."

"Well, that'll be a little tough. I don't have a wife."

"Not any more?"

"Not ever, Aggie. I've never been married."

She blinked. "How old are you? You look at least—well, you're getting close to thirty, aren't you?"

"That's it. On the button. In fact, I've been thirty for a hell of a time now."

She was aghast. "Thirty! And not *married? Never* married?"

Then she actually stood there, after all she'd said to me, blood burbling in her arteries as though sap in an ancient tree and oozing through her veins like grabbers stirring in a purple swamp, and said, "Oh, Shell, you've missed the greatest joy and fulfillment any man could ever have!"

That's what she said. Just when I was starting to like her, too, almost.

10

⁋

Something was going on near the Hamilton Building.

Whatever it was, I'd missed it. Thanks to Aggie I was seven minutes late.

The Hamilton, where I have my office, is in downtown L.A. on Broadway, between Third and Fourth Streets. Near the office is a lot where I park the Cad, and that's where I was heading—only I didn't make it. Not right away.

I was still a block from the lot when the sound of a police siren shrilled in my ears. I pulled over to the right, stopped. The car was a couple blocks away, coming toward me on Broadway, red light flashing on its top.

It was going like hell, at least forty or fifty miles an hour, which was more than plenty for crowded Broadway. It came right past the Hamilton and flashed past on my left, the siren-whine loud enough to stretch the nerves in my spine. As it faded slightly it was joined by another, the second siren wailing nearby. A counterpoint to it was a third somewhere.

There was more shrill noise and screeching and wailing than I'd ever heard in this area before. A police car skidded to a stop in front of the Hamilton. Even from a block away I could clearly hear the tires protesting on the asphalt. One officer, then another, leaped from the car and ran to the sidewalk. I could see other people running.

A crowd was gathering, milling there. There—not near the Hamilton, but right in front of it.

I put the Cad in gear and hit the gas, gunned across Fourth, swung into the lot as another car, siren howling, drew near. This one wasn't a police buggy but a long limousine, an ambulance; attendants opened its back doors as I left my car with the attendant in the lot and began trotting down the sidewalk.

As I pushed through several dozen citizens standing around and gawking, ambulance attendants made their way to the sidewalk carrying a wheeled stretcher. I was only a few feet from the focus of all the excitement, half a dozen men and women still between me and the body sprawled on the cement. It was a man, face down on the sidewalk, legs splayed and feet pointing in opposite directions.

"Excuse me," I said, tapping a man on the shoulder. He didn't want to move. So I moved him.

Not roughly, I just pushed a bit, and kept pushing, and he moved. He didn't mind. He hardly noticed. But he did turn his head and look at me, eyes bright and face a little pale. "How about that?" he said.

This had probably made his day. I don't know why it is, but the ghouls gravitate to big or little calamities, and sometimes it seems the bigger it is the better they like it. They look, a little frightened, maybe, but more fascinated than frightened, staring at the dead, the maimed, the injured, the dying. Civilized man, at scenes of sorrow.

The guy on the sidewalk looked dead.

I still hadn't made my way into the open, but I could see most of him, see his back, see the holes and dark stains of blood in the cloth of his hound's-tooth jacket, and the mess that was one side of his head.

I moved forward. "Pardon me, Miss. I've got to get through."

Another one, right in the front row—a woman, at that. Sometimes they're worse than the men. But this one was not what I'd have expected in the front row, not what I'd have expected anywhere in the area. Maybe that's because I find it difficult to think ill of gorgeous tomatoes.

And that's what she was: a gorgeous tomato. Tall, with blonde hair swooping smoothly down from the back of her head to rest, gleaming, just about level with her shoulders. I hadn't seen her full-face, only from the side; but it was the kind of profile that might have graced the temples of Troy, and the body belonged to the queen of saturnalia.

Simply dressed, pale blue sweater and darker skirt, a wide belt, white scarf tied around her neck, she was standing with arms crossed over exceptionally abundant breasts, gazing down at the man on the sidewalk.

As I touched her shoulder she turned. And I saw her full-face. And the face melted.

That's about the only way I can describe it with reasonable accuracy. She looked at me, quite calmly, for about two seconds. For the third and fourth seconds her features seemed to become—well, rigid. Congealed. Like a fixed photograph, rather than something of flesh and blood, juices and bone. But then it melted, twisted, changed.

Her eyes slowly grew wider and wider until they were enormous in her lovely face.

"Ohh-hh," she said, breath sighing from moist, warm-looking lips.

She pulled in her breath with a soft "Ah—" in three separate jerks, as though her lungs had stopped working involuntarily, and she had to pull, suck at the air, to fill them again.

Then once more the sigh, "Ohh-hh," and her face paled as I watched.

It was odd that I could notice so many things about her in those few seconds. It was a very short time. Ten seconds maybe, all told, before she was gone, before she turned and pushed almost blindly through the men and women behind us.

But I noticed that her eyes were hazel, dotted with tiny flecks of gray; that her skin was smooth as still water; and that she wore no makeup except lipstick and darkness on her lashes.

When she turned, suddenly, pushed past me and away, I watched her move, tall and slim, limber and lithe. She moved with the natural grace of a slim tree swaying in warm winds, a tree laden with ripe, heavy fruit. I would not forget that face; and I would remember the way she moved.

But what the hell, I wondered, had sent her into the small fit?

I looked down at the man before me. The attendants had the stretcher next to him now, and were preparing to lift him onto it. Another police car was sliding to a stop and I heard two car doors slam, one after another, then the splat of feet on pavement as somebody ran this way.

I recognized the injured man—dead man, it looked like. Hell, he had to be dead. I could clearly see the side of his skull now, a great ugly wound there in his white hair. Not to mention the holes in his back.

I looked at that white hair again. I'd got it by then, I think.

He was a big guy, a man named Porter who'd taken an office

in the Hamilton only a couple of weeks ago, a C.P.A. with a wife and a couple of kids. He was over fifty, more than twenty years past my thirty, but he did look quite a bit like me—from the back. Mainly, I guess, it was the white hair, cut fairly short. And the size of him.

And of course, he'd been going into the Hamilton Building. His body lay only a yard short of the entrance, blood spilled next to, and from, his head.

As I looked down at him, Captain Samson ran up, bent over the body. He must have been one of the men trotting over here from that last police car.

"Hey, Sam," I said.

He was looking at the dead man's face. So he must have known it wasn't me. But his head snapped around, as if somebody had socked his chin a good one; and he stared at me as he rose to his feet.

His face was white, not its usual healthy pink. And he appeared to have aged a bit, but not more than a hundred years.

"You sonofabitch," he said—right out in front of all those people. "You—you scared hell out of me."

I stepped over next to him, let a hand flop on his shoulder. "I'm a little spooked myself, old buddy," I said. "You know who the guy is, Sam?"

He shook his head.

I told him and he stepped to the nearest police car, radioed the info in.

When he came back he said, "I thought it was you, you damn fool." He was still mad at me.

"So did somebody else, Sam."

He looked toward the body now being lifted into the back of the ambulance. I could just see the dead man's shoulders and head.

Samson got out a black cigar, lit it, clamped his strong teeth on it, big jaw wiggling. About half a minute of that and the cigar would be on the cement, and he'd be chewing tobacco.

"Like who?" he said—then glanced around and added, "Skip that."

Too many ears around, and we couldn't know who all of them belonged to. Sam knew there would be plainclothes men mingling with the crowd, listening to comments from the interested citizens, some of whom just might be more interested than the average casual bystander.

They'd report to Sam a little later, but in the meantime we

knew a few things. Sam filled me in when we got back to the Police Building and were in his office.

I did, by the way, before leaving the Hamilton Building, make sure little Hazel knew I was not dead, and gave her a big and unmistakably enthusiastic kiss—despite her squeals and gentle fist-flailing protests. And left, smiling at her parting comment: "But I was a *virgin!*"

In Sam's office he said, "What we've got so far, throwing out the witnesses who think it was seven men in a tank"—there are always some of those, in any investigation—"is this. Two men, not on foot, in a pale-colored sedan, maybe blue, maybe brown. They pulled up at the curb, lifted the hood—like trouble, you know, had to stop."

I nodded.

"Nobody knows what happened until the shots were fired. Probably when they spotted Porter one of the men put the hood down, driver started the car; they were all ready to go. Four slugs hit Porter in the back, one in the neck, two in the head. That's not all that were fired; we figure maybe two full clips. Automatics, .45 caliber. Most likely they breezed a few blocks and switched to another car. Clean, no descriptions worth a damn. Who knew you were going to show up at your office about two o'clock?"

"What makes you think somebody knew?"

"Two things. One's Porter. He looks enough like you. I thought it was you."

"What's the second thing?"

"I got a phone call. Tell you about it in a minute. Somebody did know you were going to show." It was a statement, not a question.

"Yeah. Only I don't know who." I told him about the call to Hazel earlier, setting up the two o'clock appointment, then said "Phones are busy today. Who rang you?"

"Man, kind of whispery voice, rough, like whiskey-rough. He decided not to give me his name and address."

"What'd he say?"

Sam squinted, thinking back. "Like this. 'Hey, Papa, Shell Scott just got shot at the Hamilton. Shot and killed. That grab you, Papa?' Then he hung up, with more noise than necessary." Sam rubbed his ear, remembering.

"Wonder why in hell the guy would phone you?"

"Rub it in. Punks are getting pretty cocky these days. Might be that's all of it—or some guy who hates my guts."

"Not very fond of mine, either, I'd guess."

"Maybe he doesn't hate anybody's guts. Just hates cops, part of the stick-the-fuzz routine. S.o.p., Shell, the kookie climate."

"Yeah, maybe. What time did the call come in?"

Sam glanced at a pad on his desk. "Man didn't lose anything by tipping me. It was five after two when he reached me. Maybe a minute before the first call came in to the complaint board."

"Uh-huh. That would have been right after the shooting. When your caller figured I was good and dead. Could be the guy was close enough to hear the shots—maybe even see Porter go down."

Sam rubbed his head. "Haven't had anything like this, not downtown, for a hell of a time. They must have wanted you bad enough to take the big chance. But . . ." He paused. "If we were going to pick them up on the streets, something should have come in."

It was true. They would have switched cars, maybe a couple of times by now. Or they might be in a hotel room, strolling on the streets, sitting in a bar somewhere. Probably raising a toast to the memory of the late, unlamented Shell Scott.

I sat quietly for a minute, thinking.

"Well," I said finally, "right at first I thought maybe there was a slim chance they were after Porter instead of me. But the call you got chalks that off. And that was a hood job. Pro, or damn good amateurs, anyway. Only hoods I've been chumming around with lately is the Jimmy Violet collection of creeps."

"Yeah. I talked to Lieutenant Peterson an hour ago. I think he'd give his pension to get those punks good—Hollywood Division gets most of the action, and trouble, with that bunch."

"Those three didn't spend much time in the clutches of the law, did they?"

"Hell, no," Sam said. Not with rancor, not even wearily. I suppose he was getting used to it by now.

"What's Jimmy up to out there these days?" I asked him.

"Nothing we can prove. And even if we could—" he waved a big hand. "Oh, he's still in prostitution; got some call girls on the string. Still gets a rakeoff from the union he headed before he was sent up.

"He's still able to swing sweetheart contracts, and help call off a threatened strike from time to time. Enough to pick up pocket money. But we think he's worked into narcotics in the

80

four years since he got out of San Quentin. Nothing solid, no evidence. Just the picture the ID gets."

I'd gone through the Intelligence Division's file on Violet myself. Aside from the things Samson had mentioned, he seemed to have tried his hand at virtually anything that might mean fast and easy money. He'd picked up several new ideas during the three years he'd spent in Q, apparently.

I said, "Well, two guys in the blue or brown sedan. Add your friendly caller, who had to be part of the play in advance. So that's three, at least. Probably more. Which starts adding up to an organization. I popped Jimmy on his beak yesterday, but—"

"You what?"

"I biffed him a pretty good one on the nose."

"Why the hell did you do that?"

"It seemed like a splendid idea at the time. He was getting pretty bad-mouth with me. And breathing on me, besides."

"Will you never learn—"

"Look, so I clobbered him a little. I don't think even Jimmy would send two or three wipers after me for that—not for that alone. Oh, he'd *want* to, but if you ask me, he'd need something else, another reason."

"You could be wrong, too."

"I guess it's possible."

We talked about the Halstead killing for a couple of minutes. There was nothing new, nothing of much value, at least. I told Sam about finding Ed Walles; hit a few highspots in my activity of the day.

When I finished he glanced at his watch. "Guess we missed 'em."

"There'll be another time."

He looked at me, sharp brown eyes steady on mine. I suppose he was thinking of Porter, prone on the cement with his head open.

As a matter of fact, I thought of it every once in a while myself.

11

I WENT IN THE SAME GATE, THROUGH THE SAME LOVELY garden, over the same white gravel path.

It was broad daylight this time, but the difference was more than merely the difference between day and night. It was very quiet. Only the hum of the pool pump broke the stillness, and the water swirled gently, clear and blue.

Mrs. Halstead was expecting me.

She was waiting for me at the back door, looking quite pretty if a bit tired, sunlight saucy on her strawberry-blonde hair and the full-curved figure covered by a loose-fitting white shift. We didn't go inside, but instead sat side by side on a small, padded bench resting on a few square yards of fluffy green dichondra; two weeping willows and a clump of tall queen palms were filtering the sunlight.

I didn't like bothering Mrs. Halstead so soon after her husband's death. But she was my client, after all. Even more important, she had not leveled with me. Maybe she'd leveled in the parts she'd told me, but Mrs. George Halstead had sure left a lot unsaid. Of course, I didn't really blame her.

It was sure as hell time, however, for *all* the facts to come out. And if I had to be just a little rough on Mrs. Halstead, then that's how it was going to be.

So I started by telling her of the recent scene in front of the Hamilton Building. I made the telling reasonably detailed, and attempted to draw a colorfully graphic picture for her.

I wound it up, "Last I saw of Porter—who was, as I have

indicated, supposed to be me—was when they were putting him into the ambulance. Just before they got him in it, his head jiggled off the edge of the stretcher, and a piece of his brain fell onto the street."

She closed her big, cool, green eyes, and swayed, just a little.

"Why . . . why are you telling me this?"

"Because that was supposed to be my piece of brain, and I haven't got any pieces to spare. At least, not like that. And it's very possible, if not probable, that I'll get stupendously killed unless people start telling me all the little things which might help keep me alive."

"I don't understand."

"Keep listening. I mean I may buy it like Porter if people keep holding out on me. The way you've held out on me."

"I've told you everything—"

"When's the last time you heard from Jimmy Violet?"

"Jimmy . . . who?"

It was a hundred to one she wouldn't have answered like that if she'd ever heard of the guy. Not "Who did you say?" not even "Jimmy *who*?" Just questioning, slightly puzzled.

She shook her head. "Did you say Jimmy Violet? Like the color?"

"Yes."

She shook her head again. "Goodness, no," she said. "Who is he?"

"A hood. Never mind. Maybe there's no connection."

Mrs. Halstead seemed preoccupied. She folded her hands in her lap, rolled the green eyes toward me. "Have you found out anything yet, Mr. Scott? Do you have any idea who killed George?"

"Not so far. You might say the middle of the picture's still fuzzy, but I'm getting developments around the edges. Like, I finally figured out what Mr. Pryer meant last night when he said the Whists and Rileys dropped out. I thought he meant they came by, dropped out here for a while during the evening. I didn't realize he meant they'd dropped out of the club."

The flush was slow, but unmistakable. It would have been clearly evident from a distance of ten yards. The pink rose from her neck over her face and disappeared up past her hairline. If she'd been as bare as when I first saw her in her bedroom, I might have been able to watch the color rise from her toes clear up to her face.

"Club?" she said. After a considerable silence.

"Yeah. Sex club, swap club, health club; I don't know what the hell you call it. So the Rileys and Whists turned in their . . . well, whatever. Membership cards? Name's not Whist, by the way—it's Walles. That ring any bells? And who else is in the group besides those who were here last night? Other than the Kents and Nelsons mentioned last night, I mean."

She stood up. She played with her fingers for a while, not looking at me. Then she sat down. And looked at me.

"How did you find out? Who told you?"

"Never mind that." I wasn't going to tell her about Aggie. "It wasn't one of the group, one of your friends. I know that you, or your friends, have had enough pull—or luck—to keep the spicy details about last night from getting into the papers. But I got the background, all of it, from one of my sources."

"All right. So what?" A modicum of belligerence, that time.

"Nothing what," I said. "Just quit holding out on me, dammit. If, that is, you want me to stay on the case."

"Of course I want you to. But, oh, dear—it didn't seem important . . . germane, I mean; I didn't think it could have any bearing on what happened to George."

"Let me make up my own mind about that, will you? While I've still got it."

"I . . . should have told you, I guess."

"You know damn well you should have told me."

"Do you have to swear at me?"

"I'm not swearing *at* you. I'm just swearing. For the hell of it, O.K.? It isn't every day I'm practically killed by having my brains—"

"Don't—I understand. I forgot about that."

"Maybe *you* forgot. O.K., Mrs. Halstead. I think it would be nice if we could sit here for a few minutes while I say nothing at all, but just listen."

She cooperated nicely. I'd say she talked for three minutes straight, somewhat stiffly at first but quite free-wheeling toward the end. I figured she was telling all of it, leaving nothing out. She did, though; she left something out. Of course, I didn't know that right then.

When she stopped, either for breath or because she was finished, I said, "O.K., fine and dandy. Wish I'd known all this several hours ago—but no matter now. Question: You and Mr. Halstead had not commenced this fairly recent, ah, group activity before you met the Whists?"

"No, they were the first couple we . . . Just a moment, didn't

84

you say something about their name not being Whist? You said so many things then that I got a little confused."

"I said their name is Walles. W-a-l-l-e-s. They gave you a phoney."

"Why?"

"That's what I'm still trying to find out. In case I don't already know. Which maybe I do. The name Walles means nothing to you?"

"Nothing."

"I've met Ed, but not his wife. Not yet. I know you told me what she looks like, but describe her again, will you?"

"She's quite lovely, taller than I am, blonde hair and brown eyes. I don't know, I can't think of anything but what I've already told you."

"Any special marks, scars, that sort of thing?"

"No. I will admit, she's got about the most beautiful figure I've ever seen."

This Marcelle had to be something, I thought, because Mrs. Halstead herself wouldn't have to take a back seat to many. She was going on.

"She's just a lovely woman, that's all." A pause. "I could tell you more about Ed."

"I think I know enough about Ed. Well, O.K., Whist or Walles, they were the first couple you and your husband joined in, ah, merrymaking and frolic?"

"Yes."

"Whose idea was it?"

"Why . . . I really don't know. It just, well, it just came up. Sort of in the conversation, very light and joking at first. Then, later, not joking."

"Somebody must have made the first pitch, or pointed comment."

"I suppose. I simply don't remember. It may sound strange to you, but it seemed to happen very naturally."

"It came suddenly from outer space. Neither you nor your husband had ever even thought of such a thing, then boom, zowie—"

"I didn't mean that. We, George and I, often had long, lazy talks. And we'd discussed that sort of thing. Not so much as if it might ever involve us, but as part of the . . . sociological landscape, you might say. That is, we'd *thought* about it. To me, it was academic—I couldn't have cared less, frankly. But George, well, it wasn't academic to him. It was out of the classroom and into the playground, for George. Especially once he'd seen Marcelle . . ." She bent forward and picked up a bit of the dichondra; rubbed it between her fingers.

I found the pack of cigarettes in my pocket, offered her a smoke. She shook her head. I lit up and said, "Then I take it I've got all the names and addresses which are—germane. The ones you gave me last night."

"That's right."

"O.K., you and the Walleses—then known as the Whists—to start with. Next, the Bersudians."

"Yes, it was as if they'd been reading our minds—for weeks. George merely dropped a hint, and they picked it up and ran to the goal line. Angelica was all over George, just like that."

I smiled, a sort of sappy smile. "Angelica, hmm? I'm going right out to see her. From here, I mean. I mean, I *already* had planned to see her. Next. Planned it before I got here."

Mrs. Halstead managed to work up the best smile I'd seen on her pretty face since meeting her.

"Of course," she said, in that disturbingly squishy tone women sometimes use when inserting among the sincere syllables an inaudible "Ha-ha, you're full of baloney." But then she went right on, "A while after that Ed and Marcelle brought the Rileys around, just casually, once or twice, then as—part of the merry group."

"Yeah, but from what you've said, the Rileys were the only couple introduced into the group by the Walleses. The rest were drawn from among your friends or acquaintances. All of the others."

She looked at me for a few seconds, pursing her lips. "That's true." She paused. "You know, I never realized that before. I never even thought about it. And it was Ed—" she chopped it off.

"Ed what?"

"Just . . . nothing. Well, he and Marcelle were the first ones to drop out. Then the Rileys. And they're the only two couples who did. I don't suppose that means anything."

I didn't suppose so, either. But somehow I didn't think it was what she'd started to say.

But, enough had been said, it seemed. So after another minute I thanked her for her time, and her frankness, apologized for having to bother her with so many questions, and left.

I had already talked once with Angelica Bersudian earlier

this day, Angelica of the bosomy bosom and slumbrous eyes, but that had been a brief and fruitless dialogue. Merely a few questions, her expressed sorrow that she knew nothing that might help me, though she did wish she could be of help, she surely did—that sort of thing. I hadn't even gone inside the house, but simply stood by the door for three or four minutes asking my routine questions.

But I had not known then what I knew now.

I supposed, soon after the shock and upheaval of last night, all of the concerned couples had reached an agreement—if, as seemed more likely, it hadn't been reached long before—that none of them, under any circumstances, would say a thing about the "private and personal" matters which, presumably, could have no vital bearing on the matter of George Halstead's murder. For, should one spill, all would be in the soup.

I didn't know for sure. But certainly there'd been no peep about it until I'd gotten the inside info from Agatha Smellow.

Come to think of it, I owed Aggie a lot. Not only the lead which I was now following but the fact that her martini, her plea for "Just a little while longer," had spared me the unpleasant—if not actually fatal—experience of getting four fat bullets in my back, one in my neck, and two in my head.

The Bersudians lived in Westwood, about midway between the Los Angeles Country Club and the UCLA campus. I was driving out Wilshire Boulevard when I got that funny feeling again—while checking the rear-view mirror.

A dark sedan had been weaving in and out of traffic, keeping close but never directly behind me, usually the second or third car back. There was really nothing to connect it with the dark sedan with the cock-eyed light, which had been behind me last night. But it was a Dodge Polara. I'd noticed this buggy minutes ago, before turning west on Wilshire.

It was probably maw and paw and the kids out for a Saturday afternoon drive—"Younguns, thet thar's whar Stony Virile, the big moonpitcher star lives"—but so vivid was memory of Porter's head in my head that I was leery of maw and paw and even the kids. So I slowed, made sure I was the last car through the next light just as it turned from yellow to red, and stepped on the gas. I didn't spot the dark Polara again.

In two more mintues I was at the Bersudians' pink stucco villa, or whatever it was. A big joint, it looked as though it should have had canals around it and a gondola parked in front.

I almost felt like whistling the Venetian national anthem as I walked up the pink sidewalk to the ornately carved front door.

I almost felt like whistling something else—like *weee-weeoo* —when Mrs. Bersudian opened the door. Because she was something else.

"Angelica," I said. *"Weee-weeoo."*

"Mr. Scott." She smiled. "Hello, there. Why did you whistle?"

"Did I whistle? I thought I was just thinking. Boy, I've got to watch my thinking."

"What can I do for you this time?"

"Well, uh, there have been some more developments in the case. And how. So I figured we'd better lay our cards and things on the table ... just be frank as hell, I mean. Well, that's not exactly what I mean. I think we ought to talk about it, though, whatever it is."

"I do too, Mr. Scott. Come in, please. I hope you'll excuse the way I'm dressed. I was out in back by the pool, getting some sun."

I'd guessed she must have been doing something like that. I had for a certainty noticed what she was wearing. It wasn't much. At least, not for a gal the size and shape of Angelica Bersudian. In fact, it wasn't quite enough. Not if she was trying to hide the facts of life, anyhow. It was a polka-dot bikini big enough for three dots.

"Well, don't just stand there making that funny noise, Mr. Scott. Come on in."

I went inside and she shut the door, then walked past me, calling over her bare shoulder, "Shall we go out in back by the pool?"

"Fine. Anywhere. You go ahead. I'll just follow till you stop moving."

We walked through the house, outside into a large patio partially covered by sections of thin bamboo strips overhead, and past a stone barbecue with a portable wooden bar next to it. Near the sparkling blue swimming pool was a pink chaise longue, on which Angelica sort of arranged herself very attractively. I sat in a big wicker chair facing her, and watched her for a while.

Finally she said, "I know why you're here."

"Boy, I've *got* to watch it—or maybe stop watching—"

"Ann phoned me."

"Ann? Mrs. Halstead?"

"Yes."

"Busy girl, isn't she?"

"She told me you were there with her. And . . . what you talked about. So I guess now you know everything."

"Well, not everything. But quite a bunch."

"I hope you don't think we're terrible."

"Terrible? Did you hear me say terrible? I'll admit, you're quite a bunch. But, ah, erum . . ."

"I'm glad you came back. My husband's at his office, and I didn't have anybody to talk to."

"Well, golly—"

"And my conscience has been bothering me."

"It has, huh? Well, I suppose you could try kicking the habit. Seems sort of drastic, though. Maybe you could just kick it a little—"

"Because I did leave some things out when I talked to you before."

"Yeah, I know—"

"I don't mean what you discussed with Mrs. Halstead. Not that *other* thing. I mean, something from last night. I didn't mention it because I was afraid it would lead to the *other* thing. Of course, now you know about the other thing, it doesn't make any difference."

It didn't make much difference what she said, either. That low, humming voice of hers scratched my ears the way you do to a dog's head. I don't mean it was a scratchy voice. It was just that—well, I liked it a lot.

I said, "What other thing?"

"You know. Sex."

That was exactly what Agatha had said, using a different language. Mrs. Bersudian, whose husband was at his office, sounded like a gal who would take three or four olives in her martinis.

"Let's see if I'm getting this," I said. "Are you implying . . . inferring? Are you saying you have information relative to the slaying of Mr. Halstead which, if conveyed to me, might assist me in my conduct of this here investigation?"

"My, you sound formal all of a sudden."

"I'm trying to, Mrs. Bersudian—"

"Call me Angelica. My husband, who is at his office, calls me Angel. But that's probably *too* intimate. So call me Angelica. Will you, Shell?"

"Will I what?"

"Call me Angelica."

"Sure. Angelica."

"What?"

"Nothing. I was just calling you Angelica."

"You said something a moment ago about . . . would you say it again?"

"I'm afraid that will be impossible."

"Well . . . We don't seem to be getting anywhere, do we?"

"You hit it on the head that time."

"I know what's wrong. You're embarrassed!"

"Where'd you get that idea?"

"I mean, because of the . . . other thing. Because you know all about it now, you're embarrassed. You don't want to talk to me about it."

"Where'd you get that idea?"

"I know! Would you like a drink? Maybe a martini?"

"How are you fixed for olives?"

"Oh, I've got bottles and bottles of them. From Italy, those great big juicy ones!"

"I knew it."

"They're stuffed with pimientos."

"You're kidding."

"You haven't really told me yet. Would you like one?"

"I sure would. Probably I shouldn't, but—"

"Fine, I'll be right back, Shell."

"Where are you going?"

"To the kitchen."

"What for?"

"To get the ice."

"You've got to be kidding."

"I don't understand."

"I think you're way ahead of me, at that."

"Well, I *have* to get some ice. You want it cold, don't you?"

"Cold?" I said. "Cold? Well, wouldn't that frost you?"

"It *has* to be cold. Otherwise it's no good."

"You know, I'm swinging around to the idea that the world's going to hell. If this is what we've come to—"

"You just sit there and let me take care of everything."

"O.K."

"I'll be back with yours in a minute."

"You mean yours, don't you?"

"Do you like it sweet or dry?"

"What kind of dumb question is that?"

"Well, people are all different, Ask any bartender."

"I will not ask a bartender."

"Some people like theirs stirred a lot, and some don't like them stirred at all."

"The world is going—"

"And some even like them shaken with cracked ice."

"Yeah. Sure. Pretty quick I'll believe anything."

"Personally, I like mine very dry, and only stirred three or four times."

"Well, I'll see you around, Angelica. I've got a case out there somewhere, Duty calls—"

"Oh, Shell—have *one* drink, first. Just *one* martini. And I truly do have something to tell you about last night."

"Say that again."

"I truly do have something to tell—"

"No, that first part." I swung my head in a 180-degree arc for a few seconds, then I said, "Never mind. Just a moment."

I got up and walked back toward the stone barbecue, stopped at the portable bar, opened its little door. There I found several bottles; I selected a quart of gin and a bottle of vermouth, which I looked at long and hard. "Uh-huh," I said to myself. "How about that?" I said to myself.

Then I went back and sat down and said, "Well, better get cracking, Angelica. Round up that ice, hey?"

A few minutes later we were sipping delicious, cold martinis and nibbling big, fat, green, pimiento-stuffed olives, and Angelica was saying, "There, that's better. Shall I tell you about last night now?"

"Sure. I'd be fascinated. Lots of fun, huh?"

"I was with Mr. Halstead. Not my husband. Because, well ..."

"He was at his office?"

"No, he was, oo, talking to Mrs. Warren. Anyway, I was with George when we heard a car coming up the road. We could see the glow from its lights, too. Right then George got this phone call."

"What phone call?"

"The one I'm telling you about."

"Yeah. O.K."

"We were, oo—there's a phone outside, near the pool, you see. It's got a long cord on it. It rang, and George got up and started swearing."

I didn't say anything. I knew there must be more.

"Then he answered the phone and talked a minute or so, very softly. I couldn't hear what he was saying. But I was quite a

91

distance off, anyway, over in the dichondra. While he was talking, the car went around to the front of the house. The pool and all is behind the house, you know."

"Yeah."

"Well, when he came back, George just wasn't the same man."

"How do you mean?"

"He had his eyebrows pulled way down and was kind of beating his teeth together—he looked quite disturbed."

"I'll bet he did."

"He said he had to talk to a man—the one who'd just driven up in the car. That was what the phone call was about."

"Do you know who called?"

"George didn't say. But he said he'd settle it as soon as he could. I asked him if we ought to go and hide or something. He said there wasn't time, but when he went inside he'd turn the lights out in the garden area and pool, so nobody could—so it would be dark. Then he wrapped a towel around himself and went into the house, and I only saw him once more after that. I went inside to get an apple."

"Do all you people eat apples? I mean, is there some special—"

"I just wanted something to put on my stomach."

"You put apples on your stomach? What good does that do?"

"I wanted something to eat. We all eat lots of fruit and vegetables. They're very good for you."

"Yeah? How about meat? My blood needs lots of . . . well, blood, I guess. So I eat lots of rare—"

"I'm trying to tell you about George."

"That's right. When did you see him again?"

"After I got the apple I went back outside and was standing near the door, in the dark, when George walked down the hall from the front room and went up the stairs with a man—the one who'd driven up in the car, it must have been."

"You saw the guy, then?"

"Only a glimpse."

"What did he look like?"

"Just a man, rather heavy, heavy-set. Not as tall as George." She shook her head. "I don't really remember, and I didn't notice much. I'd probably know him if I saw him again, but I can't describe him."

"They were going upstairs? What's up there besides Mr. Halstead's den?"

"A television room and four bedrooms. That's all."

"They must have been going to his den, then. Mr .Halstead called me from there, I think. That's where I was supposed to meet him, anyway. You didn't see him—or the other man—after that?"

"No."

"This guy, was he anybody you'd seen before?"

"No, not ever. He was . . ." She lowered the heavy lashes over her eyes, thinking. "I don't know. I just didn't like his looks. After a while somebody turned the lights back on. That was only a little while before you arrived."

I thought about it. This was a very fortunate break—assuming it was true—Angelica would recognize the man if she saw him again. She might even be able to pick him out from a bunch of mug shots. That meant the big break could come merely from picking out the right mug shots.

And I had some mug shots in mind.

So I said, "Well, thanks for the info—and the martini. Stupendous olives, by the way. But I guess I've got to go now."

"You do? No time for another drink or anything?"

"No time even for a drink. I've got to get down to the Police Building in L.A. But I might be back later with some pictures for you to look at."

"Oh?" she said, suspiciously, I thought. "What kind of pictures?"

"Police shots of some unsavory characters. Hoodlums and ex-cons, that sort of thing."

"I see. When will you be back?"

"I'll phone first, but it'll probably take me a couple of hours, maybe more."

"My husband should be home by then," she said. "From the office. Won't that be nice?"

"That," I said, "will be dandy."

I told Angelica she needn't show me to the door, I'd just walk around the side of the house to the front. I figured I'd jump into the Cad, visit the L.A.P.D., and return, and maybe wrap up the case in a jiffy.

That's what I thought.

Wrong again.

It was quite a while before I even got the Cad. And when I finally did, I no longer desired to drive downtown for those mug shots.

12

~~~~

IT WAS A NARROW PATH ALONGSIDE THE HOUSE, COOL AND green, rank with grasses and small shrubs. I ducked my head beneath an overhanging branch and stepped out onto the lawn in front of the house.

My Cad was at the curb a few yards away on my right, and as I glanced toward it my gaze took in the street, other houses, a car parked nearly a block away against the far curb. It was a dark sedan, a Dodge Polara.

I tossed my eyes around the area, swung my head left fast.

I saw him then. But he'd seen me first. He already had a gun in his hand.

I went down fast and hard, one knee pounding a shallow depression in the grass, slapping my hand to the Colt under my coat. There was a sudden shout—"Lookout, Skiko!"—from behind me. From the right side of the house. Not from the little man my eyes were on. As my knee hit the lawn he let go a shot at me, high, close but high.

I squeezed the Colt's trigger twice and missed the man both times. Even so, he spun around and jumped out of sight between the house next to the Bersudians' and the one beyond it.

I dived forward, skidded on the lawn and rolled as another gun blasted. When I came up the man firing at me—the second man—was a blur in my sight, not clear, but clear enough for me to know the sonofabitch was trying to kill me.

I snapped one shot at him in a hurry, more to jar him, shake

94

his aim, than in a real attempt to hit him. But I aimed the last two slugs. And got him. Twice.

He'd fired again, maybe several times, before I hit him. I don't know; you don't count them when they're coming at you. He staggered, but didn't go down. The gun in his hand wavered away from me, but then he pulled it slowly back to point at my head.

At least it seemed to me that he moved slowly, but probably it was fast. I was still on my knees, bracing one hand against the lawn, right arm extended before me, and when I squeezed the Colt's trigger again it took a long time for the hammer to fall on an empty cartridge.

I saw the queer puff of powder and heat from the bore of his gun and simultaneously felt the blow on the side of my head. It seemed a tremendous blow, a shock that should have torn my head off, more an explosion inside my skull than an impact from without. But I was still conscious, aware of sunlight splashing green lawn, painting brilliant color on a lone hibiscus blossom blooming against the house. A red hibiscus, moving against the pink stucco.

It kept moving. House and earth and sky were moving. I felt a feathery touch aainst my left side, knew I'd toppled over, was lying against the grass. But I didn't go out, didn't lose consciousness.

I was still functioning, clutching grass in my fingers. I'd dropped the Colt. Then I was on my hands and knees trying to move toward the man near me. Even with my brain slowed, dulled, stunned, I knew I couldn't get away. It was toward him, or just wait for it.

I got my head up, vision blurred. But I could see the bastard. Thirty feet away, facing me. Still on his feet. But his arm had dropped to his side, and he was swaying. He didn't let go of the gun even then, but it hung in a relaxing hand as he took one slow step toward me, then another. His foot was in the air for the third step when he slanted forward and fell slowly and loosely, outstretched leg bending beneath him like a limb of rubber.

He thudded audibly against the grass, rolled over onto his back. He kicked his right leg forward three times, rapidly, like a man pumping brakes, then was still.

When I managed to find my gun and get to my feet I half

expected the other little guy to be cracking down on me again. But he wasn't in sight. I couldn't hear him.

I moved unsteadily to the spot where I'd last seen him. By then the front door of the adjacent house was open and a young woman was looking out, mouth open and eyes wide. She saw me and jumped back, slamming the door. My head was beginning to throb, but my vision was clearer.

The man—Skiko was his name, I guessed; that's what the other one had yelled at him—wasn't in view between the houses. Undoubtedly it was just as well. I'd fired two slugs at him and three at, and into, the man before the house. Plus, earlier, one past Jimmy Violet's ears. Six—including that extra one I'd slipped into the revolver this morning.

So it was a good thing I'd had all six chambers filled; but they were empty now. The Colt Special wasn't a gun any longer. At best it was a rock. O.K., I'd go after the bastard with a rock.

But he hadn't waited around. He was not, apparently, a man with much stomach for getting shot at. Which didn't surprise me. I've known too many hoods.

Then I went back in front of the Bersudians' pink house. A siren was thin in the air, getting closer. The man on the grass still lay sprawled on his back, staring past the sun.

Near him, out colder than a frozen halibut, lay Angelica Bersudian.

She'd fainted and fallen with something of a jolt, no doubt. Angelica lay on her side, smooth curve of ample hip accentuated by the splash of colored cloth, one swelling breast completely free of the bikini bra.

I bent, pulled the cloth up over the bulging bareness, left her lying there, stepped near the dead man. He was dead all right.

I hadn't known who he was when returning his fire, hadn't recognized him. But I recognized him now. I knew this boy.

He was Stub Corey.

I felt a warm trickle on my leg. There was a pretty good gouge in my thigh, a couple inches above my knee. But even with my head slowly revolving as well, I was in fair shape—especially compared to Corey.

I tied a handkerchief around my leg, and waited for Angelica.

About ten seconds before the police car pulled up behind my Cad, siren growling softly, she came to.

I helped her sit up.

She sat silently, eyes dull with shock and even more sleepy-looking than usual, then she glanced at the body on the lawn.

"Sorry," I said. "I didn't think I was tailed here. They probably cruised around till they spotted my car—or maybe they guessed I was coming here. I should have made sure, I guess, but—"

She interrupted me. Pointing at the dead guy, she said, "That's the man."

"What?"

"That's the man I saw last night. With George."

The police car had stopped before the house. An officer was opening the right-hand door, looking at us, the three of us.

I said, "Well, that's great. That's just splendid."

Angelica blinked up at me. "What's the matter?"

"Nothing much. I have merely fatally plugged the guy who undoubtedly killed George Halstead."

I didn't know the driver of the car, but the first officer to walk over was a man named Chuck. Chuck looked at the dead man, then at Angelica Bersudian. He looked at her a lot longer. He'd seen lots of dead guys, but few live ones like Angelica.

Finally he turned to me. As his partner walked up alongside him he said, "What happened? Corey try to drop you?"

"He and another guy gave it a good try. Corey yelled at the other one, called him Skiko. Mean anything to you?"

He shook his head. The other officer didn't recognize the name, either. Angelica was getting to her feet. Conversation stopped while the policemen watched every movement, every sway and jiggle and ripple. Don't let contemporary propaganda lead you astray. Cops are human.

Chuck eyed the blood on my head and the side of my pants' leg. "How bad is it?"

"Not as bad as it looks."

"It couldn't be. You look worse than Stub."

I told them what had happened. After that we examined the dark sedan. The registration was in the name of Wilbur Corey. So Stub's real handle had been Wilbur. There was a radiophone, similar to the one in my Cad, under the dash.

Angelica had said when George Halstead received his call last night the car had been nearing the house. I'd assumed the call must have been made either by a man in the car, or by somebody else who knew in advance exactly when it would be arriving. It looked now as if Stub, or perhaps somebody in the car with him, had made the call from the Polara itself. I checked the headlights. The left one wasn't centered, sent its beam too high.

The body was hauled away; Angelica went back in her house after telling what little she knew, and I followed the officers downtown.

There I got patched up and bandaged, took a pill, made my report, and prepared to leave. But before I left, the doctor took another look at me, checked the tape holding a white bandage against the side of my head, and said, "That'll do for now." He was a soft-faced man about sixty, with kindly eyes. "Go straight home, call your own doctor, and get into bed."

"Bed? Hell, I feel all right, doc. I've had headaches before."

"You do as I tell you, young man. You've received a severe blow on the skull."

"Yeah, but I feel pretty good now—"

"The full effects may not be evidenced immediately."

"Effects like what?"

"It's difficult to say precisely—which is why you should be in bed. Dizziness, confusion, a lack of clarity in mental processes. You might suddenly lapse into unconsciousness. It's impossible to be more specific; but there is definite trauma, and you—"

"I'll be all right, doctor. But thanks for patching me up. And for the advice."

"You'd better take that advice, young man. At least lie down and keep very quiet."

I didn't tell him why I couldn't; that there were things I had to do unless I wanted the next slug, instead of merely being a long-distance sap, to drill two or three inches deeper. Because there would be other slugs. I had not the slightest doubt about that.

So I merely thanked him once more and took off.

Back in my apartment at the Spartan, after cleaning up and changing clothes—and reloading my revolver—I turned the thermostats higher on the community tank and the bowl wherein was my sick *Microglanis*. I fed the frisky creatures, then got on the phone and called the L.A.P.D.

I got put through to Samson—he'd already had a report on the shooting in Westwood—and filled him in.

Then I said, "I don't know anything about this Skiko—if that's what Corey actually yelled. It wasn't the most important thing in my mind right then. But it does seem like I've heard that name somewhere. Mean anything to you, Sam?"

"Means you're going to get your tail shot off if you don't—"

"Sam, I've called upon you as a guardian of goodness, truth, and beauty for aid in a time of trial. And what do I get? I get an old lady, who—"

He growled something unintelligible. But loud. I guessed he had one of those abominable black cigars stuck between his teeth. Then he growled intelligibly. "O.K. I don't make the name. But I'll check it out for you. How do you feel?"

"Fine, except for the agony of my wounds."

"Anything else?"

"Yeah. Far as I know, there was never anybody named Skiko associated with Jimmy Violet. But Stub Corey sure was. Stub is the guy who almost surely caved in Halstead's head, but I fixed it so we can't ask him about it."

"You fixed it good."

"However, there was a car behind me after I left the Halsteads' place last night—looks now like it tailed me from there —and I'm sold that it was the same car Stub and this Skiko were driving today."

"So?"

"So why don't you pick up Jimmy and his gang and bring them downtown and beat hell out of them? If three or four of them confess, maybe you can get a conviction."

"You got any more bright ideas?"

"Not at the moment, Sam. But as soon as I do, you'll be the first to know."

"Thank Heaven for that," he said, and hung up.

I gave Hazel a call.

After a bit of banter I asked her, "Anything cooking?"

"Yes, you got another call from a girl with a sexy voice."

"Oh? Same one who phoned before?"

"I don't think so. At least this one sounded different—and she gave me a name. Do you know a Sybil?"

"I know two . . . three Sybils. Which one was it?"

"She didn't tell me her last name. But she said you met very recently. And you said to her—I'm not sure I got this right— something like, 'Whoa'?"

"Whoa? To a girl? That doesn't sound like me."

"I didn't think so, either."

"It must've been—Ah! It was *'Whoo!'* Spork! Ah—Sybil. Sybil Spork! Hot dog."

"That was entirely unintelligible, except for hot dog."

"I merely said it was Sybil Spork who called."

"I thought you were having a fit. Spork? I'll bet you're making these people up."

"No, she's real. I hope to tell you—"

"How do you meet all these people, Shell? Especially so many girls with sexy voices."

"Well, it's—they eat lots of fruits and vegetables. What did Sybil want with me?"

"She wants you to come to her house immediately, as soon as possible, at least. She phoned half an hour ago."

"Come out for what?"

"All she told me was that she wants you to come out to see her—"

"I'm on my way."

"—and that she's got something to show you."

"Goodbye."

"But nobody must know you're there. You'll have to park a block away, around the corner, and sneak in."

"Oh?"

"She and her husband will be inside the house—"

"She and her husband?"

"And they'll explain everything to you. They've both got something to show you."

"I don't know about this—"

"She didn't explain what it was, Shell, but simply said something terrible had happened. And it's connected with the case you're on, the Halstead case."

It rang a funny little bell. There was a kind of faint clanging in my head already, along with a kind of dull thrombling, but I could hear the funny little bell.

The last caller with a sexy voice had said the same thing. And soon after that Porter got it in the back.

"Nobody's supposed to know I'm out there, huh?" I said suspiciously. "I'm supposed to sneak in, huh? Did this lovely girl give any specific directions, like making sure to sneak in by way of some ambushes—"

"She did say you should walk in from the street behind their house—wherever it is."

"I know where it is. I was there this morning. There's bushes back there. Can you think of anything better than bushes for ambushes?"

"You're to go in the back way. And you aren't to let *anybody* know you're going out there."

100

"Splendid. Anything else?"

"Just a minute. Let me check my notebook. No . . . that's all, Shell. But she stressed it was important; it just couldn't wait."

"Yeah. They might be trying to trick me. Outwit me. Ha. That'll be the day. I'll fix them. Uhh."

"What? Is something the matter?"

"No. Just a little ache in my headache. O.K., thanks again, Hazel."

"You're sure you're all right, Shell?"

"Me? Ha-ha, of *course* I'm all right."

13

⚜

I DIDN'T PARK ONE BLOCK AWAY. I PARKED TWO BLOCKS AWAY.

Then I opened the Cad's trunk and pawed through the junk I carry in it. There's a lot of electronics equipment, microphones, bugs, infra-red gear and such, but that's not what I was after at the moment. I lifted a scratched, stained crossbow and found the extension brace and bit I was after. Then I put the crossbow back and looked at it for a moment.

The crossbow, a medieval weapon, one type of which had once been used for shooting quarrels—square-headed bolts or arrows—at the enemy. But a friend of mine had given this one to me. He was a Marine recently back from overseas. Most high-level talk was about the unthinkable atomic and H-bombs, but at a lower level, in the heat and muck of jungles, ancient weaponry was being used for waging war. My friend had used this very crossbow for silent kills. Some of the arrows he'd given me were still stained with blood.

I rummaged a bit, picked up a light but strong collapsible bamboo ladder—the kind that can be slid out or back like a fishing rod—and a roll of tape; then slammed the trunk's lid and headed for the Sporks'.

There was always a chance they were on the level, of course. But it didn't seem likely. There were too many people around who impressed me as being definitely atilt. Besides, even if they were un-atilt there was nothing wrong with taking a few extra precautions. Nobody was going to shoot me in the backside if I could help it.

Fool me once, I was thinking sagely as I neared the Spork house, your fault; fool me twice, my fault. I couldn't sagely remember what came after that, for fool me three times, four times, and so on.

I didn't go in the Sporks' back way, but through the back yard of the house next to theirs. Just in case people, expecting me at the back of the Sporks, were skulking there. To outwit me. To massacre me. There was lots of shrubbery—lots of bushes—and I kept my eyes peeled, but didn't see anything suspicious. Probably *I* looked suspicious, darting from bush to bush, but that couldn't be helped. Even though all this darting was beginning to tire my head.

Having safely reached the side of the Sporks' two-story house, I ran up my extension ladder, placed it carefully, then climbed up it to a small veranda or deck outside one of the rear rooms on the second floor. There I tried the window, but it was locked. A few yards away, however, was a door. It also was locked; but using the brace and bit it was the work of only a minute to bore a four-inch hole in the wood below the door-knob, reach through and unlock the door and step inside.

I was in a wide, carpeted hallway. I walked quietly past closed doors to the end of the hall, reached the top of a wide stairway curving down to a small room, into which the front door opened. At the top of the stairs I stood quietly, listening, senses keen and alert.

There wasn't a sound from anywhere up here on the second floor, but a soft flutter of voices rose from somewhere below. On my right at the foot of the stairs was an arched doorway, closed by blue velvet draperies or curtains. I started slowly and cautiously down the stairs, holding my brace and bit ready.

Then I stopped, cocked my head to one side.

I deliberated a moment, eyeing the brace and bit.

Then I nodded knowingly, put down the brace and bit and took my Colt Special from its holster. I started down again, gripping the .38 in my right hand.

I had been instructed to come in the back way. If there'd been evil aforethought, that meant people would be in the back of the house preparing to slaughter me. But those sounds seemed to be coming from the front of the house. What did it mean?

Halfway down the stairs I slipped off my shoes, continued in my stocking feet. Not only was my progress thus even more silent, but it appeared to soothe my head. Well, it almost *had* to,

I thought. After all, my feet were *connected* to my head. It gave me a queer feeling to realize that not once before in my whole life had I thought of that—though it was now a perfectly obvious truism. Then I had another truism: Probably a lot of headaches were caused by feet.

Right then I realized something wonderful was happening to me. My reasoning powers were being elevated to the nth degree. My mind was clearer than it had ever been before. It was getting just like glass. I was standing there thinking that maybe thinking caused athlete's foot, when those sounds below captured my attention again.

I cased the area carefully. The scene appeared a little different, now that I was seeing more clearly.

At the foot of the stairs on my right was a doored archway. In the arch hung thick blue velvet draperies. And it was from behind those draped velvetries that the sounds came, a buzzing, as of conversation. A buzzing, as of something, anyhow. I listened carefully. *Buzz-buzz.* It was a bit difficult to filter it out from the faint clanging and dull thrombling, but I filtered it. Somebody—something—was in there.

I cocked my .38 Colt Special.

My course was clear. It was either go in there—or leave.

But I couldn't leave. Not after coming this far. And spending such a *hell* of a time getting here.

No, it was in I go, quick, while I've got the element of total surprise. I would tiptoe down the rest of the stairs in my stocking feet, which fortunately were connected to my head, and pause for only a moment before those draped velvets. Then I'd part the arches with a lightning movement and spring inside. And then . . .

Then . . .

Well, I'd cross that bridge when I came to it.

When I was on the fourth step from the bottom a little reddish arrow of dizziness zipped silently, like a quarrel shot from a crossbow, from the left side of my skull to the right side. The little radish must have gone straight through my brain. Then it ricocheted, quarreling west, north, south—all over the place. What I think happened then is, I tripped. Or stumbled. That is to say, I appeared not to have everything under control.

But I continued to think very fast. Like lightning.

Well, I thought, I'm tripping, all right. But at least I'm tripping in the right direction. That's where I wanted to go, isn't it? Down there? Well, that's where I'm going. Just going a little faster than I'd planned to. But, hell, you can't expect everything to go *precisely* according to plan.

That draped archway was only a few feet away. I knew if I fell down and hit the floor at the foot of the stairs it would make a hell of a noise, and thus alert anybody in there—where those buzzing buzzes were buzzing—and my element of surprise would be lessened. According to my position, however—I was way over at an angle in the air by this time, even though I was still thinking like lightning—it was going to be impossible for me to tiptoe down as I had planned and catch the assassins—or monster bumblebees—unaware.

It was clear to me that the only sensible course left was to give a great leap and burst through those velveted curtains into the room. It was either that, or keep considering alternatives until I fell flat on my face. So that's what I did. Well . . .

I did the great leap, all right. But, unfortunately, it was in a direction very nearly parallel to the floor. In fact, I think my head was about an inch below my feet when I did the great leap. But, hell, things can't *always* go as you plan them. I was aimed right at those curtained velvets, though. Sailing through the air at them. If *anybody* can burst through those veal cutlets, I thought, it has to be me right now.

I was wrong about that, too.

Perhaps it's because I didn't hit the things squarely in the middle, where they were supposed to open. Whatever the reason, they didn't open. I could feel them wrapping around me like velvet octopuses, all over and around me; but there's always a bright side and whatever it was softened the blow when I landed. I hit with a jarring thump, skidded, rolled, and then felt something crash against me. There was eerie plinking music. And there was a geat big bang. Like a gun going off.

Muffled in my curtain-clogged ears I could hear wild sounds. No more buzzing. There was a high-pitched scream, and a low-pitched scream. Sounded like a woman screaming, and a man screaming. "Eeeeeyorrk!" the woman screeched, and "BLLAAAHK!" the man bellowed. I was kicking, yanking, pulling, trying to get out from inside the curtains.

"Eeeeeyorrk!"

"BLLAAAHK!"

It occurred to me that if somebody was going to slaughter me they couldn't ask a better time for it. In fact there wouldn't be much left to do. But nobody had killed me yet. I thought about it. I thought like lightning.

Then I stopped struggling.

"Ah, shut up," I said. "Shut up and get me out of here."

I had to ask them a couple more times, but finally they pulled themselves together and got the job done. I sat silently on the floor for a few seconds, looking up at Mr. and Mrs. Spork.

Sybil put long red-nailed fingers over her lips and turned her head a bit, and looked at me with slanting eyes.

I looked up at Mr. Spork with crossed eyes. "Have you got any bees in here?"

"Bees?" he said. "Bees?"

"Well, if you don't know what they are, you must not have any." I paused. "Mr. Spork, I suppose you're wondering . . ." I threw my hands up in the air.

"You've certainly ruined our blue velvet draperies," Sybil said.

"Is that what they were? Yeah, I guess I have. Shot a hole in one, didn't I? Hmm, didn't do the carpet any good either, did it? Ah, there's a door I'd better tell you about, too."

I got to my feet, feeling myself over. Nothing seemed to be broken. Nothing new. In fact, it appeared that when something had crashed into me—actually, I had rolled up against a piano —it had stopped some of that quarreling inside my skull. For example, I now *knew* thinking wouldn't cause athlete's foot. At least, it didn't seem likely.

I put my gun back in its holster—after I found it in the blue velvet draperies—took a deep breath, and said, "Mr. and Mrs. Spork, no matter what any of us has done, let's not criticize eath other, hey? Let's . . . live and let live. Let's not ask me why I came in here in this, ah, this, uh, this fashion. I had my reasons. Truly I did. But I should prefer not to go into them right now. Or ever. Each of us does things different ways, right? O.K.? Well, that's settled, so what was it—"

"But why," Sybil asked me wonderingly, "did you jump into the draperies?"

"Mrs. Spork," I said, "how would you like to play Russian roulette? All by yourself."

"I'm still all a-flutter," she said. "All a-twang."

"*You're* all a-twang. Huh. You don't know what all a-twang is." I paused. "Matter of fact, neither do I."

"Where are your shoes?" she asked me.

"You're full of marvelous questions, aren't you? I left them halfway up the stairway, if you've really got to know. After I bored a big hole in your door. Yeah. Bored a hole right through it. Why didn't I use my set of picklocks? Why didn't I use a five-cent key? It is possible none of us will ever know. I will say only this, boring a hole in your door seemed a keen idea at the time. I took my shoes off so my head, in which I recently got shot—see the bandage? See the big hole? Ah, maybe *that* explains the hole in your door—wouldn't make so much noise. I didn't want my head to make any noise because I was afraid the bumblebees would hear it and eat me. There, that should cover most of it. Any more questions?"

She didn't have any more questions.

A couple of minutes later we were all seated in the room—the living room it was—and I told them I knew everything there was to know, so they could speak freely.

"You don't know everything," Sybil said. "I called you because we're being blackmailed."

"Oh? By whom?"

"We don't know—I mean, a man came here this afternoon, but we'd never seen him before."

"Blackmailed how?"

"He had a picture."

"Ah. So? Chinese say, one picture—" I shook my head. "What kind of picture?" I asked her, suddenly recalling that Angelica Bersudian had asked me the same question—suspiciously—not long ago.

"A photograph of me and Hugh in bed. Hugh Pryer and me."

"Ah. In bed."

"Well . . . Not in it, on it."

"I presume you were not having a pillow fight."

"Not exactly." She reached into a handbag on the couch between her and her husband, took out a small snapshot and handed it to me. "This is what I wanted to show you," she said. "The man left this copy with us. Now do you understand?" I examined the photo—and told her, yes, I understood.

They'd been warned not to contact the police or anybody else—which was why she hadn't given Hazel her full name, and also why she'd asked me to sneak in the back way, so nobody would see me and deduce that the Sporks had called me.

"Hum," I said, handing the photo back. "Erum. I see. So, on one of the recent evenings of, ah . . . someone, without your knowledge, snapped a—"

"Oh, we knew about it. All of us did. But we thought the whole album had been burned up. The picture this greasy man

107

had today *was* burned. But only around the edges. Not . . . in the middle."

"Slow down a shake." I was starting to get the picture. *The* picture. "You *all* knew about this?" I went on. "That there was an album? And it was supposed to have been burned? In a fire, you mean, of course."

"Yes, of course."

"In this album who—that is, the photographs of what individuals were included?"

Mr. Spork joined in for the first time. "All of us."

I nodded. "You mean not merely you and Mrs. Spork, but the Halsteads, Whists, Rileys, Kents, Nelsons, Bersudians, Smiths, Warrens, and Pryers."

"That's right." He thought a minute. "In fact, you've named every one."

"Uh-huh. Why this album? Just for fun?"

"No, for our protection. That is, the protection of the group," he said. "Do you understand?"

"Not completely."

"We aren't the first group to utilize this method of insuring the—well, the discretion of each individual member. It's been done many times before. You might be surprised to know how many times."

"I suppose I would. You mean that if somebody felt like blabbing—say to a newspaperman, the law—knowledge of the existence of his, or her, compromising photograph would insure silence?"

"Not merely silence, but also very conscious discretion. Should someone feel remorse, or become angry with one or another in the group, estranged—a divorce, for example, or a couple leaving the group—the photographs would very likely prevent . . . retaliation."

"Uh-huh."

Mr. Spork pursed his lips. "Understand," he went on seriously, "we—none of us—feel we're doing anything heinous or even reprehensible. Certainly Sybil and I don't. We feel that sex, the act of sex, is much more than merely some kind of carnal acrobatics intrinsically cursed and degrading—"

"It's about the *friendliest* thing you can do," Sybil broke in.

"Well," I said, "you certainly have some kind of point there—"

"—though it is undeniably true," Mr Spork was continuing lyrically, "that sex, or rather the false aura of evil and shame
108

and guilt which has been imposed upon the word and act, is the foundation on which has been erected uncountable neuroses—"

"That's certainly true," Sybil said, "there's certainly truth in *that*—"

"—and psychoses. This monumental hypocrisy has led millions, perhaps billions, to hospitals, mental wards, the psychiatrist's couch, and to the divorce court. Yet once stripped of illusion and hypocrisy, if we can ignore the vocal victims of sexual starvation denying their own hungers—"

"There certainly aren't many things that are more *fun*—"

"—sex stands revealed in a newer and purer light—"

"I could tell you a thing or two—"

"Sybil, shut up, please."

Wonder of wonders, she smiled at him and shut up.

Mr. Spork continued, "As I was saying—"

"Hey," I said. "What about this blackmailer?"

"Yes, I was getting to that. The point I'm making is this, Mr. Scott. We members of the group feel neither shame nor guilt, but we are excruciatingly aware that our mores and attitudes, our conception of morality, is greatly at variance with that of many other members of our society—others who have it in their power to cause us, individually and collectively, great harm, frustration, and loss. Exposure of the group's—ours or any other group's—activities could bring upon us censure. Contempt. Financial and social retribution. And more, much more. There is no wrath more horrible than the wrath of the righteous —even when they're wrong." He smiled. "They conducted the Inquisition, made Galileo kneel. They crucified Christ. They burned Bruno."

I think he was about to give me a history lesson. And I'm not so hot on history. "This blackmailer," I said.

"He came here this afternoon, showed us this photograph—a copy of the original, he said. His demand is for twenty thousand dollars to be delivered to him tomorrow night. Or—well, I'm sure you understand the or else."

"Uh-huh. Also, the twenty G's—should you fork it over— would undoubtedly be only the first installment. Tell me, adding up the net worth—of all the members of your group, Mr. Spork, what would you say the total would come to?"

"I'd have to guess. I really don't know. I'm worth over a million. Bersudian's worth at least four or five. I'd guess the total at perhaps fifteen million. Might be thirty, for that matter."

"What time did this guy come by today?"

"Fortunately I noted that. He was here at twenty minutes past two this afternoon."

"What did he look like?"

"About five-six and thin. Narrow face. Rather washed-out blue eyes."

Sybil broke in, "I don't think he was more than thirty or thirty-five, but somehow he looked a lot older."

"Little pits all over his face," Mr Spork added. "Little scars."

"Bingo," I said.

14

"What?"

"That's his name. Bingo—Lester Kestel."

"You know him?" Mr. Spork leaned forward. "You mean you recognize him from our description?"

"From that and a couple of other things. I think. I'm reasonably sure it was Bingo."

"If you know who he is, I suppose we could have him arrested." Mr. Spork shook his head. "But, frankly, we can't take the chance he'd make good his threat to expose—"

I smiled. "This should interest you. If I'm right about the little slob, we had him in the can already today. Him and two other hoods. Not for long, of course—not long enough. One of those boys has since tried to kill me. Bingo apparently came out to see you. I wonder what Little Phil's been up to?" I added, largely to myself.

"Well . . . what can we do?" That was Sybil.

"I've got a couple things in mind," I said. "I'm working, as you know, for Mrs. Halstead. But you can take it for granted that I'll be working on this, too. And looking for Bingo, among others."

"We'd be so terribly grateful if you could help—"

"We'll pay you very generously, Mr. Scott—"

That was Sybil first, followed by her husband. I interrupted both of them, "Forget that. There won't be any fee. My fee, whatever happens, will come from Mrs. Halstead. We've already got that settled." I paused. "But—just in case I should get lucky enough to solve your problem and get Bingo, or any of his friends, off your backs . . ."

"Yes?"

"Maybe you'll be good enough to forget about the blue velvet draperies? And the carpet?"

"Of course."

"And, um, the door upstairs with a big hole in it."

I think I could have added, "And burning down your house," and they would happily have agreed.

"O.K.," I said. "Tell me more about this album. Whose idea was it originally? When were these photos taken, and where? Were they kept in a regular album—kept where? And how did Bingo, or whoever the guy was, get his hands on the photo he had with him today?"

Each of them answered some of the questions, or parts of them, and added bits of additional info here and there. But when I put it all together, there wasn't much.

They didn't know where Bingo had got the photo of Sybil and Hugh Pryer, but it had been taken at the Halsteads' home on the night they "joined the club," as Mr. Spork put it; and that had been about three months ago. The photos were kept—in Sybil's words—in "a regular album, just like a family album."

Neither of them knew for sure who had originally broached the idea, only that the "album" had been s.o.p. when they joined the club, and the addition of their photographs to it a prerequisite for inclusion among the select and secret membership of the group.

"It was like an initiation," said Sybil. "Besides being for everybody's protection, it did sort of break the ice. And besides that, it was lots of fun—"

"A prerequisite," drily continued Mr. Spork, who had been speaking, "in addition to approval of all other members, of course."

"Uh-huh. And those members then consisted of the Halsteads and Whists, the Bersudians and Rileys."

"That's right."

"Which means the idea of the album must have been initiated by someone from among those four couples." I thought a moment. "And I'd assume one of those couples had the album in their possession, for safekeeping."

"Yes, that was Ed and Marcelle."

112

"Somehow I'm not surprised. Didn't you hear about the fire they had in their apartment at the Norvue?"

"I was coming to that," said Mr. Spork. "That was about a month ago, just before they dropped out. They said the album had been destroyed in the fire. It was in their bedroom—"

"I know. Apparently the entire album wasn't destroyed."

"No, dammit," said Mr. Spork.

"I suppose," I said, "that one snap might have been recovered from the trash. But Bingo isn't a trash man. Or a bellboy, for that matter. Assuming it was Bingo who came here today."

We talked another minute, then Mr. Spork said, "I'm arranging to have the twenty thousand in cash here tomorrow, in case there's nothing else to do but pay the man—when I get instructions on how that's to be accomplished. I'm inclined to agree with you that the one payment wouldn't be the end of it, so we certainly hope you can help us in some way. I'd be glad to pay you the twenty—"

I waved a hand. "Forget that. I can't make any promises, but I'll do what I can. A couple of things are puzzling me, and if I can work them out . . ." I didn't finish it.

That was about all there was to say, so we shook hands and I left.

I went back to the Cad following the same route I'd used to get here—without all that darting of course—carrying my brace and bit and ladder. Hadn't broken in any windows, so I hadn't needed the roll of tape. Hadn't really needed the ladder and brace and bit, I thought sourly.

Rolling back toward Hollywood, I called Homicide and got Samson on the line again.

I asked him if he'd dug up anything on the name Skiko and he said, "Not much. No record here, Shell. Checked R and I, and there's not even a 'Skiko' in the monicker file. But there's one lead. You remember Lane from ID?"

"Sure." He was retired now, but Sergeant Lane had been in Intelligence Division for several years.

"One of his reports," Samson went on, "mentions a Skiko. That's all, no first name or last name, just included as one of the people he'd run into or heard about while putting together a folder of information."

"Information about what?"

"He was checking on hoods moving into the L.A. area from out of state then. That was a couple years ago. Want me to get in touch with Lane, see if he remembers anything more?"

"No, I know where he lives. I'll give him a call and if he's home I'm sure he'll see me. Something else I wish you would do, though, Sam."

"Like what?"

"I told you about this guy Walles. Ed, and wife Marcelle. Used the name Whist for a while."

"Yeah."

"I've a hunch his name isn't Walles, either. If you had a set of his prints, you could check them out for me, couldn't you?"

"Could. But how are we going to get his prints? If I know you, you want us to kick in some doors and—"

"Nope, just check out those prints—as fast as humanly possible—when and if I get them to you."

"How are you going to get them? I suppose *you're* going to kick—"

"Relax, Sam. Cootie owes me a favor. He'll bring the prints in, if he makes out."

"Don't tell me any more about it."

Cootie was a man who'd worked for me on other occasions. He'd been a police lab man for about six months, but hadn't been exactly cut out for law-enforcement work, and now owned a string of two gas stations. He hadn't forgotten his former skills, however, and could photograph—or lift—latent prints, which was all I wanted him to do. And which I was sure he would do, for a couple of C-notes.

"O.K., but you know who he is. Thus when and if he shows up, you'll know he's my personal representative in the continuing fight against crime, the titanic struggle—"

"I know who he is," Sam interrupted wearily.

"So, knowing he's from me, that will make it police business."

"Not likely," he said.

But he hadn't said he wouldn't run a check on the prints. I told him I'd call in later, and hung up.

Then I phoned the Edward Walles' number in Beverly Hills. There was no answer. Which was what I'd expected.

So I phoned Cootie.

Sergeant Ben Lane, retired, was a still erect and solid-looking man of sixty-odd, with bushy gray brows and deep lines at the corners of his mouth. I'd found him at home, and been talking to him for several minutes.

I got up, thanked him for his time—and info from the voluminous mental files still in head—and said, "Sounds like the
114

guy, Ben. I didn't get a very good look at him, but he was short and bald—and Stub called him Skiko, after all. Anyhow, I'll know him if I see him again."

"Try those dumps I mentioned," Ben said. "Might be he still hangs out in one of them. It's been two years, but hoods don't change much."

"Nothing that ever tied him to Jimmy Violet, though?"

"No, like I said, he was just one of a bunch moving into town. Came from Illinois, I think. Got too hot for him there. He was just a small-timer, a punk. Wasn't in with anybody else —not then, anyhow—just a loner rolling in. I never had anything on him, except he got busted a couple times back there, no convictions."

"Yeah, but the arrests were for extortion, and that's good enough for me. Let me know if I can do anything for you, Ben."

He nodded and we shook hands.

Back in the Cad I headed for La Cienega. Not the famed stretch of it known as "Restaurant Row," but another face of the Boulevard farther from Hollywood, where within a mile or so were half a dozen run-down bars, beer joints, and grandly named cocktail lounges.

According to Ben Lane, that was where Skiko had spent a good deal of his free time, where he could be a big fish in a little pool, trying to impress the B-girls and floozies who cadged drinks from the not-too-savory clientele. At least, that had been true a couple of years ago. Maybe it still was.

It was.

I found him in a joint called the Sphinx, which was at least as Egyptian in decor as the corner of Second and Main in L.A. When I walked through the dump's entrance and stood in the gloom inside, letting my pupils open up again while wishing I could as easily close my nostrils, the only familiar thing was the beer-and-sour-burp smell of the place, which was nauseously reminiscent of the atmosphere in the three previous joints I'd cased.

At first.

Three or four men, a very fat gal sagging on and over a far-too-small bar stool, and a young but wasted-looking woman were sitting at the bar on my right. The booths were on my left and all seemed to be empty; but one wasn't. The backs of the booths were high and I couldn't see into the one at the end farthest from me, but I could hear the sound of a woman

115

giggling there. It was an oddly whining giggle, as if she were tee-heeing through her nose.

And then I heard the man's voice. It was rasping but soft, or at least low-pitched. Like a loud, hoarse whisper.

I couldn't make out the words at first, but I walked closer and heard him saying, ". . .and then, doll, I just ankled away and left them all standin' there with their faces fallin' off. How about that? Don't that grab you?"

The woman was giggling all through his story, really giving her nostrils a workout. But the interesting thing to me was that male voice, the sound of it and the man's words. Because I was remembering Samson's telling me about the guy who'd phoned him right after Porter got it in the back.

As I walked along the row of booths I smiled slightly, reached up and loosened the Colt in its holster, kept my hand on it.

The conversation, and even the giggling, ended suddenly when I stopped in front of that last booth.

Little guy. Bald. I could see a faint brown blotch on one of his cheeks and a thin scar in his upper lip—marks Ben Lane had described but which I hadn't noticed when we'd met before. It was the same boy who'd been out in Westwood this afternoon with Stub Corey. With Stub and me.

"Hello, fleeper," I said. And then I added softly, "You can finish that story with the fuzz, Skiko. Yeah, I know who you are. That grab you, Papa?"

15

He'd been wrong about me twice so far.

He made it three.

Skiko could see I had my hand under my coat, obviously on my gun, even if he couldn't see the Colt itself. And he for sure knew I carried a gun. Maybe he just didn't think—or simply thought I was here to kill him. Or maybe he'd charged himself up so much selling himself to his floozie that he kept believing his lies for a little too long. Just a moment too long. But too long.

Or maybe he thought he had a chance when I took my eyes off him and looked at the woman. Maybe, maybe not; but that's when he made his move.

The "doll" seated across from Skiko was somewhere between thirty and forty years old and approximately the same number of pounds overweight, a gal with the look of decay in her eyes and pain puckered around her mouth. She was a faded blonde, dark roots showing close to her scalp. She stared at me with her too-red and oily-looking lips parted, the corners still pulled up slightly in what remained of her real or feigned amusement. Folds of dough-white flesh sagged over the low top of her dress, much as the fat gal had sagged on her bar stool.

I just glanced at her, that was all.

But in that second or two Skiko shoved his feet against the floor pushing himself farther from me while his right hand whipped up under his coat. His hand hitting the gun butt made

117

a flat sound, like a thin stick breaking, and I yelled, "Don't do it, you damn—"

But that was all there was time for.

He was yanking out the gun even as I jerked the Colt from its holster and slapped it toward him. His eyes fixed on the Colt in my hand and widened till the whites were enormous and his mouth started stretching open—but he didn't let go of the gun, didn't stop.

I waited as long as I could. It wasn't long. But the gun was out from under his coat before I pulled the trigger.

When I pulled the trigger, though, when I had to pull it, I didn't stop with one. I put three into him. A baby's hand could have covered the three holes. But not the blood that poured, with astonishing suddenness, from them.

He made a sound that seemed to come not from his mouth but from deep in his throat, almost like a gasp starting in his stomach. The hand holding his gun thudded against the table, hitting a glass and shattering it, sending splinters of glass and splashes of beer over the table and onto the low-cut dress and doughy breasts of the faded blonde.

She started to scream.

She just sat there and stared at the blood spreading over Skiko's wrinkled white shirt, crawling in a thick dark U down toward his belt buckle, and screamed, over and over and over; the shrill nerve-racking screeches were punctuated only by the strangled throat rasp as she sucked in air.

Skiko coughed. Blood bubbled on his lips.

I picked up his gun, glanced over my shoulder. The bar was emptying, last of the customers just going through the door into late-afternoon sunlight. But the bartender was behind the bar, looking at us. I jerked my head, pointed to the woman still staring and screaming at the top of her lungs.

He hurried over, took the woman's hand and pulled her away. I told him to plant her and call the cops. She stopped screaming, but kept making little gasping noises.

I leaned over Skiko. His eyes were rolling.

"Skiko," I said, "where'd Bingo get that photo—" I stopped, started over. There might not be much time, and the number-one problem was making sure I stayed alive to ask other questions.

So I said, "Who set me up for the kill at the Hamilton, Skiko?"

He moved his head a little, got his eyes on my face. They

118

weren't dull, but almost glowing, hot and feverish. I'm not sure he understood me. Maybe he didn't even hear me. He pushed his bloody tongue out and over the blood on his lips.

I put my head closer to his, looked straight at him. "Look, you knew you got Porter—didn't get me, anyway—because you and Stub showed up and tried again in Westwood. I know two guys did the blasting downtown and you phoned Samson right after that. So start there, at the Hamilton. You had to be near a phone. Who were the trigger-men?"

"Gippo," he said. It sounded as if he were gargling, but I caught the name; and I knew the rest of it, Gippo Crane. "And . . . Tooth."

"Billy?"

"Yeah."

"No brains there, Skiko. Who set me up for that kill?"

His eyes rolled again. I grabbed the cloth of his suit coat, bunched cloth and shoulder padding in my hand, holding him up. "There at the Hamilton, Skiko! *Who set me up for that kill?*"

His eyes didn't look feverish any longer. He wasn't looking right at me, but past my head. Not much juice in him now. Brain sluggish, heart slowing.

"Dilly," he said finally. "Dilly Pickle."

I blinked. He would have sounded out of his skull if I hadn't heard so many hoodlum monickers; but this was a new one to me.

"Did you say 'Dilly Pickle?' " I asked him.

He let the lids fall and rise over his eyes, moved his head as though trying to nod.

"Where'll I find him, Skiko?" I waited for him, then said, louder than before, "This Dilly Pickle, where'll I find the bastard?"

"Hidden Valley. Should be . . . by now. Lodge . . ."

"What's he got to do with Jimmy Violet? Where the hell does Violet fit into this?"

Skiko was dead.

I let go of his shoulder and his body slumped in the seat, crumpled almost out of sight below the table top.

I looked down at him for a moment, then used my handkerchief to rub blood flecks from the back of my hand. Well, he'd told me a little. Not enough, but a little.

That "Dilly Pickle" bit had thrown me for a second or two. I'd expected to hear the name of Jimmy Violet—assuming

Skiko knew at that point what I was actually asking him. He'd been pretty close to the edge.

But if it was a hood's monicker, while unusual, it wasn't of an unprecedented goofiness. Sometimes a crook's nickname or underworld handle is based on an outstanding aspect of his personality or character. Like that of a little, not-too-unpleasant creep I'd known called Viper because he was deathly afraid of snakes. Or a monicker might be an addition to, or corruption of, a man's real name. The "Tooth" Skiko had mentioned, for example. His real name was William DeKay. And he had exceptionally large and horselike choppers. It was a natural; almost inevitably he'd become known to his chums as Billy "Tooth" DeKay.

So, it wasn't merely the name "Dilly Pickle" that had jarred me, but the fact that it was a brand new one to me, and I thus had nothing on which to base any deductions about why this particular Pickle would have arranged for me to get knocked off.

Well, maybe I could ask the bastard. Ask either pleasantly or horrendously. Because it appeared the guy had wound up at, or checked into, the Hidden Valley Lodge. Skiko had told me that much, in addition to tagging the boys who'd blasted Porter instead of me: Gippo Crane and Billy DeKay.

So I was going to the Hidden Valley Lodge.

The bartender was still standing next to the chubby blonde. He'd brought her a drink, and she was quiet now, but her upper lip, under her nose, was wet and shiny.

I took the bartender across the room, gave him Skiko's .45, and said, "You call the police?"

He nodded.

"All right. I'm taking off."

I was. I didn't have time to stick around—not the time I knew would be consumed if I did.

"My name's Shell Scott." I got out my wallet, handed him one of my business cards. "Tell the police just what happened. You saw it?"

He nodded again.

"You know Skiko?"

"Yeah. He's in here all the time."

"You saw him go for his gun?"

The bartender swallowed, but nodded. "I seen it."

"O.K. Tell the police what you saw." I smiled. "But you

won't make Skiko look like an innocent citizen assulted by a big white-haired thug, will you?"

His words, and voice, and eyes, and jumping Adam's apple, said he wouldn't make Skiko look like that at all.

I pointed to the blonde. "And keep that one here to tell her story, too." Then I trotted to the Cad and got out of there.

The Hidden Valley Lodge was about as close as you could get to "country," to trees and stream and birds chirping, to peace and restful quiet, without going clear out of the county.

Only a short drive north of Beverly Hills, it was, like the Bel Air Hotel not far away, in a very woodsy setting with lots of trees and bosky growth all around, a sylvan landscape where one might expect poets to brood, but where, in fact, the high-powered well-to-do—industrialists, members of the board, company presidents, bankers, and numerous Hollywood producers, directors, writers, stars and even starlets—relaxed and played.

The rates at Hidden Valley were prohibitively expensive, but the Lodge was generally filled nearly to capacity nonetheless.

Not, however, with hoods.

So what would somebody named Dilly Pickle be doing here?

The real pickle, however, was the fact that while I had no idea who Dilly was, it was crystal clear that he knew me.

Consequently, when I walked over the wooden bridge, beneath which flowed a ten-foot-wide stream, I not only wore a hat and dark glasses but carried my own movie camera, which I'd taken from the Cad's trunk. It was a sixteen-millimeter Bolex loaded with a hundred feet of unexposed film—unexposed, at least, except for a few feet I'd shot on my last trip to Laguna Beach, when with a gorgeous tomato named Tootsie.

Not that I intended to be making any movies at the Hidden Valley Lodge. But, by pretending to be catching a few candid shots, I could hold the thing in front of my face while looking the area over. The hat and glasses would hide my too-obvious hair and eyebrows, but today I wanted every bit of help I could get. Especially since my head was aching like fury despite the consumption of several aspirins, and at rare intervals my eyes failed to focus as well as I'd have liked. Occasionally I saw two things where there was only one thing.

But as I walked over the bridge and toward a side entrance of the Hidden Valley's enormous lobby, my vision was at least 20-20 and it was one of those moments of respite when my entire skull seemed intact. I hoped it stayed thus in one piece, for I had not forgotten my experience at the Sporks'.

Ten minutes later, after talking briefly to the chief of security, and getting his O.K. for a gambit I wanted to employ, I checked with a clerk at the registration desk. Nobody named Pickle, Pickel, Peckle, Packle, or even Pickerel had checked in today, or during the last week. In fact, there had not been any guests registered whose last name began with a P. I spent another ten minutes roaming through the bars, dining rooms, and grounds outside—taking lots of "pictures"—without seeing any recognizable faces, then went back into the hotel.

I walked across the lobby holding a hand before my face, as though having trouble keeping my nose on, and stopped before thick plate-glass windows beyond which was the huge swimming pool. The sun would be below the horizon in less than an hour, but in and around the pool four or five dozen carefree guests still swam, splashed, or lolled.

Only a few feet beyond the window, reclining on a blue chaise longue with its back slightly elevated, was a gal with a body so splendid it was getting almost as much attention as a naked tomato would have received.

She was lying on her back with her arms at her sides, and a big wide-brimmed straw hat over her face, and thus concealing some of her features. But it was the other features catching the eye of the men—and women—who strolled by.

She was wearing a swimsuit, but it wasn't a bikini or even one of those brief jobs cut way up at the sides. It was a form-fitting white dandy which came clear up to her neck and over her shoulders, something like a sleeveless leotard, but it must have been made from perhaps an ounce and a half of clinging jersey, because a guy close enough should have been able to count her pores, and if she'd had a wee mole on her ribs, I would undoubtedly have been able to spot it even from here.

The smooth bare arms and legs were deeply tanned, and she looked so relaxed she might earlier have fallen asleep in the sun. I wanted to think the straw hat was covering her face because she'd decided to nap during the bright afternoon; but with a trace of unusual pessimism I concluded it was probably because she knew the body was fantastic, and thus chose to conceal a kisser virtually unkissable.

I wondered who she was. Nobody I knew, I was pretty sure.

A number of other people appeared to be wondering the same and probably other things, and it was interesting to note the varied reactions of those whose eyes fell upon her. As she breathed, the thin white jersey rose and fell, tight against the

122

skin of her flat stomach; the looming breasts swelled and sighed. And when the men strode by and glanced, or looked, or goggled, almost invariably their eyes seemed to flutter and dance, and their lips involuntarily curled, or twitched, or wiggled, or pooched.

Not the babes, though; not, not the babes.

The first gal who looked full upon the lyrelike outline and bulging bosom and taut stomach flaring sharply into hips worthy of sonnets, pulled her mouth into the round, compressed attitude of one sucking on a lemon gumdrop, and her eyes got smaller and smaller and finally disappeared entirely, or so it seemed to me. The next one gazed and yanked her head away, but the eyes—yes, narrowing, narrowing—stayed fixed and focused upon the cruelly unfair competition.

Two couples walked by, quite close to the gal in the white jersey dandy. Both guys looked and assumed expressions akin to that of alcoholics preparing gladly to leap off the wagon. You could see the cords swelling in their necks, the muscles wiggling in their eyebrows, nostrils thinning and flaring and again thinning, as might the nasal flaps of a bull ape upon scenting—after long lone days and days—a cow ape.

The first girl noted her fellow's apparent distress, and glanced about to see what horror it was his painted orbs had fallen upon. She saw. And on her pretty face grew an expression of unrestrained and total malevolence. Had it stayed there, her head could have been hung without alteration in the wax museum, suspended in mid-air below Jack the Ripper's bloody ripper, or perhaps even screwed upon Jack's neck.

But it was there for only an instant, a revelatory flicker which it is given to few men to see, and see so clearly. Fortunately. Then in a trice her features sprang back to their normal prettiness, were in fact even prettier—gay! glad! fun-fun!—as she snapped her head back toward her fellow's face, pressing closer against him, chattering and squirming in apparent ecstasy while nudging him toward the pool. Possibly to drown him.

The second girl did the same thing.

Too bad I've got to keep the old nose to the grindstone, I thought. I could stand here—or there—all day, learning about human nature, about life, about that babe in the white jersey dandy.

But instead I called a bellman over, slipped him a bill and asked him to have Dilly Pickle paged. I told him what I wanted

123

said, and that it was O.K. with the chief of security. He smiled at the bill, and walked away.

Unfortunately, the p.a. system used for paging could not be used selectively—that is, for a specific dining room only, or a bar, or the lobby alone—so the call for Dilly Pickle would be heard simultaneously everywhere, in and around the hotel. Also unfortunately, I couldn't be every place at once watching everybody; so it was unlikely that when his name boomed over the p.a. system I'd be fortunate enough to note a small or tall or thin or fat fellow go into a squat of vast surprise, clutching at his heart, or gun, or hind end upon hearing his name.

So I stayed where I was, glancing at the people in the lobby and those visible in and around the pool.

Then came the announcement over the lobby speakers. *"Will Dilly Pickle please come to the Lost and Found Section at the main desk? Will Dilly Pickle . . ."* and so on.

Several of the guests glanced around; some smiled, a few chuckled and shook their heads. Nothing out of the ordinary. The name rang oddly on my ears, too.

"Will Dilly Pickle please . . ."

I hadn't expected much from the page. But it was the only thing I'd been abe to think of which might speed this pursuit. The alternatives were either to hang around here looking, maybe for hours and even then unsuccessfully, or else forget it and go to work on some of the other angles.

The lovely with the mesmerizing curves apparently had indeed been taking a nap. Because as I glanced through the windows toward the pool I saw her stir, move slightly as though awakening, beginning to stretch, or tensing her sexy muscles.

"Will Dilly Pickle . . ."

She arched her back slightly, filling her lungs with breath, and the already amazingly prominent breasts seemed to strain toward the sky as though countdown had ended and liftoff was imminent.

They seemed to quiver in anticipation, eager to take off and fly. Maybe my mind was beginning to stray hither and yon again, because for a moment I was actually thinking of wild birds soaring to yon horizon and then back hither; free at last of their downy nests; all sorts of bird junk was winging through my brain.

But such junk flew from my thoughts quickly. Because all of a sudden several things happened. A whole bunch. And all of them very peculiar.

124

The lovely stopped in mid-stretch. Her arms still lay at her sides, but the hands suddenly opened wide, fingers stretching.

At that moment I heard thumping footsteps behind me in the lobby, somebody coming in a hurry over the carpet.

The girl sat up in one quick, almost spasmodic movement, like a Jack—or, rather—Jill-in-the-box.

"Will Dilly Pickle . . ."

In that one quick movement she swung sideways on the chaise longue, facing away from me, and swept the straw hat from her head. I couldn't see her face but she looked good from the rear, smooth golden-blonde hair still swinging heavily from her movement.

Whoever had been running over the carpet went through the twin doors a few feet to my left, and on outside. From the corner of my eye I could see him trotting toward the pool. He was a well-built man wearing a yellow silk sport shirt and bright yellow Bermuda shorts, thick-soled sandals on his feet. He was grinning, waving and yelling something, apparently waving and calling to somebody at the far end of the pool.

The girl stood up, started turning toward the lobby.

And then I recognized the running man.

It was Edward Walles. Or Ed somebody—if his name was Ed.

I took a step to my left toward the doors he'd gone through, starting after him—he'd stopped near a redheaded girl sitting at the pool's edge with her legs dangling in the water, and bent down beside her.

But that was the only step I took. I just froze there, motionless and gawking.

I even forgot about Ed Walles. Only for a little while, but for that short length of time I truly forgot about him.

Because I got a good look at the girl's face as she swung toward the lobby—and then turned quickly away.

It was a beautiful face, and my previous thought that perhaps she'd hidden her kisser because it was unkissable must have been one of my major errors of the day. It was a face that went with the body, that matched or even surpassed it, a face to conjure with and dream on.

It was also a face I had seen before. When she had been staring down at "my" body in front of the Hamilton Building.

I got it then. Or at least some of it. But at first only one thought swam in my brain. One sentence, five little words.

Dilly Pickle was a *girl*.

16

SHE WAS STILL STANDING NEXT TO THE CHAISE LONGUE, looking toward the pool, when I walked up behind her. I'd taken off my sunglasses, no need for them now.

"Hello, Dilly," I said.

She turned, raising her eyes to my face.

I waited for the shock to register, for her features to change, perhaps almost "melt" as they had a few hours earlier.

She blinked gray-flecked hazel eyes at me once, and then the reaction started. There was some shock—or at least surprise—but it wasn't what I'd expected.

The soft eyes widened suddenly. The moist, warm-looking lips parted. "Ohh-hh," she sighed, raising a hand to touch her cheek. And "Ohh-hh," again.

"Surprised, huh?"

"Ohh-hh—Shell! I mean . . . Mr. Scott. My goodness, oh, dear, my goodness." She waggled her fingers together in what seemed pretty confusion, wrists vigorously joggling her breasts, which seemed also to waggle in pretty confusion.

"Where did *you* come from?" she asked breathlessly.

"From in front of the Hamilton Building, Dilly. I guess you could almost say I rose from the dead."

"Don't—don't remind me of that, Shell—Mr. Scott."

"You might as well call me Shell, Dilly."

"I'd love to, Shell . . . Why do you keep calling me Dilly? Is that what you said?"

"That's it."

"But why?"

"What else? Clearly that's who you are. Unfortunately for both of us."

I meant the last part, especially. Because this one was truly outstanding, choice, transcendental, almost a new and improved second sex, a gal the like of which even I had rarely looked upon. And it was with sticky gob of sadness indeed, you can bet, that I realized there could never be anything between us. At least, not anything *good*.

Not even a gal as gorgeous as this one could send hoods to shoot the hell out of me and expect all to be forgiven, just because she looked sexy enough to be illegal, with a figure that could be seen and still be disbelieved, and with a love-in-the-moonlight light in her eyes, and skin smooth and warm as sun-stirred honey, and yummy-plump lips—

"I'm who?" she said.

"Hmmm? What?"

"Who did you say I am?"

"Dilly. You're Dilly Pickle."

"Di—*what?*"

The fools were still paging her.

"Will Dilly Pickle please . . ."

I should have told them to turn it off after a minute or two.

"You mean the whatever . . . the *whoever* they're paging?" she asked me wide-eyed.

"That's it. And don't try to trickle me, Di—don't try to diddle—just don't, that's all."

"But my name is Burma. I don't understand."

"Burma—hah!"

"Not Burmaha. Burma O'Hare. My daddy's Ragen O'Hare."

I looked blankly at her.

"You must know him, Shell. He's a reporter on the *Herald-Examiner*. That's how I happen to know all about you and all your wonderful cases. From him, my scrapbooks."

"Scrapbooks?"

She lowered her eyes and looked away.

"Listen," I said, "if we're going to talk nonsense, we can do it on the way downtown."

"Oh, all right," she said and smiled.

She had marvelous teeth. Perfectly even and almost luminously white, their clean look accentuated by the ripe redness of her sweetly curving lips. . . .

Why was she smiling?

"We can even chat while you're mugged and booked," I said. "This isn't actually an arrest—not yet. The police can handle that formality. So I don't think I have to tell you you're not supposed to say anything, or confess, or even feel guilty, and that you can have a lawyer, and even if you can't afford one we'll get you some. Shall we go?"

She looked at me with what seemed a great lack of comprehension in her eyes.

"Police?" she said. "What police?"

"The ones I'm taking you to. So they can jug you."

She stepped to the chaise longue, brushing past me, turned and sank down upon it. She crossed her ams beneath her breasts, reaching up to grip those smooth bare arms beneath her shoulders—at the same time lifting her bosom approximately three inches into the air. At least.

I was still thinking about her brushing past me and, at the some time, noting the remarkable things she could do with her anatomy, which she was holding way up there with her arms, when she flung her arms out to the side. Woweewow. Truly remarkable. They were alive. Birds, trapped in a downy nest, spreading their wild wings to fly—

"I don't *understand*," she cried. "What do you *mean*?"

"Just a second," I said. "Half a sec."

She pulled her arms back in, clutched them beneath her shoulders again.

"Hold still, will you?" I said.

"What do you *mean*?"

"Just hold still, that's all. Don't go flanging—"

"But—*police*? Why *police*?"

For a moment she appeared to go slightly out of focus and then the double image blended into one again, like when you're using a range finder atop a camera.

I gave my head a little shake and said, "Come off it. I saw you down at the Hamilton Building. A few minutes after two p.m. it was. You can't deny it, Dilly."

"Of course not—quit calling me Dilly, will you? Why would I deny it?"

"You took off like a scared rabbit, for one thing—one of many. Before I'd even seen that dead guy lying there in pools of blood—"

128

"Please, don't remind me. Shell—I thought it was you!"

"Yeah, that's what I figured. You and a couple other—"

"And then, when I saw you—alive!—I nearly fainted."

"Yeah, I remember. That's the very first thing that got me suspicious—"

"At first I couldn't believe it. But when I realized it was you standing there next to me, truly *you*, it was like waking up from a bad dream, from a nightmare. I was so relieved, so happy—"

"Hey, hold it. Cool it a minute. Something is cracked. How could you be relieved? You called Hazel and made the appointment with your sexy voice. You *wanted* me dead there, lying in pools of blood—"

"Oh, how cruel!"

"Didn't you?"

Her face twisted a little, and her eyes seemed to get mistier. "You know I didn't, you must know. When I saw you—him, but I *believed* it was you—lying there in pools of blood, I thought my heart would break."

"Let's go through that again. In a bit more detail, Dilly."

"*Quit calling me Dilly!*"

I looked around. Everything seemed normal. The sun was a bit lower, its beams filtering through the branches of the trees and dancing on the pool's surface. People frolicked in the water. Didn't see Ed Walles, though.

Yeah, Ed. Where had he got to?

I was going to have to get on Edward's track right away. But one thing at a time. I was having enough trouble with this one. This one, who sure didn't seem to like it when I called her Dilly Pickle. That I could understand, if it wasn't her name. Who, with any other name, would want to be called Dilly Pickle? But if she wasn't Dilly, I was going to be sinking for the third time in confusion. I'd have to start all over again.

She had to be Dilly, though. It made sense, very good sense —at least it had just a little while ago. When I'd been standing in the lobby and experienced my little revelation, when the thought "Dilly Pickle was a *girl*" swirled in my mind, it had there been swirling with at least four or five other dim elucidations which made it transparently apparent—then, at least— that he *had* to be Dilly.

Of course, if she *wasn't*, if she was really Rangoon O'Toole, or whatever she'd said, that meant . . .

Yes, it meant that my sticky gob of sadness could dissolve. It

129

meant there might yet be the possibility of something between us, something *good* between us.

I looked down at her again, musing.

She was saying, "I didn't mean to shout at you, Shell. But my name *is* Burma O'Hare. It's a *good* name. I *like* it. And if you can't call me Burma, don't call me anything."

"I guess it doesn't make much difference what I call you," I said.

She reached forward and took my right hand in both of hers —my left hand was still hanging onto that big Bolex, which was getting pretty heavy—and said, "I guess I should confess, Shell—"

"Well, it's about time—"

"—how I've felt about you all these years. I might as well get it off my chest, even if it means nothing to you."

She said a lot of queer things. Did a few, too. For example, when she'd mentioned getting someting *off* her chest, she'd got something on it instead. She'd leaned forward and risen to her feet, and somehow had unconsciously pulled my hand close to press the back of it against her left breast.

That white jersey didn't merely look thin, it *felt* thin; it felt like *nothing*. The sensation was much like having one's hand pressed against bare skin with a faint warp and weft in it.

She dropped her right hand to her side, but kept the other one holding mine against the warp and weft, and looked up at me. "But I can't tell you here, Shell. Not with all these people near, maybe listening. I'd be too embarrassed. Can we walk a little way?"

"O.K., if you'll explain what you're getting at."

We walked the length of the pool and then over a graveled path toward a small bridge arching above a narrow stream a few yards ahead. Beyond the bridge was a narrow path, a kind of "lover's lane," winding through green growth beneath overhanging limbs of densely growing trees. A few little birds fluttered and hopped from limb to twig.

As we walked Dilly explained in a quiet voice that though we'd never really met before, she felt she knew me intimately. She'd known about me a long time, a *long* time, had followed my career, read about some of my cases in newspapers and magazines. She did seem to know a lot about my cases, including some of the real good ones.

We went over the little bridge and started down the little path, out of sight of those others behind us now. Dilly was still holding my hand. And, still unconsciously I guessed, pressing its back against her left breast. I wondered if I ought to say something to her about it. But I didn't want to make a big thing of it and maybe embarrass her. She'd said just talking about this was embarrassing for her.

Burma—or Dilly, whoever she was—continued, telling me she'd thought about me often and often, even at night, lying awake in bed. She never did actually come right out and say *what* she was thinking, lying there nude in the sack—she didn't quite say nude, either, I don't believe; it was certainly the impression I got, however—but it wasn't anything hateful, I was pretty sure.

She'd actually kept the newspaper stories and such in scrapbooks, she admitted. Two were filled already, and she was working on the third one. While confessing this, I noticed she often looked behind us, and glanced all around occasionally. Probably watching the birds in the trees, I thought. She was a gal who would like birds.

Birds, I thought. What was it I'd been thinking about birds?

We were pretty well out in a reasonably authentic jungle by now. Might even be eagles out here. Possibly we should be heading back, I thought. Besides, Burma had been kind of gently moving my hand once in a while, sort of sliding it around against her warmsoftness, and within the last few seconds her unconscious seemed to have taken a turn for the worse, because —how it happened I shall really never know for certain— somehow she'd gotten my hand turned around so that not its back but its front was pressed against her soft warmnest, and anybody who didn't know what was going on might have concluded I was deliberately clutching her bird in my hand. I was pretty uncomfortable.

The thing was, because of that circumstance plus the fact that Burma and I were walking side by side and still on that narrow path, in order not to dislocate my arm at the shoulder it had become necessary for me to sort of stoop forward and twist my body a bit, thus adopting a rather spastic posture not strikingly suitable for strolling along Lover's Lane.

Burma didn't seem to notice anything unusual, however, in my somewhat hobbling and sidling gait. Maybe it was the way she always walked in the woods with guys she was crazy about.

Yeah, she was crazy about me. She'd practically come right out and said it.

She had also been telling me how, when she'd heard the shots just after noon today, she had rushed from her desk—she worked downtown. She'd even told me where. It was in a big building, down there. Down there somewhere. And when she'd seen that white-haired corpse lying there in pools of blood . . . She choked up then.

She slowed, came to a stop.

"Shell," she said, in a voice charged with emotion.

"Yeah?" I started straightening up. "Uhh—ack."

"What's the matter, darling?"

"I've, uh, got a little crick in my back and arm, that's all. There—Oh—*aah!* Think that got it."

"Shell. . ." She moved close. That is, even closer. Pretty damn close. "Do you see? Do you understand now?"

There were tears in her little-gray-fleck-flecked hazel eyes. She was weeping.

It was all clear now, clear as glass. Why, when she'd seen that poor old man plugged she'd thought it was Shell Scott. Me lying there in pools of blood. She'd thought *I* was dead. Dead—after all her dreams . . . her hungers . . . her scrapbooks.

"Shell . . ."

"Yeah?"

"You do understand?"

"Yeah. Yeah."

"Darling I want you to—to kiss me just once. Just once before we go back."

"Once? What's this once? We're on Lover's Lane, aren't we? Way out here in the wilds? All alone? Just us and the trees and little birds, right? What's with once? Twice, three times—maybe even a score, a gross—"

That was as far as I got.

She put both arms around my neck and flowed against me and up me like a warm flesh river, her lips finding mine, and then we came to the rapids. I felt her lips on my lips, knew her tongue and her fingertips, a hand strayed over my cheek, long fingernails sharp against my neck, the hand straying, straying . . .

Well, all I can say is, no matter what might have been scheduled by the Fates to follow that kiss, it was indisputably a kiss worth kissing. More than that it was to a mere kiss what one cold A and B is to the whole can of hot alphabet soup. It was as though luscious, lovelorn, Hungry Burma O'Hare had been saving up for years and years, the dear; and in one grand and imaginative moment deposited it all, plus accumulated interest compounded, on my amazed chops.

132

She moved away from me after a minute or two. Or three. Who counts? She sighed a big sigh and said, "Wait here, darling. I'll be right back."

"Back? Where you going? Here we are in the trees . . . With the birds . . ."

She was a hundred feet away already. Maybe she had a weak bladder.

No, *I* was the one with the weak bladder.

So would you have been if you could have seen what I saw and heard what I heard.

What I saw was Burma O'Hare disappearing around a curve in the path; and then coming around that same curve—coming this way very speedily—four hard-looking and apparently maniacal individuals.

Individual hoods, undoubtedly; they had the look of hoods, and they had the enormous deadly ugly guns of hoods.

What I heard was a bunch of yelling from those hoods, punctuated by two or three shots. Maybe four. Who counts?

Besides, I had a lot of other things to think about.

Burma baby, I was thinking. You must have known, huh? Sure, you must have. But how could you? Why? What about those hungry nights and all? And your scrapboo . . .

Of course. No scrapbooks. She didn't really think I was the nuts after all. She had been pulling my leg. She'd pulled it clear off, and was running like sixty, probably 3,000 yards away by now, carrying the dismembered organ with her. All she'd ever wanted was my leg. So, now she had it. Well—if I lived, of course, which didn't seem very likely at the moment—I intended to give her the foot that went with it.

It didn't seem likely I was going to live, because those enormous deadly ugly hoods were thundering this way, shooting at me, and in a trice were going to kill me.

But I stood there thinking a little bit more. There was something I had to get clear. I have a very independent mind. Which is to say, sometimes I have no control over it at all.

Burma, I thought, Burma O'Hare. She'd brought me here deliberately, inveigled me into the wilds, and—somehow . . . how?—managed to tip the hoods so they could come out here and shoot me a lot. Which, assuredly, they were going to do. But that means—sure. It meant a lot of things, many of them of more than passing interest.

But prime among them—corroboration of previous thought,

133

capstone to logic, the big, fat, sick, sad one—was the thought I had thought before.

Thought before and now thought again, but this time for good and all, for ever and ever, unchangeable through all eternity:

Dilly Pickle *was* a girl.

17

GREAT, I TOLD MYSELF; NOW YOU TELL ME.

Because those ugly hoods were now twice as close as they'd been before, and shooting something fierce. Shooting wildly so far, but in a trice they were going to kill me. I was dead.

No, not yet dead. In a trice I'd be dead.

But in half a trice I leaped sideways what must have been, could it ever have been measured, a full fourteen feet through the air, clunking into a gnarled tree trunk, which severely bruised an arm and leg, and did my head a lot of good when it snapped over and hit a boll, or knot, or embryo limb, or whatever those extraordinarily hard lumps on tree trunks are.

There was no point in running. Not with my head like that. Not on one leg, anyhow. Besides, I don't run from hoods. Not if I can help it. And I could help it. So it was four-to-one, so what? Wasn't I an ex-Marine?

Maybe there was something about the setting, too, which addled me. The darkling sky—though the sun hadn't set yet, it was getting darker—and the thunder of those guys' feet, the hiss of air leaking through my teeth, the yells in my ears. It was savage, blood-heating. I could feel my features contort into a savage grimace. I went swiftly into a crouchy squat; I sent my right hand flashing—flashing like lightning—up toward my holster. Oh—ack. My arm still had such a crick in it I hit my damn belt buckle.

Well, I'll have to do better than *that*, I told myself. I started cricking my hand up toward my holster again—and even while

135

yowling softly as the stretched and agonized muscles protested, I realized something else awful.

I remembered putting three slugs into Skiko. And not reloading my Colt since then. Which meant there were only three slugs in the gun—three slugs, and four guys out there. Four guys getting closer.

I'd even been able to recognize two of them by this time. One was gargantuan Fleck, farthest away but recognizable from his massive size if nothing else. Fleck, last seen at Jimmy Violet's gate—a meaty clue if ever I'd seen one. Ahead of him was Little Phil, pumping along after a man I didn't know. And out front, nearest me, a tall, long-legged sprinter named Harry Reil, a mobster of British descent known to the boys as English 'Arry.

English 'Arry was yelling excitedly, "Theah 'e is; theah's the bahstad?" and pooping away at me with his heat.

Long since, of course, my hand had cricked to my holster. But I was still crouching there in my squat, and I yanked and yanked, and yanked some more. What had happened was this. I'd grabbed at my holster, and that's what I'd got: my holster.

That was funny. Supposed to be a gun in there. A .38 Colt Special with three bullets in it; that's what was supposed to be there. But it wasn't. No .38 Colt Special. Not even a peashooter. How could it be?

There was a gunshot, and a slug sped past about an inch from my head. Maybe two inches. And I was standing there sort of wonderingly running a couple of fingers around inside my empty holster. Of course, very little actual time had elapsed since I'd flown through the air like a bir—like an airplane. Possibly two seconds. And I stood there for maybe one more second, during which I thought at least a couple minutes' worth.

Dilly Pickle, I thought.

Yeah. She was a dilly, all right. And she'd sure got me into a pickle. I'd had it figured backwards. Which, probably, she'd counted on.

It was all clear as glass now. *That* was why she'd been loving me up, up and down, all over the place, pressing her woweewow against me, pooching her luscious wild lips at me. Turning me on temporarily had been part of her plan to turn me off permanently.

I'd been thinking it was my savage charm—have to get *that* idea out of my head once and for all I guessed—which had

136

turned her juices into jelly. She hadn't been after my savage charm. Not even my leg. Unless it was my hawgleg. It had been my *gun* she was after.

Fury rose up in me, interfering with my usual lightninglike mental processes, as I thought of Dilly Pickle. She was a god-damn picklepocket!

No, a *pick*pocket.

No, not even that. She was a pickholster.

That's what she'd done: She'd holstered my pickle. Boy, *that* was a wrong one.

I made a tremendous effort and got it clear, lucid and shining and *right,* for once and for all: *She had picked my holster.*

What it boiled down to was that, regarding armament, I was outnumbered four guns to nothing. There they came at me. And here I stood, empty-handed.

Well, not quite empty-handed. I had been brilliant enough to carry for all this wearying time my sixteen-millimeter Bolex movie camera fully loaded with a hundred feet of film. Ah, fine, fine. Nothing like planning ahead, making provision for any conceivable contingency.

There seemed nothing whatever left to do except to turn and run. Run and run and *run.* So I did.

I got a break at that—and about time, I thought.

Dilly had miscalculated in at least one small area. Two, if we include the fact that I can run like a startled antelope when necessary. But her first miscalculation had been in choosing the spot where we'd stopped.

True, there was a long straight stretch of the path—down which those guys had been and were running—which was fine for target practice; but no more than ten feet from me the path curved sharply to the right for several yards and then curved left again with equal suddenness. So when I got to that first turn, which was hardly any time at all once I'd decided that was the way to go, I was largely concealed by numerous tree trunks long enough for me to get going. I mean, *really* get going.

Every once in a while a shot cracked out, but I hadn't been hit or even nicked yet; and along with the sensation as of getting hit with ax handles atop the head was a thought: Maybe I'll actually make it. And I started wondering where I was at.

The rate I was going, I would have passed Duesenbergs speeding in the fast lane on the Freeway, but *where* was I going?

A separate path branched off to the left at one point, but by the time I saw the turnoff I was going past it. That did remind me, though, that when Dilly and I had been strolling along it, the path had curved both left and right, but continued primarily curving to our right; and that the path here at the Hidden Valley Lodge was an irregular circle extending through the woods for approximately a mile; and that I had just passed the hunk of path which led back to the Lodge.

By then I was either dizzy from lack of sufficient oxygen in my lungs or not yet thinking with admirable clarity, because I had stopped worrying about *whether* I would get away from those men behind me and begun wondering what I'd do once I had. And, how I could fix their wagons.

Along with the thought was realization that it's getting tougher and tougher to pin their jobs on hoods, tougher to make a rap stick. For good or ill, that's the way it is. You damn near have to catch them in the act of dismembering the body ...

And I had it.

I was lugging my damned camera. Maybe there'd been a reason—besides the fact that I had some splendidly provocative shots of Tootsie in the exposed footage—for my hanging onto the Bolex. The next best thing to actually catching hoods in the commission of a crime should be a movie of them in the middle of it.

A shot of them chasing after me, shooting at me, should be enough for any court in the land, temporarily. That meant I would have to get into the film somehow, myself, while taking care that the action was merely of the boys shooting *at* me, not in me.

So, for one, I couldn't stand holding the camera, filming them while they ran down on top of me. And for another, I was going to have to run at least another mile.

But I was quite a bit ahead of them now—though a shot still rang out from time to time—so I sprinted as hard as I could for a hundred yards, the last thirty of which were quite straight, and then skidded to a stop. The Bolex was battery-operated and, once started, would function unaided until the film ran out, if I locked the shutter release down. But there was only one hundred feet of film, and that would run past the lens in four minutes. I didn't think I could be sure of running another mile in four minutes—not after what I'd recently been through. In fact, I was pretty sure I couldn't.

But there was still a way.

If I set the camera speed to expose not the normal sixteen

frames a second but only eight, which I could do merely turning a little knob on the side of the camera, the thing would run twice as long, or for eight minutes. True, when projected it would be in fast motion, the action speeded up, but that didn't matter. The faces—and guns—of those lobs would be identifiable.

The only ticklish part, actually, after adjusting the lens aperture and frames-per-second setting, was spotting a limb in the right place and at the right angle to hold the camera firmly. But I found one suitable, jammed the Bolex into place pointing back down the path, depressed and locked the shutter release to start it whirring and moved out of there. Moved not quite as rapidly this time. In part because I was coming more than a bit undone already; and in part because—now—I wanted my pursuers to get a glimpse of me. One really good glimpse to charge them up enough so they'd run that extra mile. The extra mile; that's the one that counts.

"Theah 'e is, theah's the bahstad?" *Crack!*

The slug whistled past me and ripped bark from a tree trunk yards ahead. That was enough glimpse.

A mile is not a fixed and constant length. In order to get once more around that mile-long path I ran at least forty furlongs. Fortunately I'm in excellent condition, much better condition than were those unhealthy hoods, I assumed. Thus I figured I could loaf part of the way while they dragged along behind me.

I would have been right, except for Gargantua.

I should have known. I already knew he wasn't human.

That lumbering hulk could have run all day and into the night, I think, scratching his armpits. From way back in the pack he had somehow caught up with and thudded past all three of the others, for when I imagined I sensed the earth shaking as in tumult or cataclysm, I looked back and saw, about where I'd expected him, rangy English 'Arry.

But saw also, *between* 'Arry and me—no more than twenty yards off and gaining lickety-split—Fleck. He would damn sure have killed me if he'd stopped, taken aim, and shot at me. But either he'd used up all his ammunition, or cherished the hope of getting close enough to clamp his paws upon me, which would ensure that my demise would be slower, and more fun.

I used up a lot of soup stretching the distance out to what I considered relative safety, but then I had to slow down for a while. Excellent condition, yeah. So who's supposed to run a couple of miles after an experience like Dilly?

I sprinted around the last curve in the path—maybe a bit sloppily, I confess, since I ran into a little tree and broke it smack off—then got straightened out and determinedly put one much-abused foot down after another until I spotted the white scar where 'Arry's slug had ripped bark from that tree trunk. Short of that tree I spotted my Bolex, and leaped toward it.

Well, maybe it wasn't much of a leap. I felt that I was soaring, soaring through the air; but I must have stumbled slightly since I skidded in the air a bit, on my mangled knees, before succeeding in reaching up and clutching the camera. It was a happy moment.

Before taking off like an antelope again I glanced back along the path. How could it be?

There was Fleck, and 'Arry, and even the guy I hadn't met, but whom I would meet pretty quick if I didn't get a wiggle on. Why, I'd sped down that path—so it seemed to me—and clutched my camera in a jiffy. How'd those out-of-condition hoods get so close so quickly?

Crack! Blam!

They had not used up all their ammunition.

I was really startled by their unexpected proximity. And I suppose I was also, and naturally enough, a bit disturbed by the certainty that I was, at last, plugged in the gizzard. Not the gizzard, actually; the chin, actually. Yes, there was a moment when I felt I'd been shot in the chin.

All that really happened was that I jerked my hands up for some reason. Why? How would I know why? Maybe to hide my eyes so I wouldn't see the horrible thing that was going to happen to me. And since the camera was in my hands when I jerked my hands up, the Bolex came along and the lens cracked me smartly in the chin.

But that was the only moment of . . . well, of real dismay. By the time I was running again, lickety-split down the path, I realized my chin hadn't been shot off.

I began thinking again that maybe I'd make it.

I grew sure of it.

And I did.

I sat in my Cadillac trying to get the key into the ignition. Now that I had outwitted everybody, including myself, I wanted to get the hell away from quiet, peaceful Hidden Valley.

I'd had a brief rest when I staggered and stumbled off the

path and involuntarily flopped under a little bush with long evil spines sticking from it. But the speedy reverse route up the path and then along the turnoff leading to the Lodge—after my four apparently dying pursuers had passed wheezing and honking by my hiding place—had left me with a bone-weary exhaustion approximating rigor mortis.

I was not about to go back to the Lodge, even had I been certain Fleck and 'Arry and Little Phil and the fourth murderer would continue running stupidly around in circles—as I had done for a couple of circuits—until the sun rose in splendor. Dilly alone could have licked me in a fair fight and she didn't fight fair anyhow.

So I kept wobbling my key around until I got it into the ignition, started the car and zoomed away, a center of peril not only to myself but to every other living thing in the area.

But, as I headed once more for Mrs. Halstead's home, I felt pretty good. Despite the ache in my lungs, the misery in my head, the charley horses in my legs, and the pain in my—well, a real and abiding pain—I felt pretty good.

Because it was over now.

At least the whole thing was clear, the picture developed, all the bits of the mosaic in place, crimes pegged, cases solved. That is to say, the thinking part was over.

The only thing left was the wrap-up part, the denouement, the concluding scenes of the drama. Only the part requiring strong limbs and stout heart, vigor and energy, and zip and zing. Only the *action* part.

Yes, I thought, as I wobbled and careened down the highway, that was all.

But even though I felt as if each of my individual muscles had been opened up and gutted like fish in the market, if what I had just been accomplishing was the *thinking* part, I could hardly help but look forward to the action.

18

ON THE WAY TO MRS. HALSTEAD'S HOME, I PHONED SAMSON and caught him in the Intelligence Division.

"Did Cootie get in to see you?" I asked him.

"Yeah. We've checked it out and got the kickback already. But Cootie wouldn't tell me where he lifted the prints; said he was just a delivery boy."

"That's what I told him to say. Well, I'm glad he got the job done."

"I hate to say it, but I am, too. You sure these are from the man you call Edward Walles?"

"Sure enough." I'd told Cootie to let himself into the Walles house in Beverly Hills. But I was pretty certain Samson wouldn't want to know that, so I didn't tell him.

He was going on, "We've got a want on this Vanda ourselves. He's also wanted in Nevada and Arizona."

"Who? Vanda?"

"Yeah, Edward Walles isn't his name, either. Probably has a dozen aliases. Real name's Kermit Vanda, and he's one of the slickest confidence men operating in the Western States."

I smiled. "A con man. Well, that's the cork in the bottle. It's perfect Sam. I'll buy you a box of cigars. *Good* cigars."

"I don't *like* good cigars," he growled. "We checked out the address in Beverly Hills, but the place was empty. The house is being kept under surveillance."

"Call the Beverly Hills boys off, Sam. He won't be back, not for a while, anyway. Last I saw of him was out at the Hidden

142

Valley Lodge. But he won't be there now, either. Incidentally, you say the L.A.P.D. has a want on him? You mean Homicide wants him?"

"Not us. Bunco—con game; he's never gone in for the heavy."

"Not personally, maybe. He lets other guys handle the heavy for him. Guys like Jimmy Violet's charmers. What's the rap here?"

"Vanda and his partner—female—took an old couple for sixty G's last year. Variation on the wire. They dropped out of sight. We identified him, but never made the woman."

"Her monicker's Dilly Pickle, Sam. She may or may not be Vanda's wife."

"Where'd you get this?"

"You might say from them, indirectly. Any sex angle in the confidence games they've worked so far?"

"None we know about. No more than the usual. They work damned clever and up-to-date variations on the standard con games though."

"Yeah, they would. Well, you can add the sex bit now—and conspiracy to commit homicide, among other things. Like extortion. This Dilly Pickle—"

"I thought that was what you said."

"—set me up for the murder try that wound up with Porter getting it. I doubt that she and Vanda had much contact with the real heavies before their latest escapade. Anyhow the boys picked to do the job on me knew her by that monicker or nickname, and that she made the call to Hazel that was supposed to put me at the Hamilton around two p.m."

He was silent for a few seconds. "Can you prove all this?"

"I will when I come in, Sam. I'll be down pretty quick to fill you in, and also to show you a movie that'll knock your eyes out. You're going to be proud of me, old buddy."

"Not likely. What do you mean, movie?"

"Just that. Film's being developed now." I gave him a hint of what was on the film and added, "I'll bring it in as soon as I can—"

"You get in here right now, Shell. There's a local out on you."

"On me? Oh, you mean—"

"Yeah. You can't leave dead guys lying around in the city. Not even in crumby bars."

"That was Skiko—the boy who phoned you today, Papa."

"Oh?"

"Yeah. The hoods who knocked down Porter were Billy DeKay and Gippo Crane."

"That's good news. But we'll need a little more than just your say-so before we can pick them up."

"Skiko told me himself," I said. "Moments before he died. So it was straight from the hearse's mouth. Give me half an hour, O.K., Sam?"

"What for?"

"I've one stop to make, then I'll come straight in. I won't even wait to pick up the film; I'll have it delivered to the squad room."

"Tell me more about this film."

"Patience," I said mysteriously. "You'll see."

He told me to get to Homicide by eight p.m. or he'd jug me himself. I had a hunch he would too.

"I'll be in," I said. "One more favor, if you will. Have somebody check the monicker file for 'Dilly Pickle,' and call me back, O.K.?"

He grumbled a bit, but said he'd do it.

He did. The call reached me just before I parked at Mrs. Halstead's home in the Hollywood Hills. And the info from the monicker file added one more small piece to the picture, one more bit I could give my client.

Mrs. Halstead and I had been talking five minutes when I said "O.K., that ties it in a ribbon."

"I still don't understand, Mr. Scott."

"That's because I've been asking questions instead of telling you the score. But I'll give you all I can now, Mrs. Halstead. Some of it I know is accurate, and some is deduction subject to later corroboration. But I'll bet my bottom dollar what I'm going to tell you now is very close to the way it was. And before the night's over I've a hunch I'll have proof of the parts I can't guarantee as accurate just yet."

"Do you know who killed my husband?"

"Yeah, a man named Stub Corey who works for a hood named Jimmy Violet—the guy I asked you about earlier."

"This man . . . who killed George. Will he be arrested?"

"No. I killed him this afternoon."

She moistened her lips and the green eyes widened.

"It was self-defense." I touched the bandage—still on my head but getting a little loose. "He gave me this at the time.

Anyway, he's dead, and consequently his guilt may not ever be proved positively. Maybe it will—but at least Stub isn't going to be walking the streets."

She pressed her lips together, looking down at her hands. Then she glanced up at me and asked "Why? Why did he kill George?"

"Well, let's go back a little. You've just told me the idea of the album—from which I mentioned the photo of Sybil Spork and Hugh Pryer came—was Ed Whist's idea. The guy you know as Ed Whist, that is."

She nodded. "It seems ... unwise now. A little. But at the time it appeared to be an *exceptionally* logical and desirable procedure. Obviously we all had to be very careful; it was only common sense to make sure that nobody . . ." She let it trail off.

"I can understand that," I said. "I can also understand, better than most, how convincing Edward can be. Ed and his partner."

I stopped. This wasn't going to be pleasant for Mrs. Halstead. It's never pleasant to realize that someone has led you down the garden path, that you've been a prize sap. I should know.

"Well, I'll simply lay it out for you," I said, "without pulling any punches. It begins with the couple of high-class con artists whom you knew as Ed and Marcelle Whist. Who are in fact Kermit Vanda and his wife—perhaps—Dale, born Dale Jill Piquelle, and called in kidhood Dilly Piquelle by the kids, and in adulthood Dilly Pickle by the hoods. And even by me for a while."

"Con artists? Hoods?"

"They're a confidence team. You know what a confidence man is? Or a con game?"

"Well . . . a little."

"You know quite a bit now, believe me. From first-hand observation. A con man always chooses his marks—the suckers, or victims of the con—with care. And—we'll call them Ed and Marcelle, since that's how you think of them—those two artists picked the Halsteads. Don't kid yourself; that was no chance meeting in a bar—they planned it. And everything else."

"Oh, dear." She looked distressed. As well she might.

But I said, "Don't kick yourself too much, Mrs. Halstead. Any con man worth his salt is not only of the criminal elite, but a consummate actor, a practicing psychologist, a student of human emotions—and weaknesses. They're usually brilliant,

145

but warped, and almost invariably *totally* without a trace of conscience. They're freaks, true; but this team, take it from one who's known plenty of them, is the cream of the elite. To put it simply, they combined a new twist on the old con game with an old extortion play, and from the beginning had blackmail in mind. Hence the blackmail album. You can be sure Ed knew there are other clubs, other groups with similar albums. He just decided to choose his marks—marks with money—and make up his own album. With the willing, maybe even eager cooperation of the marks he meant to bleed later, which seems a nice touch."

"Oh, dear," she said again.

"It could be they had a good-sized group in mind from the beginning, or maybe they started with you and your husband and let the thing build, grow naturally. All the couples but one came from among your friends or acquaintances, you'll remember. Well, when Ed and Marcelle were ready for the payoff they 'burned' the album which was in their possession. At least that was their story, and they even faked a fire in the Norvue so there'd be corroboration if you checked."

She frowned. "Why would they do that? And go to all that trouble if—"

I smiled. "Not trouble. Simply part of the routine, the s.o.p. In the con man's phrase, they always try to 'cool out the mark,' that is, they not only attempt to keep the mark from ever knowing he *has* been the victim of a con, but also cover themselves so they won't draw any heat if there's a rumble. Some con men never spend a day in jail in their lives, simply because they go to all that trouble, as you put it."

"Then the pictures never *were* burned? I believed Ed when he said—"

"Sure, you did. Doubting Thomas would have believed him. What I think—what I'm almost certain—they did then was turn that album over to Jimmy Violet. Either for a flat, and undoubtedly fancy, chunk of cash, or perhaps in expectation of a cut from the later profits."

"Profits. You make it sound like a business."

"That's what it is. They simply farmed out the physical labor of extortion to a guy with the men and muscle appropriate to the act. One of whom visited your husband here last night."

"The one you—killed?"

"The same. Stub Corey. We know a copy of one of those snaps from the album, burned a little to fit the tale, was used to hit the Sporks today. But I think that must have been the second blackmail try. The first being when Stub came here last night."

"You know he was here?"

"Yeah. More important, I know they went up to your husband's den. There's where Stub most likely gave him the pitch, complete with photo of George and a lady—or you and somebody's husband—maybe even both for all I know. Anyway, Stub named his price. When your husband phoned me he was upset, speaking softly; asked me to come over as soon as possible. Obviously he wouldn't have phoned from the den if Stub was still around. I'd guess he left Stub there—maybe on the pretext that he was going to get the money, or part of it, and used the outside phone near the pool for the call."

Mrs. Halstead stared at the wall, then nodded slowly. "Then you think this man followed him out, and saw or heard my husband phoning . . . and killed him."

"I do. He very likely heard part of the conversation. Stub's IQ wouldn't have put him in the genius class, but if one of the marks wasn't acting like a mark, and was calling in the law—or even a private investigator—Stub would have known the man couldn't be allowed to blow the whole operation apart by spilling the beans. Maybe Stub acted on his own, without instruction from higher up so to speak, but he grabbed a rock and that was it, right or wrong."

She bent forward a little, pressing the fingers of one hand against her forehead.

"It happened very soon after Mr. Halstead phoned me," I said. "Had to. Immediately after that—if he could have—he would certainly have called off the party. Before my arrival, I mean. But he didn't."

"Yes. I see. Have you proof of all this?"

"Not all, but some. I hope, with the help of a lot of police officers, to get more proof before the night's over. For example, there's no question in my mind that the entire album still exists —except of course, for any shots of Ed or Marcelle. Those *will* have been burned by now. But the others, I'd bet my life, are in Jimmy Violet's possession."

There wasn't much more that Mrs. Halstead needed to hear, so after another minute I got up to go.

At the door she said, shaking her head, "I know you must be right, Mr. Scott. But it's hard to believe. They seemed so nice. And Ed was . . . so *completely* charming."

"I'll bet he was," I said. "And so, I have no doubt, was Marcelle."

When I walked into the Homicide squad room just before eight p.m., Sam was filling a paper cup with coffee from the ever-present pot, and there were half a dozen men with him from other departments—a couple from ID, two from Burglary, one each from Forgery and Narcotics.

"We having a party?" I said, to nobody in particular.

Sam turned from the coffee pot and smiled. "Remains to be seen," he said. "Some of the men heard about a few of your less exciting exploits today and this movie masterpiece, or whatever it is, so they dropped by for a lesson in proper police procedure."

I smiled, myself. I knew why they were here.

There is a rather rough camaraderie among the men of the L.A.P.D., many of whom—including all those present—are friends of mine. They are not, as a general rule, however, the kind of friends who act particularly friendly. Nothing would give them more real, sadistic pleasure than to catch me with egg on my face. Well, no egg tonight, I thought. They would have to wait for another day.

So, smiling, I said, "Splendid. The Shell Scott Academy of investigation, ratiocination, cinemation, and several other ations, will be open to eager seekers after the truth in a very few minutes. I shall be overjoyed to give you all a few minutes of my time, and the benefit of my vast experience—"

There were some hoots and catcalls, and a six-foot-four-inch, two-hundred-and-sixty-pound sergeant named MacCraig made a vulgar noise with his lips.

"—in the hope of making better human beings of you. Thanks for your applause. Just be patient, men."

I turned to Sam. "But first, a brief conference?"

As we started into Sam's private office, Lieutenant Rawlins came into the squad room, and Sam waved him in with us.

Bill Rawlins, a damned fine detective, and also a very good-looking so-and-so. If I had any desire at all to be a handsome chap, which I don't any more, I might choose to look like Rawlins. Tall and slim with good shoulders, he had wavy black hair and long-lashed movie-lover eyes, and his expression usually reflected the jollity and good humor inside him.

Rawlins sat against the wall and I straddled a chair as Sam got behind his desk. For several minutes we went over every-

148

thing from the Halstead killing to my plugging of Corey and Skiko, and I repeated to Sam all I'd told Mrs. Halstead, and more.

Then I said, "How about letting me borrow about a hundred of L.A.'s finest for the purpose of dropping in on Jimmy Violet tonight?"

"And how do we justify invading a citizen's private property?"

"How? Hell, I've just been telling you, Sam. It's eight to five the album's out there. Not to mention Gippo and Tooth and—"

"Eight to five isn't good enough."

"So make it a hundred to one."

"Not on what you've told me."

"I'll tell you some more, then. Also . . ." I smiled, thinking about it. "When that film is delivered here you'll see three men whom we all *know* work for Violet, plus another guy who undoubtedly does. You'll see them trying—unsuccessfully, of course—to kill me. That should help excuse our calling on Jimmy, shouldn't it?"

"Maybe."

Rawlins chimed in, "I heard a rumble about that, Shell. You really have got some kind of film of Jimmy's hoods?"

"Not *some* kind, Bill, but assuredly a masterpiece of its kind —of which it happens there is only one of a kind. These hoods will not be able to say, 'Gun? What gun?' Or, 'Officer, I ain't done nothin'; I was in Chicago.' This is evidence which will convince judge or jury, a silent witness which cannot be coerced or intimidated—"

"You were going to tell me some more?" Sam asked sweetly.

"Take Stub Corey—he's dead, sure, but you know he worked for Jimmy. Mrs. Bersudian places him at the Halsteads shortly before the time when Halstead phoned me. A car—the same Dodge Polara Corey and Skiko used the next day—followed me from the Halsteads to the Norvue Hotel. I just happened to check that address first, true, but since it was where Vanda, registered as Whist, had been living, it must really have shaken the boys up that I went *directly* there from the scene of Halstead's murder. Because Violet and his boys knew the truth about Whist-Vanda, they almost certainly must have assumed I knew at least a little myself, certainly more than I actually did. After all, there were several other couples in the group I might have visited, but where did I go right away? Why, straight to

Vanda's. And since we conclude that Vanda turned over the album to Jimmy Violet—"

"*You* conclude."

"If he didn't, how in hell did Jimmy's boy Corey get the picture he must have shown to Halstead last night? And if you won't buy that, how did Jimmy's boy Bingo get the photo we *know* he hit the Sporks with this afternoon. The timing is cute, too, but I'll get to that in a minute."

"Suppose we assume, for now, that Vanda turned the extortion material over to Violet."

"O.K., Violet was already twitchy about me getting close to Kermit Vanda—and so were Kermit and his Dilly, because they were all keeping in touch. They got twitchier the next day when I not only checked the Beverly Hills Hotel but later located Vanda himself in Beverly Hills. Even before I actually got to Vanda, though, Jimmy was wetting his pants—his boys, including Stub Corey, picked me up, you'll recall."

"Circumstantial. Highly."

"But it gets damned convincing, Sam. Let's get to when I *did* find Vanda, right after leaving Jimmy with his sore beak. Vanda explained beautifully why he'd used the name Whist with the Halsteads and that bunch. He told me just enough of the truth to make it believable, while still keeping himself covered. He didn't expect me to live past two p.m., anyway."

"Come again?"

"Well, he couldn't have known the hour then, but he soon did. Because it's clear as can be to me that his lovely Dilly was in the house with him then, was *right then* making her call to Hazel and setting me up. I'd say she made the call and immediately phoned Jimmy Violet to tell him I'd not only located Kermit, but would probably be entering the Hamilton at around two p.m."

"Why right then?"

"Because when I left and phoned Hazel she told me the sexy-voice call had come in twenty minutes before. And that placed it at the time when I'd just started talking to Kermit Vanda in his home. Ergo, Dilly wasn't downtown getting her hair done."

Samson shrugged. "Or Jimmy had some babe make the call for him, and it happened to reach your office while you were talking to Vanda. You'd left Jimmy's place not long before, Shell."

"Either way, that makes it Jimmy Violet. And if he had some

babe do it, it was Dilly. Hell, check the next bit, the timing of the extortion play at the Sporks. I was supposed to get hit at the Hamilton at two p.m., only I was a few minutes late and Porter got it. All the important characters *thought* I'd been killed, however, for a while. So the go-ahead was given to put the bite on the Sporks—no need to worry about Shell Scott getting close to Vanda, now that Scott's dead—and Bingo was sent on his way. In the meantime the much-involved 'Marcelle Walles' of the friendly club—Dilly Pickle to us—took off in a flap about two-ten after eyeballing me, not down there on the sidewalk in pools of blood, but right next to her and not even anemic. The Sporks were contacted at two-twenty p.m.—before Dilly could get word to them, or more likely to Violet, that I wasn't the guy who got killed. Anyway, Bingo hadn't got the word."

Sam scowled. "Even if I bought everything you've said so far —and I'm not saying I do—we still couldn't go piling in on Violet and tearing the place up. Except for what you've told us, there's nothing solid and concrete that ties him in."

"Hell, you've got records on Vanda and Dilly. I've told you how they started and built up the group, developed the album idea, pulled the fake fire. Then Violet's men turn up with the photos, his boys grab me, Jimmy himself leans on me, they kill Porter instead of me and try for me again a couple more times —the last time, by the way, without question at the request of Vanda himself."

"How's that?"

"Well, I didn't go into detail, Sam. That was out at the Hidden Valley Lodge." I hit the high spots as quickly as possible, adding, "A little while ago I phoned the chief of security at the Lodge, asked him to check around for me, and he found one old geezer who'd been at the pool keeping most of his attention on Dilly—which you'd understand if you saw her. This guy heard what Vanda said when he ran past Dilly and what she answered."

"Slow down. Ran past her?"

I'd skipped over much of that sequence, since I didn't feel I had come out of it too dashingly, but I explained to Sam about Vanda running out of the lobby, waving and apparently yelling to somebody at the far end of the pool. "He wasn't yelling, though," I went on, "just making it look like he was. Maybe that's one reason the old geezer remembered exactly what they both said, because Vanda must have looked more than a bit peculiar."

151

"What was it he said?"

"Vanda, wiggling his mouth and waving, softly said as he passed Dilly, 'Zex! It's Scott in the lobby ridin' the Earie!' And she said, 'Hell and damnation. O.K., Sweet, you tip the boy and I'll boost his heat.' The geezer thought it was some kind of poem, not Vanda telling her to look out, and that I was the guy paging—"

I stopped, because Rawlins was laughing, getting a big kick out of the story. "I wish she had," he said.

I ignored him. He knew "boost" is a pickpocket's term for stealing, or pocket-picking. "Anyhow," I continued to Sam, "it's clear that while I was with her, he was rounding up the goons who chased me for, it seems, approximately fifty miles."

"It's not good enough."

"What the hell do you want? A picture—" I smiled.

Sam wasn't smiling, though. "Look," he said, "you know what we're up against. I don't doubt you're right, Shell, but it isn't enough just to bring these punks in, or book them. We've got to have enough for indictment, arraignment, trial—and conviction. Otherwise it's a waste of time. For us *and* the D.A.'s office. Worse than that, if they go to trial and beat it, they're cleaner than before. We can't try 'em again. That happens a couple times and the punks start thinking we can't touch them, and they get worse. Cockier, bolder, big-headed, more reckless, more dangerous. Why not? They beat the last rap, didn't they? And the one before?"

He cut it off, grinding his teeth together, big jaw wiggling. "Shell, what I mean is, you can jump to conclusions. We can't. You can do things we can't do. You can have a hunch—I know you and your fool hunches—but we've got to have facts. Concrete evidence. The whole package." He paused. "If I knew that album you talk so much about was at Violet's, or any other solid, certain evidence of crime, we'd get a warrant and go look. But it can't just be a hunch, or reasonably logical deduction. I've got to be damn near certain there's conclusive evidence of felony—or we blow the whole case."

He was just a bit heated, and I knew frustration gnawed at him from time to time, so I smiled and gave it the light touch. "Hell, I was being pessimistic when I asked for a hundred cops, Sam. I'll go out there by myself, and once I've found the clues and evidence and fun pictures and dead bodies and guns and grenades and such, I'll write you a formal letter requesting—"

Sam didn't let me finish. But he did lift his upper lip in a small smile. Lifted it about a sixteenth of an inch. "We get a little information ourselves here and there. Like we know right now Violet and eight, maybe nine of his men are at that house of his on his little lake. Don't know yet if it's normal procedure, or the start of a new Apalachin."

"He's always got three or four of the lobs there with him."

"More than that this time. It's barely possibly that, while blundering around in your usual comatose fashion, and shooting people here and there, and there, and there, you may have stirred up the animals."

I let the comment pass because something else had come into my mind when Sam spoke of shooting people. "Say, can you fix me up with a gun?"

"What's wrong with that .38 you're in love with?"

"Well, uh, when this Dilly was . . . saying hello to me, just before she said goodbye—I kind of mentioned the way she took off there in the woods, didn't I? Yeah, I remember mentioning it. Well, she kind of took my gun with her. That's the real reason I didn't shoot all those hoods to death—"

Rawlins howled. "Took your *gun*? That petted and pampered Colts?—Shell, you mean she *did* boost your heat? She lifted it right off you? How in hell—"

"Bill, cool it, hey? You haven't met this lady genius. Take it from me, pal, I'm extremely fortunate that she didn't steal my shorts—"

"Stole his gun!" He smacked a fist into his palm looking at Samson. "That's the best news I've heard since they got Dillinger outside the—"

"Bill, if you value our friendship, our long, rewarding—"

Samson cut it off. He stood up and said, "Come on. When's this precious movie of yours supposed to be here?"

"Any time now. I left word to bring it straight to the squad room, soon as possible."

"O.K. Come on up to SID with me. I'll show you a gun. Not for you to use, however—we're testing it."

"When we stepped out of Sam's office the squad room was even more crowded than before. I spotted another man from Burglary, one from Administration, a couple from Auto-Theft. Must be a slow night, I thought. Rawlins stayed behind while Samson and I went up to the fourth floor. I didn't think anything about it. Probably that should be: Like a *fool*, I didn't think anything about it.

In the Crime Lab Sam spoke to a technician who walked to a

case against the wall, unlocked a door, and took out a fairly large box and brought it over to us. Sam opened it, exposing several boxes of cartridges—new boxes to me—and the damnedest looking pistol I'd ever seen.

It had a row of holes in each side of the barrel, an oddly-shaped grip. It appeared to have everything a pistol should have, including sights and trigger, but I couldn't see any hammer.

"What is it?" I asked. "A water pistol?"

Sam grinned. "Well, it *can* be fired under water, but it packs more wallop than the little .38 you have—used to have, I mean. More than a Magnum, for that matter. Great semiautomatic action, too."

"Where's the hammer?"

"Up here." He pointed. "In front of the magazine. Hammer hits the front of the cartridge—little rocket's what it is—and bangs it back against the firing pin. That sets her off, and she whooshes down the barrel, cocking the hammer again on the way."

"Rocket? Yeah—a rocket pistol. I remember reading about these things. Something in *True* magazine a while back, wasn't there? Called a—a Gyrojet?"

"This is a special model we're trying out. Who knows? They might become official equipment." He was handling the thing like a kid with a new toy. He spent a couple more minutes explaining how the gun—or little rocket launcher—worked, and showed me some of the cartridges, all of which had four little holes in the base. The escaping gas shot out those little holes, Sam said, and pushed the whole shebang along.

There were three or four different kinds of rounds for the gun. Some were copperplated and a little bigger than a .45 caliber slug, and another box had metal-piercing slugs in it. The prettiest, with a colored tip, were about halfway between a tracer and a midget napalm bomb, the way I got it. At least they were incendiary and hotter than hell wherever they hit, so Sam said.

I asked him to let me fire the thing, but he shook his head and handed the box back to the lab man, commenting that he felt I had done enough shooting for one day.

Then we went back down to the third floor and into the Homicide squad room.

And my hour of trial, of nausea, of sheer, unadulterated misery, began.

154

19

The film still had not arrived, but I called the lab and learned it was on its way over. Learned also, to my decided satisfaction, that the film was beautifully exposed considering the failing light when I'd shot the roll. That had been the one thing I was a bit worried about.

And I will confess to a feeling of real relief at that point, for had the pictures been of the inside of a lens cap it would have been quite anticlimactic, since the squad room was now crammed with what could have passed for a small town's entire police force with possibly half of the fire department included. A projector was set up at one end of the room, silvered screen at the other, and apparently the word had spread that something conceivably of unusual interest was going on in Homicide.

In fact, one of the men asked me, with obvious interest, what we were about to see, so while waiting for the film to arrive I let myself be persuaded to speak a few words of explanation, and self-praise.

There was the usual raillery and vulgar comment—crude "man" talk, but rather stimulating nonetheless. Jolly good fellowship and all that, even though some of the raucous comments were quite blunt and, at least, uncouth. But that has to be expected on occasion from men who live on the seamy side of the day, and as some wise man said, to know all is to forgive all. Besides, I did think I gave back as good as I got. At first.

After a brief explanation of the setting in which the film had been made—that I had been pounced upon by four huge, armed, murderous hoodlums while alone and far from aid of any kind, with nothing but my wits as weapons; I went on, "Truly, men, this film must surely be one of the investigative triumphs—"

Somebody—I didn't spot him immediately—said, "Nothing but your wits, Scott? You mean you were unarmed?"

"—of the century. A film, a real . . ."

I paused, looking about. "Unarmed?" I said. "Well, um, ah . . ." I'd skipped over that part about losing my gun quite neatly, I thought. But . . .

I spotted Rawlins, laughing behind his hand. Lots of other guys were laughing behind their hands. Some weren't even using their hands.

"Why, you *sadist,*" I said to Rawlins.

There was a little more amusement, and some comments which do not bear repeating.

I went on, "Yes, unarmed. Only my wits—"

I paused, scowling. Probably I should have got that tasteless crack a bit sooner. But, hell, I'd had a pretty wearing day. Even been shot in the head. These jolly good fellows should make allowances. They, of course, would not.

"So, thinking like lightning," I said, and went on to explain what the men would see. "This unique document, then," I said, "at the birth of which you are privileged to be midwives, is a film, a real moving-picture film of four hoods *smack in the act of attempted murder!*"

It didn't go over with the impact I'd hoped it would have. But at least some of the men were nodding as though in approval.

I continued, "It required a bit of daring, of course, but also luck. I was simply lucky enough that it was *I,* instead of, say, J. Edgar Hoover, who managed to bring this coup off."

I went on for a bit, telling them how dangerous the men were, especially huge Fleck and English 'Arry, and perhaps I got a bit carried away.

At any rate, one of the officers, a lieutenant from Burglary, said, "Scott, if you really do have those guys on film—especially the ones you named—I got to hand it to you. But letting them shoot at you is one of the dumbest things I ever heard of."

"Dumb?" I said. "Where is the line between magnificent courage and stupidity? Can you tell me that?"

"No—and now we know you can't, either." He grinned.

"Well . . . It's not as though I *invited* them to shoot at me.

They were bound and determined to shoot at me. In fact, that's all they were there for." I paused. "I merely took *advantage* of the opportunity."

Fortunately the delivery boy came in then, bearing the film in a tin case.

I threaded it through the projector with some satisfaction, thinking this would silence the Burglary lieutenant, and the rest of these guys, for that matter. As the Chinese say, one picture worth ten thou, and so on. I mentally savored my approaching moment of triumph. Such moments don't come along very often. Then with everything ready I moved my wooden chair near the table on which the projector sat, put a finger on the starting switch.

I had already dwelt at some length on the four men, stressing that two of them, at least, were truly big sonsoguns, veritable behemoths, and that Fleck alone was the size of two, three big guys. Bigger than English 'Arry, who himself was huge and all over muscle. After explaining that because I'd started escaping away from the camera and would not be seen until completing one lap of the track, I finished setting the stage.

"So the first person you'll see will be Fleck, or Gargantua, whom I'm sure you all know by reputation, if not sight."

I nodded to Rawlins, who was standing by the light switch, and he flicked the lights out. Then he picked his way through policemen sitting on folding chairs, which had been brought in, and others sitting on the floor, and plopped down in a vacant chair next to me.

"This better be good," he said. "Kind of crowded here— maybe we should have run it downstairs in the auditorium."

"Perhaps we will next time, Bill," I said airily. "Probably SID and the Intelligence Division will—"

There was a sudden, explosive roar. It sounded like— laughter? Yes, I was looking at Bill Rawlins and he was bellowing at the top of his lungs.

I turned my head toward my movie. "What's so fu . . ."

On the screen was a little boy. No mistaking it.

He was about four years old, running over a white sand beach toward the camera, fat little legs going like windmills. In his right hand he held one of those little celluloid propeller things on the end of a stick. It was spinning around and around in the wind as he ran, and when he neared the camera the little boy smiled slobberishly and pointed the stick at it.

Some clown in the room yelled, "Bang! Bang!"

There was already so much stupid noise I shouldn't have been able to hear the guy. But I heard him—and, of course, so did the others in here.

Rawlins actually slid off his chair. He was down on the floor on his fanny, beating both palms on the floor and making ridiculous snorting noises.

I reached numbly for the switch and shut off the projector. "Well—" I said in the darkness, using a word I rarely use unless under titanic stress. "Well—" I said again. I waited to speak further until there was relative quiet—for quite some time afterwards any quiet was only relative.

"Friends," I said icily. "Idiot friends. I merely forgot that I had exposed a few feet of the film in my camera on *another* day, before taking the rest of this movie which—if you can contain yourselves long enough to watch it—will impress you, I have little doubt, as a high point in the entire field of criminalistics. And perhaps even in the history of *Hollywood,* the film capital of the *land."*

I was laying it on too much now—and maybe earlier as well —but I couldn't stop. A kind of verbal diarrhea was afflicting me, and besides, I couldn't backtrack after laying it on my jolly friends so heavily. Jolly friends—they were certainly jolly now.

"Come on, Shell," Rawlins said, getting back onto his chair. "Let's see the rest. Maybe we'll enjoy the main feature more now we've had the short subject. Get it—*short* subject—"

I quickly flipped the projector on again before my moment of triumph could become a shambles. I'd forgotten shooting that brief bit of the little kid. I should have remembered taking a shot or two that day at Laguna Beach, when Tootsie and I had . . .

Ye Gods! Tootsie!

But once again I was in the midst of howling, hoots, and whistles. Tootsie was already on the screen, doing a little dance for the camera. Behind her, as in the poem, the lone and level sands stretched far away. There wasn't even a seagull in sight, not another living thing.

But Tootsie was a living thing. She was five-feet-eight living inches tall, with a thirty-eight bust, twenty-four waist, and thirty-seven hips, not a little girl. No, there was a lot of Tootsie, and she was wearing a striped bikini over only a little of it.

That is, she would be for about another three seconds. But

Too late.

Rawlins grabbed my right wrist, yelping with glee, and as I pulled back my left to sock him somebody on the other side got that one. Pretty quick two more thugs had me in several viselike grips. Don't let any of this contemporary jazz about cops fool you. There's a lot of bad in some of them.

Helplessly, I watched the dancing tomato dance, first in the top and bottom of her bikini, and then only in her bikini bottom, realizing once again that there was much less bikini than bottom.

But nobody had grabbed my mouth, and just before the top half of the bikini came off I yelled, "Listen, you—you fuzz. This isn't what you want to see. We want to see *hoods*. That's only Titsie—Titty—Tootsie!"

Hell, it could have happened to anybody. I was watching the screen and it was right after I yelled "*hoods*" that the bikini bra flew off. Anybody might have got a little tongue-tied.

I felt sick.

But not these slobs. If laughter is good for the health, none of these guys was going to be sick for a couple years.

My swell film of the four hoods was on the screen now, but even though they truly did look quite fierce—and jerky because of the two-times-normal speed of the action—and you could see the guns, and there was even one fine shot of English 'Arry firing at something unseen up ahead, the impact of their initial appearance was lost entirely.

Because guys in the room were still whooping and yelling things like: "Yoo-hoo, Titty!" and, "Ba-haybee, be *my* Titsie Titty Tootsie!" and, "Oh, my hotsy-totsy Tootsie," and a lot of other dumb junk.

I just waited, sourness gathering in my bloodstream. It was awful. I had to live with these guys, and this was ruining me. But there was plenty of time for the men to calm down, because there was quite a while after the hoods went by the camera when nothing happened.

Absolutely nothing.

We performers were all running around in a circle, to be sure, but all the camera caught was a bunch of trees growing. You could not, of course, tell they were growing. Nothing stirred. There wasn't even one of those little birds hopping from branch to twig.

It was excruciatingly boring. But the men did quiet down except for an occasional chuckle.

And there was, as well, time enough for me to sort of gather my strength again, to spring back. I realize, crude fun or not, the salient—and actually reasonably important—part of the film was yet to come. And certainly there could be nothing funny in four guys trying to kill another guy. Especially when I was the other guy. I even began looking forward to my own appearance on the screen.

I knew, naturally, that it wasn't going to be *quite* as dramatic as my build-up. But, still, it was bound to be fairly gripping, especially to these men who knew Fleck and Little Phil and the others, knew them and their records of thievery, violence, and mayhem.

I was almost smiling in anticipation, feeling pretty good again and certainly less down-in-the-mouth than when it started. Because I remembered, because I had *been* there, and because it began so suddenly, the start of it damn near lifted me up off my seat.

There I came! Yes, there I was! This was keen.

I came speeding around the curve in the path, way up ahead there, turning and sprinting . . .

No, I wasn't turning.

What was happening? Who was that creep? Whoever he was, he looked even from way off like those cartoons of guys lost in parched deserts.

He wasn't turning; he was just running—well, sort of lunging staggeringly—right off into the woods. Wait—there was a pretty-good-sized tree smack in front of him, and the imbecile was staggering lungingly straight at it.

This wasn't the way I remembered it.

Yeah, I did recall smacking into a tree about there. But it had been just a little tree, more of a branch, as I recalled; I'd snapped it right in two. But that thing on the screen looked maybe six inches—oh!

He—I—some idiot—smacked right into it with a tremendous wallop. The tree bent over, and maybe cracked, but didn't go down. The guy did, though. Only not immediately.

He sort of reeled back into the path and stood there, arms held rigidly out and angled down from his sides at about a forty-five-degree angle. Then his legs began moving stiffly and jerkily as he moved right, left, forward a bit, left, right. He looked like nothing so much as those comics who do imitations of Frankenstein's monster.

It was bad enough any way you looked at it, but since the

160

film had been taken at only eight frames a second the action was speeded up tremendously. Somehow that made it quite a lot worse.

Then—there he went.

He flopped down onto the ground and lay as one dead. No, he was still twitching. Ah, there, he was getting up. Crawling forward. Staggering to his feet. Flopping as one dead again. Up, on his feet, running, weaving. Close to the camera now.

Close enough for individual features to be seen—and now behind him came the first hood. Big Fleck. Tearing along like a goddamn machine. Didn't look like he was even breathing hard. But the other one, the guy now reaching out with one hand toward the camera, *he* was breathing hard.

His mouth was stretched into a caricature of the theater's mask of tragedy, with his tongue projecting astonishingly from the middle of it. He was reaching, reaching, for the camera. Reaching while still at least fifteen feet away from it. Then he disappeared. Just fell down out of sight.

That at least left the field of vision clear—and, mercifully, removed that contorted face from view—and now behind Fleck could be seen two more men, then another, the last of the four pursuers. It was evident that one or two of them were shooting at something near the camera. Something—there he was. I had to face it: There I was.

Now, this was pretty serious business, make no mistake about it. Those were real hoods out there, with real guns, and they were shooting those real guns at me. But from the noises and near-screams these dumb cops all around me were making, would you have thought it pretty serious business? No, you would not.

The dump cops were cracking up, laughing and howling and hammering on their thighs and heads and even on other dumb cops.

Part of it, surely, was the fast-action, the jerky Keystone-Kops-pursuing-the-bandits effect. But, to tell it true, another part had to be the not entirely dashing and devil-may-care picture which I myself presented. I, and the rather astonishing —and all horrified—expressions playing over my chops.

I was up again, heading for the camera, bound and determined to get that bloody camera, chin stuck forward so far it appeared to be sliding out from under my face like the drawer in a cash register, lower lip peeled down to expose lots of teeth and even gums. Every once in a while my eyes squeezed shut and simultaneously my tongue stuck out and then popped back inside. If I'd been a lizard you'd have sworn I was catching flies.

The Homicide squad room was in an uproar; it was bedlam; it was a goddamn lunatic asylum. It was now clear as could be that those four hoods were Fleck, English 'Arry, Little Phil, and another creep who now could easily be identified, that each of them carried a pistol, and that two of them were at the moment employing their pistols feloniously in an attempted assassination.

But did the assembled forces of the law give a hoot? They did not. Not that kind of hoot, anyhow.

It had to end. At last, I had grabbed the camera. There was a big hand blocking out everything, then swirling earth, trees, sky. All over, at last. All over . . . All . . .

Nope.

The worst, in some ways, was yet to come.

There had been that final moment when I thought I'd been shot. The simple truth was that I had merely yanked up my hands—clutching the still-filming Bolex—and clanked myself on the chin. But the last few frames had captured me—since the camera was held in my hands and the lens had been aimed, as though by Satan himself, smack up at my chops—looking down the path at those lumbering, thundering, too-speedily-approaching hoods. It was not to be expected, then, that my expression would resemble that of a man completely unconcerned.

It didn't.

In the first of these final two shots my mouth was again open, though not more than nine inches, and my tongue was sticking out to what surely must have been its utmost length and a little bir more, and my eyes appeared literally to be popping from their sockets like corks from broken champagne bottles.

The second shot of my face was the same, except that it had been taken from much closer, as I'd yanked up the camera. Naturally in the extreme close-up my image was out of focus and quite fuzzy, which helped a lot. It merely made me appear to have a long, fuzzy tongue and hairy eyeballs.

When at last the sounds of great festivity ceased ululating from the now brightly-lighted Homicide squad room and echoing throughout the L.A. Police Building, and conceivably three-fourths of Los Angeles, Rawlins wheezed and choked and sighed a bit more, then got control of himself.

162

"You want us to pick 'em up, Shell—or do you want to go get 'em yourself?"

"I have *nothing* to say," I said loftily.

And he was off again.

Ah, nuts, I thought. How am I going to get help from the Los Angeles Police Department when all the cops are batty? I *will* do it myself. That's the ticket. Like the old saw, if you want something done yourself, do it right. I'll do it myself, whatever it is—I didn't remember at the moment. I was in a kind of daze.

Even Samson, my buddy, kindly old Sam, turned against me.

With his eyes still streaming he said, "Shell, I *wanted* to use your murder movie as an excuse to try tagging Violet. But I can't do that now. Who—who—" he was choking up again.

"I'll do it myself," I said. "I'll go out and see Jimmy, and . . . something."

"Something, yeah. They'll kill you half a dozen times."

"So? What have I got to live for?"

"Well, you can't expect the police to go there, not merely on this . . . this—" he started to strangle and tee-hee some more—"this evidence. Can't show this to anybody; nobody'd believe it. Especially not in *Hollywood*, the film capital of the *land*."

Samson was only kidding of course. The fact is, he seized the film as evidence. Anyway, he seized it for something.

I got up to leave. Then I sank down in my chair again, only now beginning to realize what long, lonely days lay ahead of me. In through the door had walked—or maybe wiggled is a better word—that burly, six-four police sergeant named Mac-Craig. Ordinarily, he was bald, but now he had on a woman's wig, undoubtedly borrowed from a police woman. He had his pants on, but no shirt, and around his bare chest—in front, at least, there was a string extension in back so it would fit—was a paper-stuffed brassiere of rather remarkable dimensions. Looked like it had the whole *New York Times* in it. In one big hand dangled a submachine gun. In the other was a pair of white Jockey shorts.

No initials on the shorts. No name. Nothing on the gun, either. Nothing was needed. It seemed evident that Rawlins had spilled his guts about *everything* he knew and some things he'd only guessed.

I sat there, gazing in ill-concealed disgust at the disgustingly ill-concealed exhibition MacCraig was making of himself. Cops have a very crude sense of humor. They're very crude human beings. What more can you expect when they're all the

163

time around slobs and jerks and crude things? Actually, they don't have much of a sense of humor at all. They laugh at things like people getting caught in undertows and old ladies getting snagged in power mowers.

I stood up. "Well," I said to MacCraig. "That's a pretty dumb exhibition." The cops were having a screaming good time. Laughing at Mac Craig, I supposed. "What's so funny?" I asked them. "You guys must be sick. *I* can't see anything so funny—"

I don't know why, but that set them off as much as anything else so far. Dumb—boy, you think of a better word, use it.

"That's pretty dumb," I said again, unable to think of a better word. "We need men like you, MacCraig. In the Sanitation Department. Or possibly you could give enemas in the zoo, or to restaurant oysters."

I couldn't win. Just didn't have it any more. I had lost, lost, I thought, sourness bubbling in my bubblers.

I gathered up all the dignity I could find to gather, which was approximately as much as you could insert into a gnat's—oh, a gnat's ear. I walked to the door, turned and, smiling like a man with rabies, surveyed the howling loonies whom I now thought of as the L.A. Fuzz Department.

A fuzz near me, still chuckling, said, "Ah, Scott, I don't know what we'd do without you."

"That's splendid," I said, in splendid control of myself. "It's splendid to know I'm splendid for your morale."

I'm not sure anybody heard my brilliant exit line.

As I left they were starting to run the film again.

I stalked down the hall, moving much as had that fellow I'd seen hit the tree. A hot plan was forming in my mind.

And all around the plan, splendid words were dancing:

"Kill! Kill! Kill!"

20

I WAS STILL IN A SORT OF DAZE AS I WALKED DOWN THE HALL from the Homicide squad room.

Dizzy trauma was going to be with me for a good hour, and when I finally concluded that my hot plan was a not-so-hot plan, why the bullets and arrows and heat and lead were flying, and it was too late to do much about it.

Until then, however, everything went swimmingly.

Like the first step.

I walked into SID with the laughter and bubble from Homicide faintly audible clear up here a floor above. I was laughing and slapping my thigh.

When I caught sight of the lab technician who'd gotten the rocket pistol for Sam, I said, "Gimme that crazy heater, will you?"

"The Captain wants it?"

"I—ha, *hoo!*" I broke up again.

"What the hell's going on down there?" he asked me. "That in *Homicide?*"

"Yeah—hey, that rocket gun, quick. Man, there's not much time."

Shaking his head, he went to the case and unlocked it and brought the box to me. I took it, turned and started out, then stopped and went back. Just as he'd started to say something, I think.

I leaned forward, opened my mouth, but then broke up

165

again. Then I left while he stared after me, still shaking his head.

It wouldn't be more than a minute or two before he stopped shaking his head and began wondering. But by then I expected to be long gone. And I was.

I was wetter than hell.

Covered with a bunch of muck, too.

I wasn't in the best mood of my life, either.

But I was inside the fence and about to crawl up out of the lake onto the fairly spacious grounds surrounding Jimmy Violet's house.

I had my crossbow. And arrows in a homemade quiver dangling from the crossbow. And my Buck Rogers rocket gat. And little rockets with the four holes in back. I'd brought everything I needed except a kayak.

Getting over the fence—which, to my surprise, didn't electrocute me, and didn't even set off any clangorous alarms—and then across the lake to the slanting bank where I now lay gasping and full of swamp water, had been very easy, peculiar to say. I'd expected guys armed to the teeth, lightning shooting through the fence, that sort of thing.

But there hadn't even been anybody guarding the gate when I'd checked it after getting inside. As for getting inside, I had merely climbed over the fence, ripping my ankle and my butt, and then fallen into the water and begun to drown. It bothered me: It was too easy.

Perhaps there'd been no guard at the gate because Jimmy assumed nobody would come over that high fence tonight and swim through the lake, which maybe was full of piranhas, and then attack the house when there were nine or ten criminals in it. If so, that just shows how wrong he could be.

I felt like throwing up.

Everything seemed sort of dippy around here, as if the air was thick like muck, clogging my ears, eyes, nose, all kinds of clogging. I opened my mouth and spit out some muck, which I began to consider a clue.

I crawled up onto the bank, got onto level ground with grass on it. Then I put down my bow and arrow and pistol and bullets and dug into my ears and nose and got the muck out.

I felt better instantly. But only for a moment. Then I started feeling worse again. I really didn't feel well at all even though I could now see and smell and hear again, which was an improvement. Hadn't felt splendid for at least the last hour. During that time I'd made my preparations.

I knew where there was a roll of thick soft-lead sheeting in the Spartan Apartment Hotel's garage, so I'd taken it, along with the crossbow and arrows from the Cad's trunk and some nuts and bolts, up to my rooms.

There, after feeding the fish and raising the water temperature some more—it takes lots of heat to knock that Ick—I cut part of the lead sheeting into twelve sizeable rectangles. Twelve, because that was the number of arrows I had. Then I wrapped the soft lead around the front ends of my arrows, molding a big lead gob enclosing a few assorted nuts and bolts over their sharp, lethal points. Already that "Kill! Kill!" idea was losing favor with me.

I suppose the idea had occurred to me because earlier, remembering Stub Corey's slug banging my skull, I'd thought of it as not lethal but merely a long-distance sap. So it had seemed to me a crossbow and weighted lead-pointed arrows might, while even less lethal, serve equally as well for my purpose.

I'd soon know.

In the faint light from a crescent moon I could see the bulky shadows of cars in and on this side of the garage, which was on the lake's edge and beyond the front of the house. With the gun in my right-hand coat pocket and rocket clips in the left, and carrying the bow and quivered arrows, I moved over there as silently as I could, most of the noise produced by my shoes squishing. There were two cars in the garage, two more parked outside of it.

I took the lead sheeting from one of the arrows, poked two holes in each car's gasoline tank, then put the foil and nuts and bolts back over the arrow's sharp point as the fuel began glug-glugging out onto the ground and the cement floor of the wooden garage.

I had them all trapped here now.

But that's not why I did it.

A tiny point of light glowed back at the far corner of the house. Then another brightened and dimmed near it. Two guys smoking cigarettes, maybe out merely for a breath of air, or perhaps on guard. The reason wasn't important; they were the two guys I could start on.

I pulled back the bowstring to the string's notch and locked it into place, trigger beneath the bulky weapon cocked, placed an arrow-sap into its groove atop the crossbow. All I had to do was put the stock against my shoulder, aim, and pull the trigger. And then maybe run. Run and swim. Because I'd only fired the thing a couple of times before, and then not with these much heavier—front-end-heavy—missiles. Consequently I hadn't the faintest idea how much extra elevation I should plan on when aiming. I hadn't ever anticipated doing this.

I took my time, plenty of time, moving closer to the men. First I went over near the front door of the house, made sure nobody was there. Lights were on in two of the front rooms, but the curtains were drawn and not much spilled out here.

So I turned my back to the entrance, and, hugging the wall, edged closer to the two men. I could see the glow of only one cigarette now, but I could hear the mumble of voices.

I figured I could be reasonably sure of hitting a man in the head from a distance of thirty feet. My targets were still fifteen yards away, so I moved forward with the crossbow held ready, butt of the stock against my shoulder, finger on the trigger. Ten yards. I could see their bulk, shadowy, not distinct. But I could tell where their heads were, which I supposed was all I needed, really.

Well, they hadn't noticed me yet. Might as well make sure. I moved closer, an inch at a time. My heart started thudding more heavily, and I could feel the steady pulse in my throat. Enough. I couldn't miss from here.

Not much.

I aimed just above the hairline of the man farthest away, facing me and talking to the other guy who had his back to me. The one looking my way was about six inches taller, and if I had to choose between them I preferred to get the bigger guy out of the way first. Especially since I was fairly sure, because of his size, that he had to be Fleck.

I sighted, squeezed the trigger.

There was a soft, kind of velvety *spung*.

I'd failed to consider the sound the bowstring would make snapping forward. But I was worrying more about getting a second arrow out of the quiver and into place on the bow.

By the time I did, several things had happened.

First of all, I missed the big guy entirely. Also I learned something new about this weapon. The arrow—perhaps due to wind whistling around the not-very-smoothly-wrapped lead sheeting—hummed a little as it flew through the air and over the heads of the two men. It wasn't so much a hum as a faint, sighing *psoo*. Whatever it was, I didn't see how those guys could miss it.

They didn't.

The big guy said, "You hear that, Tooth? Kind of a *fong* and *psoo*? What kind of thing makes a *psoo*?"

It was Fleck, all right. He had the *psoo* pretty close, but the *fong* was way off. It had definitely been a *spung*.

Tooth said, "Why do you ask me dumb questions?"

I had my second arrow in the groove, string taut and in its notch. Fleck had turned around and was looking toward wherever that thing had gone.

I was getting pretty nervous. Especially after that clean miss. So I took a big step forward and then aimed at the back of the smaller guy's head, partly because Fleck had called him "Tooth" which meant he was Billy DeKay, but mainly because he was two feet nearer. I was losing much of my confidence in this weapon. Actually, I'd never really had a whole lot.

I fired.

Sung-psoo-*clonk*.

Just about like that. Got him right in the back of the head, and he went straight down. Didn't wobble or stagger or let out a peep or anything. Just straight down. Which took care of Tooth DeKay for a while. Try to kill me at the Hamilton Building, would he?

Fleck heard that, all right. Only a totally deaf man would have failed to hear it.

"What wazzat?" he said.

Then he turned around, saying, "What's goin' on? I swear I heard a *clonk*. You hear it, Tooth? Tooth?"

He was staring right at the airspace where his buddy's head had been. "Where'd you go, Tooth?"

While he was staring I got another arrow ready, string cocked, all that.

Fleck looked down at his feet. "Tooth?" he said.

Clonk.

Straight down, just like the other one. Got him smack on top of the head.

I walked past them, around to the rear of the house, waited silently for a few seconds, listening. Just as I started to move forward again, the back door opened. A man stepped outside not more than ten feet away, and the door slammed shut behind him.

I reached for the gun in my pocket—already loaded with the

169

color-tipped incendiary rockets—but changed my mind. The noise would bring others out here, and I wasn't prepared for that. Not yet.

The crossbow was ready for action again. Readier than I was. But I lifted it, tried to sight over the arrow at the man's shadowy bulk.

Then a light flared. He had a cigarette in his mouth, was holding a lighter to it, the flame clearly illumining his features. It was the man who'd met me at the door on my first trip here earlier this day, a tall guy, sharp chin, ledges of bone over his eyes.

Clonk.

I was getting pretty good with this thing. One miss, then three bull's-eyes. And that meant three down. I couldn't know how many of the enemy might be here, but whatever the number, there were three less in action now.

I continued on around the house to its front without seeing anybody else, then took up a position to the right of the door, my back to the wall. Another arrow was ready to go on the bow, but this time I pulled the lightweight rocket gun from my pocket, aimed at the garage.

Samson had explained how to fire the gun, and it was simple enough: Just point and pull the trigger. But this would be the first time I'd fired the thing, and I was glad the initial target was something as large as a garage.

I aimed, pulled the trigger.

There was a solid flat crack. Hot gases shot out both sides of the gun above my hand. The sound didn't come from the gun itself, but from a few feet in front of it. According to Sam, that was when the little rocket broke the sound barrier. A ripple of mild heat washed back against my face. There was hardly any recoil at all.

But there were sure a lot of results.

I could see the incendiary projectile zip through the air like a supersonic firefly, and when it hit the gasoline-filled garage there was a great *whoom* as the fluid ignited, fire rising toward the garage's roof and belching from the open door.

Suddenly there were flames over that entire area. The gas had spilled all over the cement floor, onto the driveway beneath and near the parked cars, into the grass near the drive, and some had even spilled into the lake. As I watched, the thin film on the water caught, and fire spread in a blunt tongue of wavering red over the lake's surface. The wood of the garage caught almost immediately in the intense heat and was crackling angrily—as the first man burst through the door near me and started yelling.

That's what I'd been waiting for.

The rocket gun was thrust under my belt—where I could reach it in a hurry—because I knew soon I'd be using it again. But at the moment I had the crossbow ready once more.

Another man charged through the door and then let out a shout, skidding to a stop ten feet away. It was tall, rangy English 'Arry. The guy who'd come outside first and was now running forward waving his arms and yelling was the man whose name I didn't know, the fourth guy from my movie. He was wearing a gaudy sport shirt now, but he was one of the s.o.b.'s who'd chased me all that way, occasionally tossing unfriendly pills at me.

He stopped ten or fifteen yards from me, near the lake's edge, holding both hands before his face to ward off heat from the blaze, heat I could feel clear over here by the door. There was a fluttering boom and flare of red as a car's gas tank exploded.

I aimed the crossbow at 'Arry's head, held my breath, started to squeeze the trigger, then waited as feet pounded inside on my right. This time it was a man I didn't know who raced out, ran past 'Arry and stopped, staring at the garage. I didn't recognize him, didn't know him, but it was enough for me that he was one of Jimmy Violet's chums.

I'd held my aim and let out my breath as the third man came outside, then sucked it in and held it again. I let the arrow fly.

Fourth bull's-eye in a row. Cross off English 'Arry.

But that was the last chance I had to use my trusty crossbow. It was fine when guys would stand still and let me leisurely sap them from afar; but it wasn't worth a damn for fast action or a moving target. And from now on, it appeared incontrovertible, the action was going to be speedy and the targets moving. Yesterday's weapon had had its day; now it was time for tomorrow's.

I dropped the bow, grabbed for the gun under my belt as two things happened simultaneously. The lob in the gaudy shirt, one of my movie stars, turned and spotted me. There was plenty of reddish light, enough so he lost no time coming to the conclusion that I didn't belong here—and, presumably, was responsible for the fire. As his eyes fell on me a fourth man came running to the door but stopped barely outside, staring to his right at the blaze—and, fortunately, away from me.

Immediately he turned and ran back inside yelling something I didn't understand.

Maybe I understood it with part of my mind, but it just didn't penetrate because the gaudy-shirted lob was jumping aside, crouching, grabbing for a gun at his hip. I flipped the rocket gun toward him, fired and missed. But missed by not more than an inch—I could see the slug fly past barely to the left of his neck.

The nearer man had turned, was looking at me. But he didn't have a gun in his hand and gaudy-shirt did, so I kept the gun on him and fired a second time—and the second one wasn't wide. It hit him dead center as he triggered his gun.

The boom of his gun and crack of the bullet into the side of the house near me came at the same time. But that was the last slug he was going to toss. The impact of the small rocket in his chest threw him backward and spun him, as if he'd been clipped by a car. His gun arced high into the air. I didn't watch it start to fall.

I slapped the gun left, toward the man near me—but he wasn't near me long.

He'd been staring at me, staring at the gun in my hand, and he had seen the slug's fiery glow as it sped from me to the man even now spinning in the air, not yet on the grass.

He let out a yell of sheer panic, spun and raced away from me. I can't be sure, but I do believe he thought my strange little gun with its hot pills had caused that large conflagration all by itself. Whatever he thought, he wanted no part of it, not desiring to be cremated. He raced toward the lake and left his feet in a very ungraceful dive, hit, splashed, and disappeared in the water.

I stood there for no more than two seconds longer, then slammed the door open and jumped inside the house. But those two seconds were long enough for me to note a few things I'd been unaware of during the just-concluded action. Things like the sudden, almost painful dryness and tightness of my throat, the too-rapid hammering of my pulse, queer cooling of skin, throbbing of temples, and the thudding ache in my entire head, as if my brain was alive and trying to escape to a less agonized place.

Then I was in the carpeted hallway which stretched ahead of me to the back of the house. On my left, a door stood open. Light poured from the room into the hall. I jumped to the door, but the room was empty.

172

Light spilled through another open door down near the end of the hall—that room where I'd been with Jimmy Violet and his men yesterday. I ran toward it, gun gripped tight in my right hand, head feeling as if it were going to split open.

But it was no time to stop or even slow down now. Maybe he who hesitates isn't always lost; but he sure would be this time. So I ran full tilt down the hall, slowed skidding, and jumped through the wide double doors, catching the whole scene with one quick swing of my eyes around the room.

I let my knees bend, crouching as low as I could, gun held forward and parallel to the floor, swinging my body left.

There, on my left, was Bingo. And of the four men in the room he was the only one with a gun already in his hand. It was either the same gun he'd held on me in my Cad this morning outside the Beverly Hills Hotel, or one just like it, a .45 caliber automatic. Shock bloomed on his thin pockmarked face.

Near him, two men were throwing papers, books, something into what looked like a big hole in the wall, a big square hole. It was a safe—or rather a vault; the heavy door swung open and back against the wall. It had obviously been concealed by paneling when I'd been in this room before, but it was open now—already open, open for me, if I lived through the next few seconds.

One of the men before the vault was Little Phil, the short but meaty-faced and hook-nosed hood who'd been driving the car for Stub Corey this morning, and, later, chasing me in the woods. And next to him, hands full, was my buddy, cadaverous, with his usual air of ghastliness accentuated by his sprained expression as he swung his head toward me, and by the size of his swollen discolored nose. Jimmy Violet. Whom I had recently popped on the beak. Who had been doing his level best to get me killed.

One more man was present. He was on my right, seated in a chair near the bar. Tall, round-shouldered, potbellied Gippo Crane. He was seated, but moving, leaning forward and coming out of the chair.

Bingo fired before I did, but he missed and I didn't. There was so little kick to the gun that it wavered hardly at all when fired, didn't pull the gun off target; and I squeezed the trigger twice, both slugs slamming into his chest high and on the right. The double impact knocked him clear back to the wall.

Jimmy Violet and Little Phil had dropped whatever they were holding and their right hands were moving, Jimmy's to his shoulder and Phil's to his belt; but I could see Gippo Crane, up out of that chair now, see the gleam of light as his hand moved, the glitter of light on metal.

There wasn't time to turn, to swing my body toward him, so I just snapped my head right as I swung arm and gun around, still balanced on the balls of my feet but facing away from Gippo.

The gun was still moving when I squeezed the trigger, but I hit him. Low, down around his hip, but he hadn't been able to get his gun on me yet. He flopped back onto the front edge of the cushion in the chair behind him, but the snub-nosed .38 was still in his hand, and I had my own gun steady on him now. I put a second shot into his chest.

Remembering that he, along with Tooth outside, had left white-haired Porter flat on his face on Broadway—I felt like putting one or two more into him. But I didn't. Even while the thought spun briefly in my mind I threw my fist back toward Phil and Jimmy Violet, finger heavy on the trigger.

But that was all.

All the shooting.

All of it.

Jimmy's hand was still not out from under his coat. Little Phil's gun was in his hand, still moving, but he simply let go of it—much as Jimmy Violet had dropped his shiny little pistol when I'd been in this room before. Phil threw his arms up over his head, stiffening them, fingers splayed and thrusting toward the ceiling.

I glanced at Gippo Crane. The snub-nosed revolver had fallen to the seat cushion by his leg. His head had dropped down and turned sideways, chin on his chest. He was still moving, bending forward.

I looked at Jimmy Violet. "Go ahead, Jimmy. Do something. Pull that heat out the rest of the way. Cough, sneeze—do *something*."

I straightened up, lifted the gun higher, sighted over it, carefully aiming at a spot between his dull, dark eyes.

"Go ahead, Jimmy," I said.

He always looked sick, but he looked sick unto death at the moment. Those cupid fat lips grew slack, turned down at the corners. He didn't say anything, but he licked his dry lips and held his left hand toward me, palm out, then—slowly, slowly— used it to pull back his coat so I could see his other hand on the butt of his chrome-plated pretty. Continuing to move very slowly, he lowered his right hand, let the gun drop from it. Without being told he nudged it toward me with his foot.

I backed toward the corner of the room, stood near the wall. Gippo slid forward that last fraction of an inch, and his weight pulled him out of the chair and onto the floor. He hit with a thump. That was the last time he moved.

I carefully aimed the gun again, between Jimmy Violet's eyes. "How many men here, Jimmy? It could be I already know. In which case, if you lie, I'll have to kill you, I guess. How many all told, including you, Jimmy?"

He swallowed. But he didn't hesitate in answering. "Ten," he said. "That's all."

"Name them."

He named them. I did a little mathematics in my aching head. Usually I can take addition and subtraction or leave them alone; but this time the mathematical labor was a pleasing thing, so pleasing it seemed even to help the ache in my head. The addition came to ten, all right; but the really rewarding part was the subtraction.

Four here. Fleck and Tooth cold in front and the doorman cold in back from my first tour outside the house. That was seven. English 'Arry with a lump on his head, and gaudy-shirt the movie star, shot. That was nine. And the tenth man was either still running, or still swimming, or drowned by now.

For the first time I relaxed a little. But when a man is wound as tightly as I had apparently been wound, it is difficult to relax just a little. When I sort of let go, my knees actually bent. I sank down about an inch, gun wavering. But then I tightened my leg muscles, straightening up, but feeling those muscles beginning to tremble.

I wasn't so tired or weak, however, that I couldn't handle the little remaining to be done.

I sighed, took a deep breath, and said, "Well, let's see what we've got."

〜❧〜

"SAM?" I SAID INTO THE PHONE'S MOUTHPIECE. "SHELL HERE. I've, uh, got something to tell you. Yes, quite a story to tell you.

"Oh?" Sam could put a lot into just an "Oh?"

"Yeah," I said. "Now, let me tell you the whole thing before you crack up—before you say anything. O.K.? That's the only way you'll be able to appraise the total situation and arrive at a calm and reasoned—"

"What have you done?" If anyone thought Samson could put a lot into an "Oh?" he should have heard those four words.

"Well. I—it's wonderful news. From your point of view, I mean. I've wiped out the Jimmy Violet gang. That is, they're—"

"What? *What?* Wiped *what?*"

"The Jimmy Violet gang. This is a great victory for law and order, Sam. I'm calling from Jimmy's place now, using the phone in his den, matter of fact."

I glanced around. It was rather an appalling sight, even to me. Jimmy Violet and Little Phil sat on the floor with their hands tied behind them—I'd had Jimmy tie up Phil, but had made sure of the job on Jimmy myself.

And near them, heads against the wall and feet toward me, lay seven bodies. Two dead, one still alive despite a pair of little rockets high in his chest, and four out cold with lumps on their skulls. On the carpet near their feet was a collection of guns, knives, and saps marvelous in its variety.

There had been silence from Samson. Now he said, "You're out there? Wait a minute. I just got a report there's a fire in that

176

vicinity. Engines on the way there now. But I had not allowed myself to think, even to *dream*—"

"Not this vicinity, Sam. Right here, this is it. I had to burn down his garage."

"You had—"

I could recognize the tone, so I hurried on. "It was the only way, Sam, the *only* way, otherwise they would have killed me. I had to divide them to conquer, or something like that."

I could hear him yelling, shouting muffled things. The sound was muffled because he apparently had his hand over the mouthpiece while yelling and shouting things.

But I knew he would still be listening, so I sped on. "Besides, I had to do something dramatic, something *big,* Sam. You can see that, can't you? After all, my life was ruined, wasn't it? All my friends, laughing, *laughing*—it had to be a real humdinger—"

"What have you done?" The words came out slowly, heavy, dropping into my ear like hot lead.

"I'm trying to *tell* you, Sam. And this is, um, sure going to make you happy. Certainly makes *me* happy. After all, I don't think so many people have tried so hard for so long to kill me, ever in my life. Justice had to be done. So, I done it."

"Yes?"

"Here's the picture. I came out to Jimmy's, and there was quite a fracas, you might say. But I've got them all here in a package, waiting for you."

"All?"

"All that were here—except one, who ran, or swam, or maybe passed away. Haven't seen any more of him. But I've got Jimmy and eight of his men. Now, two of them are dead, that's true—but it worked out very nicely. They're the slowpoke from my movie, who turns out to be practically a mass murderer, a *real* mean one—and Gippo Crane, who helped knock Porter off, as Tooth DeKay will be able to testify when he comes to. If ever anybody deserved—"

"When he comes to, huh?"

"I had to knock four of them out, Sam, or I wouldn't have had a chance. I mean, sap them. From a distance, that is. Naturally I couldn't just walk around clanging them on their skulls, so I used a bow and arrow—"

"Stop."

"Sam, I have to get this said; I haven't even got to the good part yet."

177

"I'd say not." He paused. "Are you truly trying to tell me you've killed, or maimed, or somehow ravaged Jimmy Violet and a bunch of his hoods? There were—how many?—nine of them?"

"Nine of them left. The tenth one got away."

"The tenth one got away," he echoed, his voice flat. "Why did you let that happen?"

"Sam, I know you're probably a bit ... uneasy about this. But have no fears. All these guys are, ah, pacified. I think four of them may have fractured skulls, or at least concussions; but they'll be all right. In time."

"Uh-huh." I didn't like his tone. I didn't like it at all.

"Sam, old friend," I said, forcing exuberance into my voice, "I knew you'd be tickled to death. It's really swell, just *great* how it's worked out. Tooth can tell you about him and Gippo Crane, which wraps up the Porter homicide. Bingo Kestel has a couple little rockets in him, but he's going to live; I'm reasonably certain of that. And he can tell you about hitting the Sporks with that blackmail picture of Sybil, among other things. Little Phil was with Stub Corey in the car last night when he went out to put the bite on Halstead, which will be corroboration for some of that. And Jimmy Violet can tell you about all of it—including getting the album from Kermit Vanda and Dilly—since he was on top of all of it. In fact, Jimmy's just been telling me any number of things. He thought I was going to shoot him between the eyes. Of course, I wouldn't have, but—"

"You mean he's confessed. After you arrested this small community of citizens, naturally you advised Violet of his right to remain silent while you shot him between the eyes, and his right to counsel, and determined that he was voluntarily answering your questions as you shot his eyes out—"

"Don't be ridiculous, Sam." I laughed lightly. "I know the Supreme Court decisions as well as you do. I understand the care with which hoodlums—innocent citizens must be handled. But it's all right. I haven't even put them under arrest yet. Didn't even make a private person's arrest, see? But there's clear evidence of felony here—"

"Uh-huh."

"—and therefore the official police representatives can legally place these hoods under arrest and advise them of all sorts of things. I merely stand in the wings, so to speak, a private citizen concerned by the ghastly upsurge in the crime

178

rate, since the Supreme Court decisions such as the Mallory decision way back in nineteen fifty-seven . . ."

Silence. I didn't like that silence.

"And *Mapp versus Ohio . . . Preston versus U.S. . . .*"

I could hear him breathing. Breathing heavily, it sounded like. Getting a little faster.

I went on, slowing a bit, "*Gideon versus Wainwright?* And we can't forget the Escobedo case, can we?"

He'd stopped breathing. That was bad.

"And then there's that little beauty, *Miranda versus Arizona* . . . Sam? Sam, I'm merely showing you I had the law clearly in mind, what's left of it." I laughed lightly again. "I mean, what's left of the *law*, not my mind. Sam?"

Finally he spoke. His voice seemed to come from a great distance. "You didn't arrest them. Nobody arrested them. You merely ran them through with bows and arrows, beat upon them, shot them, coerced and threatened them, set fire to the countryside—the flames were seen from the corner of Hollywood and Vine!—entered illegally, probably raped the housekeeper—"

"I did burn up four automobiles, now you remind me. But, Sam, everything's *swell*—"

"I assume, in addition to the rest, you're dripping big gobs of blood onto Mr. Violet's expensive carpet."

"Blood? No, no, Sam. I didn't get a scratch."

There was a pause. Then he said faintly, "There ain't no justice any more. No, there just ain't no justice." Another pause. "Did you chance upon any physical evidence out there? *Physical* evidence? Anything that won't instantly be tossed out of court?"

"Tons of it, Sam. There's so much I wouldn't be surprised if it falls under seventeen different sections of the penal code. But on the case of immediate interest, the murder of George Halstead and the blackmail operation, not only is there now proof it was worked almost exactly as I described it to you earlier, but the album is here. The photos of the Sporks, Halsteads, Bersudians, and so on—the blackmail album."

"Well . . ." He paused. Then, grudgingly, "That should help a little."

"There's more. And this part I personally found highly interesting. Not only was Jimmy tossing the album of our immediate interest into his concealed vault when I got here, but

179

in the vault were two *other* albums. Not one, but three in all. Three of them, identical in conception and execution."

"Oh?" It had a somewhat different sound this time.

"Yep. In one of them there were fourteen photos depicting twenty-eight different individuals, none of whom I recognized. But the third one might be primarily a political group. It's a smaller album, only six photos, twelve people, but two of them had faces familiar to me. And you. One is a member of the California Legislature. And one, by golly, is a Superior Court judge."

He whistled. No words, just a soft whistle. But I found its note encouraging.

"Jimmy has told me," I went on, "that these two albums, also, were supplied to him by Kermit Vanda and his wife—they've been married, by the way, something like four years—in return for a staggeringly substantial payment of Jimmy's cash. The blackmail con with sexy frosting has been going on for two years and a bit now. We just happened to get into this one when the first pitch in the operation was tossed." I paused. "No wonder Stub clobbered Halstead last night. These creeps had a big operation to protect. If we can believe Jimmy, they've already hauled in over half a million bucks. And I think we can believe Jimmy."

Sam asked me what else I'd found in the safe, or elsewhere on the premises, and I covered some of it briefly. Then I turned again to the Halstead case and said, "Vanda and Dilly were building up one group while getting ready to drop out of another, which helps explain all their addresses. It's eight to five they've right now got another con going we don't know about—maybe based at the Hidden Valley Lodge, for all I know. Plenty money and bigshots there." I paused. "Sam, about those two, have you any lead to where they might be?"

"Not yet. We've got a local and an APB out and word to every informant available. Something should come in soon."

"I hope so. That babe still has my gun. If she didn't throw it away. Or melt it."

"By the way," he said sweetly, "What did you use to shoot all those citizens with?"

"What?"

"Didn't you say one of your victims has a couple ... what was it? Little rockets in him?"

"What? Speak up, man. Don't mumble—"

"DIDN'T YOU SAY LITTLE ROCKETS—"

"*Sam,* ouch, hey, oh, my ear. Well . . . rockets?"

He knew. Of course he knew. He'd known for a long time. He just hadn't known I was launching the little rockets. At least, he hadn't been *sure.*

So, finally—with the phone on my other ear—I said, "I did borrow that zippy little pistol. I did, all right. Yes, I did. It's a great little weapon, Sam, the only way to let fly, a regular Fun-Jet. I have, you might say, field-tested it, and can certainly recommend that it be adopted without delay—"

"You've gone too far," he said quietly. Not venomously, not angrily. Sort of sadly, I thought. "Too far," he murmured again.

I didn't say anything. I had a hunch I'd said enough.

After a pause Sam went on, "I have already sent a car to Mr. Violet's for you, Shell. In the car is Bill Rawlins and his partner. You wouldn't shoot an old friend like Bill Rawlins, would you?"

I thought of Bill sitting on his behind in the Homicide squad room, pounding the floor with his hands. And holding my wrist in a viselike grip. "Well, I'm not sure," I said.

"They have been instructed to bring you in. Please offer no resistance, and come along quietly."

"Why, of course. I'm a peace-loving man. Besides, I've got no resistance left in me. Hell, you didn't have to send a car out for me."

"I thought it best. Sheldon, don't you realize, don't you *realize,* that we, the police, were preparing to visit Jimmy Violet? *Later* tonight? Armed with legal documents and proper authority, based on evidence we have developed, and even that movie film of yours . . . are you listening, Sheldon?"

I listened a moment. "I hear sirens now," I said.

"Probably the fire engines. But Lieutenant Rawlins will not be far behind. Wait there for him."

"Yes, sir. I don't think we'll need the fire engines. Fire's practically all over now."

"The fire," he said gently, "has only begun."

Then he hung up.

I wonder what he meant by that? I thought.

What he meant was, he was going to clap me in jail.

That's the impression I got from Rawlins and his partner, a young sergeant, when they arrived. At least, Bill placed me under arrest.

The formality was taken care of after they—followed by at least half a dozen other police cars—arrived at Jimmy Violet's home and surveyed the carnage. And after the police work, photos, gathering and disposition of evidence—and hoods—was consummated.

Bill told me, smiling, that I was under arrest, then took out his little card and read, "Mr. Scott, I must advise you that you have the right to remain silent. Anything you say can be used against you in a court of law—" and on through the whole bit.

When he finished I said, "You've got to be kidding."

He smiled.

"O.K.," I said, snarling for his amusement, "so I take a fall. But I'll beat this phoney rap, you dirty rat. Hell, I'll confess quick before you can get to an attorney, you dirty—"

I stopped, and smiled. Then, not snarling, I said, "Bill, I've *already* beaten it. I'm home free. You can't do a thing to me, not a *thing*."

"Huh?"

"It's beautiful. I've already confessed! Not to a mere lieutenant, either, but to the Captain of Homicide himself. The brute. And he led me on, entrapped me, illegally coerced me. He didn't tell me a single *one* of my rights—in fact, all he told me about was my wrongs. He's clearly unconstitutional. So, take these cuffs off and I'll go."

I went. But with Bill and the sergeant.

His partner drove the car, and Rawlins sat in back with me. He'd taken the handcuffs off—actually, that had been his own warped idea of jolly fun. He had a very warped sense of humor. As I already knew. But he wsn't all bad, not by a long shot. Because when we were on Sunset, heading toward the Hollywood Freeway, he imparted to me a cheering bit of news.

He had phoned Samson two or three times from Jimmy Violet's house, and the last time, Bill said, was less than a minute after Sam had received certain information. Information on a matter which turned out to be the last major development in the case.

One of the informants had turned the trick. Kermit Vanda and Mrs. Vanda had been located.

Rawlins went on, "I asked Sam if we could take them into custody on the way in. It's a small motel farther down Sunset, past the Freeway." He paused, looking at me. "We've got enough to hold them on now. You want to come along when we pick them up?"

"Do I? I hope to shout I want to."

"As an observer. Nothing more. You are under arrest, you know."

"Yeah. I'll be good. But I'd hate to miss it, Bill. That babe may still have my gun. If she does, I want it back."

"O.K. But be on your best behavior."

"It's all I've got left."

The motel was a small one on Sunset, set back from the street. Not plush, a far cry from the expensive home, the Beverly Hills Hotel, the Norvue—or the Hidden Valley Lodge. How the mighty have fallen, I thought. And these two were going to take a big fall very soon.

I should have felt more exhilarated about it, I suppose. Maybe I was just tired from all the activity during the day. Especially that long-distance run, after I'd seen Dilly for the last time. Disappearing around a curve in the path. Maybe that was it.

The last major development was almost a mess.

When we walked into the motel's small lobby a man was getting cigarettes from a machine against the right wall, and the man was Kermit Vanda.

But when he saw us he merely got rigid for a moment, a second or so, then relaxed and stepped toward us, smiling.

"Anybody got a match?" he said agreeably. "I seem to have left my lighter in the room."

Rawlins put the cuffs on him, anyway. And left them on.

Room 22.

That's where Mrs. Vanda, or Dilly Pickle, born Dale Jill Piquelle, and possessor of probably a dozen aliases besides Marcelle Whist and Burma O'Hare, was now preparing for a good night's sleep. Which she was not going to get.

The sergeant was in the car with Vanda. Rawlins and I walked to Room 22. He had Vanda's key, but the door wasn't locked.

At the last moment, I said softly, "Bill, I'm on my best behavior. But you must have—despite the chuckles—an idea of what this conscienceless tomato did to me. Aside from helping to ruin my life, I mean."

"Yeah?"

"I'd sort of like to be the one who lets her know. Besides, I want to get my Colt Special back from the fiend, if possible. I guess, too, I just want to be the one to let her know that, even though she played me for a mark, I'm the last man she'll con for

183

a while. And, I suppose, that although maybe she conned me once she could never do it again. Something like that, anyway."

"She stuck you pretty deep, didn't she?"

"I bled, friend. But I have stopped bleeding. And I'm just mean enough to want this babe to know that."

He nodded, amused. "O.K., go on in. I'll be right behind you."

I turned the knob and stepped inside.

The lights were on in the room. The bed covers were turned down.

Dilly—somehow I would always think of her as Dilly—apparently slept in the nude. At least, that's what she was wearing. She was standing by the bed, and as we came in she turned toward us.

There was just a flicker of surprise, and perhaps shock, when she saw it was not her husband coming gayly to join her in the sack. Then her expression smoothed. She sank gracefully down onto the edge of the bed.

Dilly didn't make any effort to hide her nude body, to cover any part of herself with fluttering hands. She just placed her palms flat on the bed at the sides of those sonnet-worthy hips, leaned forward an inch or two, breasts swinging slightly, and looked at us from the melting, hazel eyes.

And, for a moment, I stood still, looking at her.

Even after the time I'd spent gazing at that body in the thin white jersey swimsuit, at the lovely face and eyes and brows and lips and smoothness of her, the sight of her was something which entered the nerves and loins and heart more than the eyes. Even aside from the nakedness of her flesh, seeing her once again had a newness, and might always have something of that newness. Maybe there's a better word. But it was the kind of newness Adam might have felt on discovering that Eve was not a boy.

O.K., I told myself. She's still beautiful, gorgeous woweewow, with a body not real, that can't truly be real, with a warmth and vital glow and an almost-sweet heat a man could feel from clear across the street on a drizzly day.

O.K. And so what? You know the real Dilly, I told myself. You know what's inside her, the dark pools, the emptiness, the —call it evil, to sum it up in a word. And you sure enough know what she did to you. Not once, but twice.

But fool me once, fool me twice, and so on—I was cured. I'd bleed no more. With all that in my mind, I knew she'd never be able to turn me on again, never be able to dazzle my eyes and brain with mere beauty and artful wile.

She smiled. "Hello, Shell," she said. "Believe it or not, I'm glad you got away." Then she looked past my shoulder and went on, "And who's your handsome friend?"

Well, *that* did it. Cool as a cucumber, wasn't she? Well, so was I. If I'd needed any additional little bit more just to be *sure*, that was it. I was cured, all right.

I took three long steps toward her, cool, calm, fully rational at last. Savoring my triumph, I stopped before her, looked down at her.

"Dilly Gun," I said, "I have come to get my pickle."

Hours later, I smoked a last cigarette, and decided to get some sleep. Try to get some, anyway.

The case was wrapped up, over entirely. Except, of course, for the attorneys, the D.A., courts, testimony, the legal denouement. Just the frosting on the cake, but the cake was cooked. I'd been running it all through my mind.

I was glad it was over, pleased with the way it had worked out. With most of it. Not all.

Ordinarily I might have tried to forget the bad parts and unwind a bit more by going out on the town with a gorgeous tomato. Some food, a few drinks, a bit of this and a bit of that.

But not tonight—I didn't have anybody in mind, anyhow, nobody in particular. Certainly nobody available. Most of the pretty girls I'd met lately had been married, for one thing. Too, I was a little tired. In fact, I was damn tired.

No, not tonight. It was common sense to relax a bit, conserve the old energies, build up the *élan vital*.

And I'd spring back soon, I knew. Things would work out for me. They always had; they would this time, too, no doubt. No doubt about it.

Yes, I would stay in tonight and get a good rest. For all the common-sense reasons I'd been thinking of.

And, of course, for one other reason.

But a man—especially one who knows all will work out well —can get used to anything, I figured.

Even jail.

So I lay back on my cot and—in about another hour—fell asleep.